Island of Wings

Karin Altenberg

W F HOWES LTD

This large print edition published in 2012 by
W F Howes Ltd
Unit 4, Rearsby Business Park, Gaddesby Lane,
Rearsby, Leicester LE7 4YH

1 3 5 7 9 10 8 6 4 2

First published in the United Kingdom in 2011
by Quercus

A CIP catalogue record for this book is available
from the British Library

ISBN 978 1 40749 547 7

Typeset by Palimpsest Book Production Limited,
Falkirk, Stirlingshire
Printed and bound in Great Britain
by MPG Books Ltd, Bodmin, Cornwall

for Robin

THE BIRDS DECLARE IT

that wing white and low
that also leeward go
   go leeward to the tor-lands
where the tin-veins maculate the fire-rocks
The birds
   have a home
in those rocks.

David Jones, *The Anathemata*

The swan's blare
my seldom amusement; for men's laughter
there was curlew-call, there were the cries of
   gannets,
for mead-drinking the music of the gull.
To the storm striking the stone cliffs
gull would answer, eagle scream
from throats frost-feathered. No friend or
   brother
by to speak with the despairing mind.

The Seafarer, translated by Michael Alexander

To cry to the sea
that roared to us;

1

*to sigh to the winds, whose pity, sighing back
again, did us but loving wrong.*

The Tempest

PART I

JULY 1830 – ARRIVAL

The young woman rose from her berth almost before she heard the knock on the cabin door. 'The Reverend asks for you, ma'am,' called the deckhand. 'He wants you to come up on deck.' The English was awkward on his tongue.

She could not remember how long she had been lying there, fully clothed. Her new travelling dress of light tweed was unpleasantly damp from the salty air and she felt queer and sad as if she had missed part of a day – or a life. Had she been asleep? She had been deeply immersed in something, a drowning or a dream where mythical sea creatures had been calling to her from the deep. She leaned against the worn timber of the cabin wall as she let the last of the nothingness dissolve around her. As the nausea cleared she squinted and looked around the dim cabin. There was a chipped enamel bucket half-full of sickness on the floor next to her feet; she looked away in humiliated disgust as she decided not to accept it as her own. Grateful to be alone with her shame and this filth she made a mental note to ask the lad to wash it out before her husband noticed. She attempted to smooth her uncompromising hair but knew, even without a mirror glass, that she was ugly.

The boy called again. The cabin floor was still at an angle and the timbers were moaning, but everything seemed to be relatively stable. She recognised a few of their possessions which had been strewn across the coarse floorboards and wondered about the child inside her; what must it be like in there? The baby was floating in its own ocean, which would have been very choppy indeed as the seasickness set in. She smiled wryly as she made for the companion ladder, hoping her child was a better sailor than herself.

The wind had died and the rough sea had softened, a dark flickering of mercury upon the swell. The skies rested heavily on the horizon, gravid with rain that would not fall for days, not until it reached the Long Isle and the world beyond: the world that was still real to those who had stayed behind. Somewhere in the west a thin band of light was breaking through the North Atlantic mist, dyeing it the colour of old sheets.

The grey uniformity of the world around the ship was almost as nauseating as the rolling waves of some hours ago – but this time, as she reached the deck, she managed to steady herself. They were two days out of Oban and it was on leaving the Sound of Harris and Pabbay behind early that morning that the sea had roughened and sent her below decks.

Her husband, the Reverend Neil MacKenzie, was standing with Captain MacLeod and Mr Bethune, the taxman's representative, by the starboard. The three men had removed their hats and were scanning the sky in boyish excitement. Mrs MacKenzie stumbled across the deck to join them and breathed again as one hand grasped the bulwarks, the other one protecting her stomach.

'Lizzie – look, look out there!' said her husband pointing eagerly as he saw her by his side, and then, embarrassed at the exposed intimacy of his exclamation, he started again in a more sober way, 'Can you see the big bird out there? It's a mollymawk, an albatross blown here by yesterday's southerly storm.' She followed the line of her husband's index finger and looked up through the rigging and the canvas, which was limp and passive now where before it had bulged and shuddered. The sky was milky and the light hurt her eyes at first; and then she saw it – a lonely cruciform shape high above the mast. Suddenly it dropped and swooped alongside the length of the ship, its huge white wingspan and black-backed body slashing the mist in a soundless dive.

'Ah,' she gasped as the majestic bird with its beautifully domed head seemed to look at them from under dark brows. 'What is it? I have never seen such a bird before; will it hurt us?' Captain MacLeod looked at her and laughed. 'Don't you worry, Mrs MacKenzie. It is the king of the ocean travellers. Some seamen say it is the reincarnated

7

soul of a lost sailor who watches over us living ones.' The Captain lowered his voice to a theatrical whisper. 'They say it should be hailed in God's name or it could decide to bring bad luck upon us.' He made the sign of the cross and winked at her.

'But did you see its eyes, Captain? They look so stern and displeased,' she replied anxiously as they watched the bird glide elegantly over the top of the waves.

'Only a superstitious fool would believe that the bird carries a human soul,' said the Reverend with a short laugh.

'Perhaps,' agreed the Captain, 'but the lore of the sailor is as ancient as the sea. We may do worse than to let it serve as a reminder of the burden of humankind, of all our sins and shortcomings.'

The Reverend looked up after the departing albatross, his gaze suddenly dark and distant. 'Yes, in this you are right, Captain, we must always be prepared to recognise a source of penance and the possibility of redemption.' Lizzie winced at the unfamiliar tone of her husband's voice, and Captain MacLeod examined the Reverend's face with a serious expression.

They were all quiet for a moment as they watched the albatross bank westwards. 'I believe it is taking our course; it has come to guide us to the islands – it is a good omen indeed!' said Mr Bethune to ease the mood, and the Reverend, suddenly sweet again, looked up and laughed with him, 'Indeed,

Mr Bethune, indeed.' But Mrs MacKenzie remained serious as she said, 'Let us hope also, Mr Bethune, that it brings some fortune to the natives of this island – I hear they are poor and wretched.'

'Poor, madam? The St Kildans want for nothing. Their bairns are better fed than any of the children on the Long Isle and their clothes are warm and tough,' answered Mr Bethune. 'But they could do with some spiritual guidance that is for sure. Your task is truly noble, Reverend,' he added dryly, and spat over the side.

The Reverend did not seem to have heard the light tone of sarcasm in Mr Bethune's voice. His earlier spell of bad mood seemed to be gone. 'My friend the Rev. Dr John MacDonald of Ferintosh, who has visited the islands several times, tells me that they are a fine people, remarkably innocent but closer to the ancient soul of the Gael than to the moral codes of our civilisation. They carry the simple faith of the peasant,' said the Reverend importantly. 'I knew as soon as I heard about them that they were my calling,' he added with poise.

'Well, I say! That call must have been mighty strong to be carried so far on the Atlantic winds,' Mr Bethune said gleefully. 'There is no other place in the Empire as remote as St Kilda, and the inhabitants are as savage as the naked blacks in the King's territories in Australia. I know nothing of their faith, but I tell you this: I'm happy as long as they pay their taxes so that my Lord of the Isles can sleep well in a feather bed.'

'You occupy yourself with the material life of the St Kildans, Mr Bethune. I have been chosen by the Society for the Propagation of Christian Knowledge to deal with their spiritual life, and I will not let them down,' the minister said firmly, hoping that his steady gaze would convince the rather impudent older man of his formidable authority in the matter.

'Let us hope that your calling will be as spiritually satisfactory to the missus when the winter storms set in,' Mr Bethune muttered coarsely in reply, and turned to cross the deck.

'I must be grateful to you, Mr Bethune, for your encouragement and concern.' This time it was MacKenzie's turn to sound sarcastic as he addressed Mr Bethune's departing back.

Lizzie studied her husband, who was deep in his own thoughts. She did not like the way in which Mr Bethune had spoken to him – and the revenue man had a most disagreeable countenance. Her husband, on the other hand, was a handsome man. Even with his dark hair tousled and matted by the sea air he looked elegant in his black minister's coat and white cravat. He was taller and leaner than the Captain, who remained at his side, and the scholarly pallor of his skin made him look dignified. To think that she had married a minister! That she was a minister's wife, and that they were sailing towards their manse. She could hardly believe it. Her sister, Annie, had laughed when she heard about the engagement, saying that Lizzie would become as dowdy as Mary Roberts's sister Peggy, who had married the minister in Kilbride. Peggy was no longer allowed to come to tea parties or the Hogmanay dance, and she wore dark dresses with high collars and long sleeves even at the height of summer, but, worst of all, her hair had gone all dull and greasy as she wasn't allowed to wash it in vinegar on a Sunday morning. Her minister husband had told her that if she didn't stop her vanity she would be dancing in the fire of Gehenna next! Lizzie had shivered a bit for the fate of Peggy Roberts, who had had such beautiful hair at school, but she told Annie that this Neil MacKenzie was not like the minister of Kilbride – he was modern, and both handsome and courteous. Her cheeks coloured as she recalled how he had looked at her when they first met at the house of Mr Grant, where he had served for a while as a tutor to the younger children. Perhaps Annie was just a bit jealous of her; the thought struck Lizzie for the first time. Annie was two years older and maybe it was not easy to have a younger sister who was getting married to a handsome minister, who had studied at the university in Glasgow – a sister who would soon be the mistress of a manse!

Lizzie had seen Annie kiss James Hamilton, the publican's son, in the alley at the back of the pub in Love Street, like a common factory girl. She wondered if Annie was in love with James, who was as strong as his father and could carry a barrel of beer on his shoulder. He was a charming and cheerful fellow, and they had known him all their lives, but surely Annie could do better? Their own father had made some money in the recent building boom, and they had both been given schooling. Their household was respectable, Lizzie reckoned, yes, quite respectable, and even the Mayor's wife had called on them once or twice.

She thought of her husband again. She had overheard Dr John MacDonald, the man they called 'the Apostle of the North', telling another man at the ordination ceremony the previous year that 'MacKenzie has the zeal and mind that will make him go far'. She suddenly thought of her own inadequacy – she was ignorant of most things, she suspected, and, although she had never told anyone, she was not sure if she could believe in God in the right way, if at all. She was changing too fast, like the world that she observed around her. How could she not be ignorant and uneducated when everything that she learned altered the constellation of the things she already knew? The nature of her thoughts was her greatest weakness, Miss Gilchrist had told her at school; they made her mind spongy as they whisked around. She must learn to separate the real world from the world of her imagination. She had tried to tell Miss Gilchrist that she was afraid that her life would be too dull without the romanticising, that life would never be quite good enough if she was just herself – that somehow she would always be found wanting.

She was not sure if her husband knew of her weaknesses. She tried to hide them as best she could. Sometimes she would agree with things he was saying although she did not know what he was talking about, and on occasion he had looked at her as if the thoughts she expressed were not her own. Ah, she was painfully ordinary! And then there was the matter of her appearance – her hair was impossible, curly and unmanageable, not at all shiny and sleek like Peggy Roberts's had been before she married the minister of Kilbride. She was quite sure that her complexion was not as fair as that of the ladies her husband would have encountered in Glasgow, but, on the other hand, Annie said she had a fine figure and he seemed keen enough to hold her in the dark. Lizzie sighed unhappily; would anyone ever be able to find beauty in her?

However, she must not forget that she was fortunate all in all, and she carried his baby – their baby – a creation of both their bodies. At that moment, as if in response to her thoughts, she felt the baby move inside her and she reckoned that she may yet begin to understand her purpose in this marriage.

The Reverend was staring hard into the melancholy grey air. The lull of the vessel as it moved slowly through the limitless seascape was making him sleepy and his thoughts were retreating deep into his head. He had not been at sea for over ten years, not since the night when William MacKillop drowned. He did not wish to think of Will now. He had met Will's father in Lamlash the previous April as the *Caledonia* left for Canada. Old MacKillop had come from Glen Sannox, along with the other families that had been cleared from their village by the laird, who had turned the arable land into grazing. MacKenzie had not told his relatives that he would be at Lamlash to see the ship off, but old MacKillop had spotted him in the crowd and come up to greet him.

'I know you favour the modern ways now, son, but we are going out there to Canada to continue living the life we know. Our kin in Megantic County tell us that in spite of the name the old language is spoken in Nova Scotia and the traditional ways are honoured. This old land of ours is for the sheep now, they say, and man has no place in it.' He laughed bitterly.

MacKenzie did not reply, and after a moment's contemplation the old man added in a softer voice, 'Pray for my boy's soul, minister. I leave young William behind with a bit of my heart.'

MacKenzie nodded mutely and avoided his gaze. The old man sighed and stooped to pick up a bundle at his feet. As he stood up again he seemed taller than before and his shadow fell over MacKenzie as he said in a low voice, 'He was a good sailor and a good swimmer too, my lad. You were the last one to see him alive and the only one to know how he died. Aye, you can pray for his soul – you who lived to be a minister with a fine black coat and all.'

The Rev. Alexander MacKay, who had escorted his congregation to the ship, preached a sermon as the group from Glen Sannox boarded: 'Casting all your care upon Him for He careth for you.' Neil watched from a distance as the last of his kin embarked and left Scotland forever.

But their exodus had nothing to do with him – had he not left the village a long time ago to spread the Gospel? Neil MacKenzie had read *The Wealth of Nations* and knew well that in order to build a new society for Scotland it was vital to remove the obstacles that hinder the natural progress of economic change and social order. This is what he had been taught at university, and he believed that it was the only way to a modern society based on moral and scientific achievement. The new world would be created to make way for advanced human happiness. He himself would like to add faith as one of the founding pillars of that new society, and it worried him that his teachers had not seemed too concerned with it, nor did it feature much in the *Edinburgh Review*, which must undoubtedly be the reading matter for any man with ethical and intellectual aspirations, such as himself. Perhaps the great intellectuals in Edinburgh considered faith to be such a basic principle of society that it was not worth mentioning. The thought was comforting and he felt encouraged by his own reasoning. *There was nothing I could do to stop it.*

But he had felt strange that morning last April at Lamlash quay, hiding from his own kin. As the

Caledonia was towed out of harbour he had said a prayer in the old language. He had prayed for the land of his ancestors, for his family, for Will who had been young and fair when he died with all his life ahead of him, and at last he had prayed for his own redemption, but by then the words stalled in his swollen throat.

It was shortly after that day that he decided to marry Miss Elizabeth Crawford. He was pleased with his choice of wife. She had grown up in a town and understood the mechanisms of society, and he was sure she would understand his mission. She had enough schooling for people to believe she was intelligent, this he was sure of, and she had a strong and healthy figure – he liked the way her dresses fitted her well. Her older sister Annie was probably prettier, he thought, but the giggle which often rippled over Annie's face was unsettling, and Lizzie had seemed to be the more serious of the two. There was something quite remarkable about her eyes, although he could not yet put it into words. She was not above his status, nor would she pull him down. Once her folks would have been above his; as tradesmen they had made some money while he had grown up a miller's boy. But he had his wits and his determination, and these faculties had brought him to education and into the society of a different class of men. His family was gone, he had no past, and while her kin remained tradespeople he had risen as a respected minister of the Church of Scotland.

He had explained his mission and the nature of his new parish to her and to her father, a decent man – not an intellectual of course, but hard-working and moral. Mr Crawford, who was a builder in Paisley, was proud and delighted that his daughter would be marrying such a prominent man, he had said, and although he could not offer much in terms of a dowry, he was sure that his daughter would be a good wife in whatever climate and on any barren island – Mr Crawford had winked at this point – and she seemed to like the minister well enough so who was he to oppose the match?

After Will's accident, Neil MacKenzie, who was still a young man, knew he needed to engage in something that was bigger than himself. The years at university had changed him; he was different, and better, and he had found a mission at last. He was a confident student, fired on by his many, often private, aspirations and after his ordination he had told the Presbytery that he would like to preach the Gospels in the most godforsaken place they could offer – he had suggested Newfoundland, where he was sure he could do a world of good. In the end, the Society in Scotland for the Propagation of Christian Knowledge had asked him to go to St Kilda – the furthest inhabited islands in Britannia.

His mentor, the Rev. Dr John MacDonald, who had visited the islands on previous occasions, had been so horrified by the low level of religiosity amongst the St Kildans that he had travelled, preaching, all around the Highlands and Islands in order to raise money for building the new church and manse. The starving Highlanders, generous as ever to their own kin, had been more than willing to offer what support they could for the spiritual salvation of their cousins on St Kilda.

The islands had become a near obsession to Neil MacKenzie over the last year. *St Kilda*! – he had repeated the name like a charm to himself over and over again. This is where I will be tested, he thought. His mind often travelled ahead of him to the islands and endowed them with the sublime grace of a Utopia. He had been chosen to relieve the islanders of their backward ways and show them the rightful path as drawn out by God and paved by the Church of Scotland. On other days, when his modesty was greater and he could not keep the fallible man in him at bay, he merely thought that these were the islands where he would find goodness, peace and redemption.

As the sea and the wind and the air were holding their breath around the ship, the Reverend returned from his thoughts, only to find he was looking at a mirage floating on the horizon. His eyes were fixed on a dark shape that balanced in and out of focus. At that moment he heard the lad ring the bell and the Captain's cheerful call of 'Land ahoy!'

The Reverend turned to see his wife beside him. She looked a bit pale, he thought. Her eyelids were thin and dark, the lashes thick as she looked down into the water. He had been conscious of her rather serious discomfort that morning but had been discreet enough not to mention it in front of the crew. He believed that had been the right thing to do, and she was strong enough to take care of herself. He suddenly felt a rush of unreasonable happiness when he thought about the baby inside her and about the island in the distance. There was a son waiting to be born to herald his quest. 'Are you quite comfortable, my dear?' he asked, his voice warm now, and put a protective arm around her. 'Oh yes, I'm fine now that we can see land again,' she answered as she leaned into him, grateful for his sudden affection. The couple continued to stand like that for some time as the ship was slowly approaching the islands. If she wasn't exactly aware of the nature of her husband's thoughts and affections at that moment, Lizzie reflected, at least their souls were resting comfortably against each other.

The archipelago grew out of the low clouds like bad teeth in a weak mouth, the rugged sea cliffs bleakly lit from behind by the sun, which was setting somewhere far out in the west. Gradually the islands took on individual shapes in prehistoric shades of grey. Captain MacLeod pointed out the different islands: Hirta, the largest and the only one that was permanently inhabited; Boreray about five miles to the north-east, with its threatening stacks – Stac Lee and Stac an Armin – the highest sea pinnacles in all of Britain, he said; Soay, about two hundred yards to the north-west of Hirta, was still out of sight. The Norse-sounding names rolled off the Captain's tongue as softly as a snowfall. The lofty peaks and sheer sea cliffs of Hirta were covered in cloud, but as the ship approached through the dull swell the wind grew stronger again and the mist started to clear.

A myriad of seabirds were circling the ship now, and the noise of their calls was deafening to the sailors who had heard nothing but the silence of the sea all day. There were gannets – white-washed and graceful with heads that looked as if they had been dipped in custard – and fulmar, skilfully skimming the surface of the waves. The lonely albatross that had overtaken their cutter earlier in the day was nowhere to be seen. To their left they could see the ridges of Dùn. Captain MacLeod pointed out that the name indicated an ancient fort, and the crown of the ridge did indeed look like the terrible battlements of the castle of a dark lord. As the rock sloped steeply towards the sea it gave way to low grass, and the sailors could soon make out the shapes of innumerable nesting puffins. Their clown-like appearance was greatly enhanced by the tragicomic sound of their old man's laughter, which rode eerily on the waves: ho, ho, ho. In one place the sea had gnawed a narrow portal through the rock. It looked like the eye of a needle, and the wind which threaded through it whispered a tune which, when it joined the song of the birds, put a peculiar feeling in the hearts of the mariners.

Lizzie drew closer to her husband. She was speechless and did not know what to make of this island which was so unlike any other place she had ever seen or even imagined. How could anyone live in a world as strange as this? she wondered. It seemed utterly impossible to man and beast alike, and then it struck her – how would *she* be able to live here?

They drew up towards the wind and turned into a wide bay where the treacherous black rocks gave way to a shore fringed by a narrow shingle beach, sloping gently up towards a hamlet surrounded by green pastures. Behind the hamlet the ground rose gradually at first and then steeply to the slopes of Ruiaval, as the Captain called it, to the south and the rugged face of Conachair to the north. The many colours of warm earth, fresh sorrel and young heather were at once pleasing to the sailors' eyes, which had grown accustomed to a dreary palette of black, white and grey. In the lee of the wind the evening seemed suddenly warm and agreeable. They were beginning to hear new, more vibrant noises carried from the shore – dogs were barking through the cacophony of birds, and Lizzie thought she could hear the mounting voices of excited children.

As they looked closer the MacKenzies could see little stone structures spotted across the hillside above the village. They seemed almost organic, as

21

if they were growing out of the rough ground like boils. These were *cleits* – Mr Bethune explained – where the natives would dry their turf and store their food and feathers. The absence of trees was striking. Lizzie had never seen such a barren place.

On the right side of the bay the sea cliffs, covered in short grass and crawling lichen and littered with more of the strange stone structures, rose steeply towards the high mountain, partly hidden by a great cloud of woolly mist. Small sheep with coats of a blackish brown were clinging to the sheer cliffs, their hooves aptly finding footholds in the most impossible places. Some of them looked up as the cutter drew nearer, chewing in stupid curiosity.

MacKenzie suddenly gasped as he laid eyes on his church and manse at the foot of the hill to the right. The whitewashed buildings shone brightly against all the brownish green and he was surprised that it had taken him so long to spot his new home.

The crew were presently busy tying down the lowered canvas sails and preparing the rowing boat. The anchor was dropped into the startlingly clear water and struck sand.

The MacKenzies waited anxiously as the rowing boat was lowered. It tugged furiously at its ropes and ground against the side of the cutter as a couple of the crew jumped in and turned to receive MacKenzie and his wife. The crew were rather surprised to see that the minister, who had seemed

22

such a land-born gentleman during the crossing, was as steady as any of them on entering the dinghy. Mrs MacKenzie, however, was another matter; she seemed to be in a sort of trance: pale, silent and stiff as Captain MacLeod helped her over the gunwale towards the outstretched arms of his crew below. The hem of her skirt caught on something, and for a terrible moment her petticoat was blown up against her thighs to show her stockinged legs. The skirt freed itself, but the keen arms that caught her as she landed in the rowing boat seemed to the Reverend to hold her tightly for a fraction longer than necessary.

MacKenzie, embarrassed by his wife's exposure, was further humiliated to notice that she did not appear perturbed by the incident; indeed she seemed strangely detached, he thought. How could she be so vulgar – and in full view of the sailors? What must they think? He did not have time to dwell on it for too long as the rowing boat set off towards some shelving rocks on the right, evidently used as a landing place. As he looked up towards the rocks which separated the village from the sea he saw a group of male natives running down to greet the boat. Further up the slope a group of women and children were shyly holding back.

The crew expertly rowed the boat alongside the landing place, and as the vessel reached the rock a group of four or five young native men quickly grabbed the prow and hauled it and its crew on to the shelf in one powerful motion. Strong arms supported the Reverend and his wife on to the slippery rocks and steadied them as their sea legs wobbled briefly on stepping on the unyielding, rough ground.

Lizzie felt her kid boots slip on the seaweed and was grateful for the support of the unknown man at her side. She felt quite numb, dazed by the terror of seeing her new home so barren and strange, but as she stepped on to dry land her senses started to return. She was aware of much noise and commotion and there was an overwhelming stench of something which reminded her of rotten shrimps. She sensed that there were people all around her but she kept her eyes turned down, hoping that her new neighbours would not notice her dishevelled looks and torn skirts. In fact, at this moment, she hoped that no one would notice her ever again. Displeased with herself, intimidated by the hustle and bustle and humiliated by her inappropriateness, she forced her feet to move on to the island, and in this manner, step by step, she arrived.

MacKenzie in the meantime was striding up a path towards a low stone wall. 'At last the firm ground of Hirta, our lost Eden!' he exclaimed triumphantly, then remembered his wife and turned around to see her, head down, walking towards him. He turned back and caught her hand. 'Are you all right, Lizzie? It must all be a little overwhelming for you, but you will get used to it, don't you worry.' He squeezed her hand and she looked up quickly. 'I am sure you are right, my love,' she lied.

At this moment they were approached by a short man with a great beard partly covering a weathered but kindly face. He held his soiled flat cap in one hand and addressed the minister in the old language while extending his other hand in welcome. The rest of the natives were quiet during this address and there seemed to be a breathless pause before the minister summoned his authority and greeted the ruddy man in Gaelic. The greeting was extended to those standing around the MacKenzies and then, inspired by the enormity of the situation, the minister beckoned to his new congregation to kneel as he said a prayer in gratitude for the safe deliverance of himself and his wife to their new home: 'Praise the Lord for His great goodness in preserving us on the mighty waters, and bringing us to this much wished-for destination.' The natives, still on their knees, seemed to be waiting for something more. The minister was not quite sure what he ought to do next, so in order to further establish his position amongst them he decided that it would be a good thing to bless them. After all, his mission was to enlighten their spiritual darkness, and as he raised his hand over their bowed heads he could indeed feel the light of reason radiating from him. As he asked his flock to stand up again he knew that he had done the right thing and he hoped that the people were cheered by his arrival.

Lizzie, who did not understand a word that was spoken, was confused by the scene in front of her. She knew, of course, that her husband's first language was Gaelic and that the natives spoke no English, but she had not heard him speak his mother tongue before. The soft words spilled out of him to form beautiful sentences which ran like water through the air. His voice sounded clearer and more youthful in this language, and she realised that this man who spoke Gaelic was not the English-speaking husband she knew. He seemed inspired and his authority appeared undoubted. She resolved to try to learn something of this tongue as soon as possible. It was essential that she got to know her husband on all levels – but how could she be curious about the dirty, foul-smelling men, women and children kneeling in their insufferable clothes on the rough ground around her? She took a step closer to her husband and gathered her skirts to protect them from the grime on the ground around her.

The minister looked at his new congregation and, if he did not find them quite like the noble savages he had expected, he still understood that there was a lot of work needed to raise them in the scale of thinking beings. The natives were well built and generally fair, although not altogether clean. Some of the young men and women could be considered quite handsome, and many of the bairns had hair the colour of straw. The men wore outfits not unlike those of the fishermen on the Long

Isle: coarse woollen trousers and dirty-white woollen jerkins with jackets of the same material as the trousers, generally dyed dark blue or brown by indigo and lichen. The women, on the other hand, he observed with apprehension, were very badly dressed indeed. Their shifts resembled sacks with simple sleeves and a cut-out hole for the head. Their gowns were of a peculiar tent shape, fitted around the body with two girdles; one above the breasts and one around the waist, where some had tucked up their skirts to be able to move more freely. This strange fashion made the women look segmented, a bit like large insects. Most of them were barefoot, he noticed, to his dismay. The men in particular had strange claw-like feet with strong ankles, perhaps the result of climbing the rocks for sea fowl. Everyone's feet were filthy.

The man who had greeted them motioned for them to walk with him up the path, past a large building which looked like a storehouse or a tithe barn, to the kirk and manse. These were respectable-looking buildings with slated roofs; the manse looked out over the bay, whereas the kirk was built in an east-facing position behind it. They were joined by a narrow passage which would allow the minister to enter the kirk without getting wet even in the foulest weather. The builders had only just finished their work a couple of weeks earlier, and the whitewashed houses dazzled the newcomers. The workmen had been supplied, along with the master builder, by MacLeod of MacLeod, the laird at Dunvegan Castle. The plans had been drawn by none other than the great lighthouse architect Robert Stevenson.

It was obvious that the natives were very proud of the new buildings, remaining silent at a respectful distance as the minister walked swiftly up the stone steps of the porch and opened the door for his young wife.

Mrs MacKenzie entered her new home and the minister looked at the back of her neck, which seemed dreadfully thin as she removed her bonnet. Perspiration had formed around her hairline and small chestnut-coloured curls had broken free from the coil at the nape of her neck and rested on the high collar of her travel gown. He was suddenly annoyed that she showed so little enthusiasm for this moment that was so important to him. Why could she not enjoy it for his sake? She had been so quiet all afternoon and she had not shown any kindness or friendliness to the natives. He had, over the last year, introduced her to the educated classes and she had absorbed their manners quickly enough. She could carry herself with polite aloofness but surely it would have been more appropriate to show some caring and compassion for their new congregation, like he himself had done. He watched her dispassionately as she looked slowly around the room, taking in the freshly plastered walls, the carpeted floor and the few pieces of furniture generously provided by the laird. She inhaled quickly as she turned towards him, smiling wanly. 'It is a pretty house,' she said, breathing out. 'We will make it our own and it will be as good as any manse on the mainland.' Encouraged by her own words, she linked her arm with his and together they walked through the remaining three rooms: first a study with a heavy desk by a window which faced the bay; the next room was a small bedroom, with two narrow beds against opposite walls; lastly they walked into another bedroom, with a large bed and in a corner a small cot with delicate flowers around a sprig of juniper carved into the headboard. She looked at it greedily as if the cot alone could restore her sense of normality and order. 'I had it ordered specially,' he said, almost shy now. 'It is lovely,' she answered quickly, and added 'Thank you!' with a smile which, for once, reinforced her words. He loved her again then and drew her close to him. 'As soon as our crates and boxes are loaded off the cutter you can start to make it homely.' He could feel his excitement growing again. 'It will be very comfortable in time for the birth of the child.'

Somebody had lit a fire in the grate for their arrival, and Mrs MacKenzie returned to the first room to heat some water for tea. Through the window she could see the islanders still lingering outside. She turned her back to them and busied herself with the kettle. Its cool metal surface seemed reassuring and she gripped it hard with both her hands for a moment. She wanted to speak, to say something normal and appropriate for an occasion such as this, a young woman moving into her new home, but her throat was thick and she feared her voice would not carry.

Neil MacKenzie opened a heavy door at the end of the hall, which led through the short passage, past a storeroom and a dairy, into the kirk. He entered in the east end by the raised platform where the pulpit stood. It was a simple room with plastered walls and a high ceiling, the rafters still bare. The last of the evening light was falling through four lancet windows on to a double row of rough pews. The earth had been packed into a slightly slanting floor. Although the kirk had been built by hands far from home and not skilled in ecclesiastical architecture, the minister was pleased with the austerity of the room, which reflected well the prevailing fashion of Highland churches. He stood at the pulpit and looked out of a window at the mackerel sky above the bay. Suddenly overcome by pious emotion he sank to his knees, his dark hair falling over his eyes as he bowed his head and thanked the Lord for the opportunity which had been presented to him: 'Gratitude be to the Lord who affords us constant reason for gratefully recognising His protecting care and unmerited kindness.'

★   ★   ★

The glorious morning sun was painting Lizzie's face as she rested on the porch. She felt her cheeks glow pleasantly as she drank in the scent of honeysuckle and deep sea carried on the summer breeze. She found it difficult to comprehend that this island had been her home for barely two weeks now – already it felt like an eternity. The days were growing heavy with her pregnancy, but at this moment her world was close and comfortable around her. The new life she carried stirred occasionally under her heart and she wished that it could see through her eyes the emerald hills sparkling with dew and the still sea of the most beautiful velvety blue. A couple of seals were asleep in the bay, their bodies drifting like drogues in the water while their heads bobbed on the surface like shining black buoys.

Her husband had been busy with his ministerial duties. He had visited all the houses in the village and he had preached two sermons which had been attended by all, though the level of concentration amongst the congregation had been somewhat low, Lizzie reflected. She herself had not visited the village yet. She had been exploring the glebe and the outhouses, but she had not yet ventured far from the manse. The only reason for this omission, she convinced herself, was that she had been so busy with unpacking their crates and boxes, brought ashore from the cutter before Captain MacLeod and Mr Bethune set sail for Pabbay again.

A steady stream of natives had been visiting them in the manse, bringing gifts of *gugas* – young gannets, dressed and prepared for eating – along with eggs and milk. She had stood by her husband's side while he greeted the guests and thanked them for their gifts in that soft language that separated her from him. Her face had strained with the expressions of hospitality and gratitude she had worn for the natives as they smiled kindly and curiously at her. One of the families had brought a puppy, a small dog of no particular breed. It was playing now at her feet, and she smiled as its clumsy paws prodded suspiciously at a shell recently dropped ashore by a gull. It was not a pretty animal, with its short legs and long black body. It had a brown face with pointed black ears. She could think of no name for it at present, but she liked it enough to realise it deserved one. Annie would have known what to call it, she thought, and reminded herself to ask her sister in the letter she had started the other night. Mr Bethune, who had not been satisfied with the rents supplied by the natives for their laird, had said that they could expect another boat from the taxman before the end of the summer. Supplies ordered to last the natives through the winter would be delivered on this occasion and Lizzie hoped that the taxman could bring her letters to Annie and her parents back with him to Harris.

The puppy was licking her hands now, its eyes revealing a pathetic yearning for something which she failed to interpret. Instead she blushed as she remembered the hot eagerness of her husband, who had lain with her last night. His kisses were still burning on her skin like a fever. He was very careful these days out of respect for the baby inside her, but he was as ardent as always and she was pleased that their bed was so warm and close, although it sometimes worried her that the tenderness kindled there was often lost in daylight.

The minister was sitting at the desk in his study. His gaze would occasionally rest on the beautiful view of the bay outside the window. He was thrilled with his new parish but concerned about the state of the congregation; he was particularly worried about the quality of their accommodation and the nature of their faith. He was writing in his notebook:

Eight years ago my friend Dr MacDonald wrote in his report to the Society that the St Kildans had 'some knowledge of the chief doctrines of the Bible, but that their knowledge was of a traditional and theoretical rather than of a scriptural and practical character'. This statement seems to be true still. In fact I myself have noted a serious lapse in their understanding of moral obligation. The St Kildans seem to have been very attentive to Dr MacDonald's powerful sermons although I suspect that they were mainly charmed by his great eloquence and energy but had not enough knowledge or insight into the Scriptures to be able to follow the arguments. I have noted a similar distraction when I have preached. I fear that they are too ignorant of the leading truths of Christianity and the practical effects thereof to profit from my sermons. Something must be done, under the influence of the Spirit of God, naturally, to make the doctrines of Christianity enter into their hearts and minds. I am planning to hold meetings every Wednesday evening to teach them, clause by clause – indeed word by word, if necessary – the shorter catechism.

He leaned back in his chair and flipped the pen between his long fingers. Perhaps they would also benefit from being able to read and write, he thought. Very few of them seemed to have mastered these skills. He would need to set up a school. The teaching would have to be conducted in Gaelic but perhaps his wife could help to try and teach them some English – that would perhaps bring her out of herself. He sighed as he pondered the monumental task that lay ahead of him.

There was also the issue of the hygiene of the members of the congregation. It was difficult to accept that there were Christian souls in these modern times who lived in such filth. Their dwellings were not much better than the burrows of the puffins, and many of them only owned one set of clothes so that they had to borrow garments from their kin on the unusual occasion when they wished to wash their attire. He had even noticed that some did away with this altogether. He returned to the notebook with a disgusted look on his face:

The St Kildans live in oval-shaped houses which are more like hovels than human dwellings. The houses are covered in grass and rubbish and can from afar be mistaken for burrows. They live close together in a clachan without any apparent structure to it. The walls of the build-ings are as thick as they are high, about seven feet, and hence there are no windows to let the light in. The only source of light is a hole where the straw roof meets the wall, which also serves as a smoke outlet. Due to the thickness of the walls the wooden door opens on to a passage which leads into the byre end of the house. In order to reach the living area you have to make your way, in complete darkness, past the animals which dwell there in the winter, to the living area shared by men and dogs. There is no furni-ture as such, just a few utensils such as a couple of iron pots, a wooden chest or two, a few wooden plates and an iron lamp fuelled by fulmar oil. The beds are dug out of the thickness of the walls and the entrance to these grave-like beds is two by three feet. Ashes, dirty water and far worse are spread daily on the earth floor and covered every few days with more ashes. This way, they tell me, the thickness of the floor accu-

mulates over the year so that by the springtime, before this human manure is dug out and spread across the fields, the inhabitants have to crawl around their houses on their hands and knees. What is more, they literally dive down into their beds at night, as the level of the floor is higher than the entrance to the 'grave'.

They tell me also that it can at times be very difficult to enter the building in wintertime. This is due to the fact that in front of the doorway, and extending well into the tunnel, is a hollow into which are thrown all the portions of the birds not used for food, the entire carcasses of those not edible, and all and every abomination you can imagine. I do not wish to think about the horrors I will have to crawl through in order to visit my parishioners when winter comes. God almighty! How can people survive under such circumstances? They do not seem to be too bothered by the standard of their living and maintain, in the most laconic way, that their ancestors built these houses and lived in them for a thousand years which in itself proves that they are good houses. But they do wonder why it is that they are not as strong as their forefathers appear to have been! I thank the Lord that my olfactory senses are so poorly developed.

It was no wonder, the minister thought as he put down his pen, that the stench around the natives was so unbearable that it made his pregnant wife nauseous. He was suddenly ashamed of himself for thinking such negative thoughts of his own flock and added a paragraph to his notes:

All praise be to the God of mercies, who has brought me hitherto, and permitted me to see the little group of mortal beings who inhabit this sequestered spot.

Pleased by this magnanimous comment he decided that it was time for a break and went in search of Lizzie. He found her on the porch, her eyes closed against the sun and an untroubled smile on her face. He noticed that her cheeks were stroked in a pretty shade of pink. Her hands lay idle and cupped in her lap – they seemed to be gathering sunlight under her swelling stomach. He watched her quietly for a while and realised that he was at that moment raised to a level of happiness that could not possibly last. In her he celebrated the unearthly beauty of the morning. She reminded him of everything in life that he had denied himself since Will's death all those years ago, and for the first time he allowed himself to recognise his dead friend's likeness in her unruly hair and frail temples. Could he dare to own this new space that she had created for him? How skilled he had become at avoiding tender emotions! Could he love her? He shuddered at the thought. There were times when he had wanted to diminish his own humiliation by hurting those he loved.

She looked up at him then, startled to find him

so close. The light that entered her eyes seemed to flash an instant before it settled into dark pewter. 'How is your work going?' she asked, and stretched her back. 'It is such a beautiful day. I think I will go for a walk.'

'A walk?' he echoed anxiously. 'Is that really wise? You know these rocks can be quite treacherous, and you have not been anywhere on the island yet.'

She laughed at his concern as he went on, 'At least wait until I have finished my work so that I can walk with you.'

'Don't worry, my dear, I want to go on my own,' she replied cheerfully. 'I will walk up the spot you told me about the other day, the place where I will be able to see the other side of the island.'

'*Bearradh na h-Eige*,' he said. 'It means the edge of the Gap. You must by no means walk all the way up there on your own.'

The week before, the natives had showed him the spot where the hill ends and the sea cliffs take over. The cliffs were about six hundred feet high and, if nothing else, the view would surely give her vertigo, he thought.

'Well, I will only walk as far as the ridge up there –' she pointed towards a ledge above the hamlet – 'as I would so like to see the view of the bay from above,' she said reasonably as she heard the concern in his voice.

'But you are really not in a fit state to walk up a hill,' he insisted.

Lizzie could feel a vague irritation rising within her. 'The baby is not due for another few months, and if it makes you feel better I will bring him along.' She pointed at the bewildered puppy at her feet.

Now it was his turn to laugh. 'All right, with such a champion at your side I cannot deny you the pleasure of the view from the hill; it is indeed stunning! But remember not to walk any higher than the small glen with the stone enclosures.'

She rose and kissed him. He let it happen although it was full daylight and they were easily visible from the *clachan*.

Soon the puppy was bouncing ahead of her on the gentle slope above the glebe. It seemed to be chasing a fly or perhaps a more obscure creation of its own mind. She smiled and waved at her husband as she started to climb the steeper ground, her petticoats stirring up the smell of fresh grass and white clover. The sound of the sea was everywhere, but as she ascended the hill the cries of the fulmar became even louder. High above the huge granite dome of the east fell starlings were playing their summer games. Lizzie thought herself lucky to be able to walk as freely as this. She thought of her home in Paisley, where the smoke from the coal fires hung thick in the air and the factories were growing fast. She wished Annie could have been here with her to see so much beauty. She had never thought it possible for grass to be this green and for the sky to be this blue. The ground seemed to be illuminated from below as if some ancient, golden treasure had been buried there.

She passed a number of cleits, used to store turf or a catch of birds, and she thought they looked like a bad rash in the landscape. It was as if the natives had built themselves into the surface of the island and it was sometimes very difficult to distinguish between man-made structures and natural features. Nor was it possible to distinguish the ancient from the new. Time was no longer linear in this place where no one could remember who built the houses, cleits and dykes and where the seasons were marked by the comings and goings of the migrating birds. The ancestors were near the living, and the world of men was closely linked with the rock, the sea and the birds with which they shared these elements. Time and space seemed suspended, so that here and now was always and everywhere.

When she reached the glen with the magnificent drystone enclosures Lizzie turned to look down at the bay and the village. Far below, the sea was so still and clear that she expected to be able to see the fish swimming in the shallows. A fine line of white foam where the surf hit the shingle beach adorned the water's edge like a rope of pearls. There was no smoke coming from the huts in the clachan. Fuel was scarce on the island, which lacked both substantial trees and peat, and during the summer months it was used for cooking only once a day. She could see some fields of barley, lit now by the midday sun. The meadows, yards and stock-pounds were empty as the cattle and sheep were enjoying the summer pasture on the other side of the island. From the manse she had watched the women as they set off, twice a day, to milk the cows that grazed the fine grass of Gleann Mòr. It was probably a long walk, she thought, as the women would be gone for many hours at a time. They were often singing together as they walked, and their tunes, which sounded ancient and alien but pretty enough, were sometimes carried on the breeze across the bay where they would echo in the air above the glebe.

The puppy had slowed down ahead of her and was fighting bravely against a passive cluster of speedwells which grew next to a drystone dyke. Its ears were pointed and it growled threateningly as it stared into the innocent blue eyes of its opponents. Lizzie suddenly laughed and stretched her arms as if to embrace all the beauty of the day. She felt like a girl again, her feet were so light that they did not seem to make a dent in the grass and gone were her anxieties and her feelings of inadequacy. The frightening magnitude of her decision to marry the minister and follow him to this place was replaced by a relieving insouciance. She was Lizzie, she was her own self, and Mrs MacKenzie was no concern of hers! She felt light-headed and hot and pulled off her bonnet to let the sun and the wind dry the perspiration from around her face. How she wished she could walk with the girls of the village to Gleann Mòr; she would sing their songs and learn to milk the cows and live as close to the rocks and the sea as they did.

She resumed her walk; youth was in her step and in the flush of her cheeks and she could see no harm in climbing a bit higher. The slope was steeper now and the grass gave way to rocks covered in lichen. A couple of willows were crouching beneath an outcrop – they had been forced by the wind and the weather into submission. Lizzie was delighted to see a young boy of eight or nine years old coming towards her from the higher ground ahead of her. He was fair and pretty and looked an image of health although his clothes were tattered and filthy. She thought how beautiful these children would be if only she could wash them and clothe them in proper, fashionable garments. She greeted the boy cheerfully in English, and he looked up in alarm as if he had only just laid eyes on her. *'Cia mar tha thu,'* he answered shyly from under his fringe. His voice was branded by the characteristic lisp of the St Kildans. The mutual greetings were followed by an awkward silence as they both realised that the conversation could go no further. Lizzie smiled at the boy and indicated with her hand towards the ridge; then she waved and turned to go. The boy was suddenly alert, the shyness all gone. He gestured towards the high grounds, shaking his head as he spoke quickly and eagerly. His pale

42

eyes were the colour of freshly caught herring and he looked quite worried. Lizzie, touched by what she interpreted as concern for her welfare, laughed and said teasingly, 'You are as bad as my husband.' Then she added coquettishly, 'I wish you men would stop worrying about me. I won't go near the edge of the precipice and I will be very, very careful.' She ruffled the boy's hair and turned to go, but he grabbed her sleeve and repeated some of the words she had heard him say before. Lizzie felt a spark of irritation and pulled her arm away rather too brusquely. The boy looked even more agitated and she thought she could detect tears of frustration welling in his eyes before he turned abruptly and ran down the hill towards the *clachan*.

Oh dear, she thought to herself, I did not handle that very well. Her gay mood was gone, but her determination to reach the ridge remained as strong as before. She wondered how long she had been gone from the manse. She was beginning to feel thirsty and tired, but the summit of the ridge was close now. At that moment the puppy barked pathetically at a couple of large brown skuas nesting amongst the rocks. Lizzie rushed towards the dog as her husband had warned her about the hot temper of the nesting birds. Too late she grabbed the puppy by the neck and slapped its nose, but the birds were already roused and once in the air they started diving towards her with mounting aggressiveness. She screamed in horror as one of the birds swooped close over her head. Its partner, however, dived even deeper and caught a strand of her hair in its claws. Livid with fright, she beat her arms in the air and started running down the hill, stumbling on the scree. The birds were relentless; their shrieking war cries rang through the air and Lizzie screamed again as one of them hit her face with its wing and tore a thin line of blood along her cheek. She slithered and hobbled down the broom-covered rocks. She tried to lean back to stem her speed and stop the inevitable fall, but her legs got caught in her petticoats and she tripped. She was lucky to fall on to a patch of grass, but as she stumbled forwards and rolled down the slope she felt a sharp pain where her left shin hit a stone. At least the stone stopped her fall and she got up, panting, on her hands and knees.

Lizzie looked up; the fulmars were still dotting the sky above her, but the skuas were gone. She pulled up her skirts to examine her leg. The stone had cut a hole through her stockings and she was bleeding, but she was able to move the leg all right. Her palm had been slashed as she tried to stop the fall and the wound was dark with dirt. The puppy came up to her and tried to lick her face. She hated it now: a stupid mindless creature which had stirred the nesting birds. She shooed it away, cursing.

As she started her slow descent she could feel that something was not right. She felt weak and she noticed that her underthings were wet and sticky. A new terror possessed her and she tried to speed up her steps. Oh please, God, don't let this happen now, she begged. The time is not right! When she reached the glen with the enclosure she was already exhausted and stopped to rest her back against a stone wall. The bright day was blackening in front of her eyes and she tried to steady herself with both hands holding on to the wall behind her. It was all terribly wrong – she could feel that things were not as they should be. She tried to call out for her husband but knew it was in vain, and in any case her voice was too weak to lift on the wind. And then she screamed as the most excruciating pain tore at her intestines. 'O God,' she cried in a hoarse voice at the silent skies, 'please help me.' She had never experienced such agony and bent over when another wave of torment broke through her.

As the pain subsided she could not believe that this was happening to her. She thought she heard voices and stumbled forwards a few steps to call out. But when the pain returned, the world around her darkened again and she made out the face of the boy she had met earlier and behind him a short, bearded man running towards her.

When she awoke a candle burned low on a small table beside the bed. The room was quiet and long shadows fell into the corners. Lizzie was aching but she could not have said where – she felt calm and sedated. Her throat was dry and she was desperate for a drink of water. As she turned her head on the pillow she saw an old woman in a chair next to the bed. The woman got up and moved closer. Her eyes were blue and her hair was grey under the white frill of her cap. She smelled of unwashed clothes and fulmar oil and her hands were claw-like in the candlelight. Lizzie tried to protest as the claws moved closer and pushed her gently back on to the pillow. The old woman held a cup of water to her mouth and Lizzie surrendered and drank greedily. The drink seemed to clear her mind, but as she started to remember she closed her eyes hard in an effort to forget. But she could not ignore her limp body under the sheets; nor did she need to touch the pain to know the empty wound under her heart.

'Where is my baby?' she asked the old woman. 'Did my child live?' she added urgently, her voice thick with dread. Lizzie looked into the pale blue eyes of the old woman as she was told, in a language which she could not – and would not – understand, that her child was dead.

The next time she woke the old woman was gone and her husband was holding her hand. For a moment, before he noticed that she was awake, she saw the dark sea of grief on his face. Then she stirred and he held her close saying, 'Oh, Lizzie, I am so, so sorry.' She clung to him desperately and after a while she managed to ask, 'Our child – was it a boy or a girl, Neil? Was it complete like a child should be?'

'It was a beautiful little boy,' he answered, his face turned away. 'He lived long enough to hear the sacraments and be baptised into the Christian faith. But he was too small to see the world; he never opened his eyes,' he added weakly.

They held each other quietly but without being able to share much comfort, destitute even of each other, until she realised what she had forgotten to ask: 'What name did you give to our son?'

'I called him Nathaniel, as he was a gift of God,' her husband answered, and she repeated the name once or twice to herself. He looked at her and cleared his throat. 'Our little boy was not allowed to stay with us. He is with God and we must be happy for him.' His minister's voice sounded impersonal as if he was not talking about his own child, but then he added, almost inaudibly, 'Although it is hard to accept that we let him slip away.'

She cried then, and for the first time since setting foot on the island she allowed self-pity to over-come her. She cried for the boy Nathaniel, who had slipped out of her and whom she had never seen, she cried for the ache in her swelling breasts and empty womb and she cried for her impossible loneliness.

It was almost dawn when Neil MacKenzie left his wife asleep in their bed and went into his study.

He sat down at his desk and looked out the window at the bay which was barely distinguishable between the night and the day. He was trying to understand the events of the previous afternoon. Had God wanted to punish him? For what – for Will's death? Had he not tried to redeem himself by giving his life to the Church, by coming to this place where no one else was willing to go to preach the Gospel? He sighed and pulled out a leather-bound notebook from one of the desk drawers. In the ashy morning he dipped his pen in the well of Perth ink and drew a horizontal line. Below this he continued to draw two vertical lines next to the margin. He paused before making his first entry of birth and death into the parish book of St Kilda: '*1830*,' he put next to the margin, and just below, at the top of the first column, '*July 18*,' and in the next column, '*Nathaniel of N. MacKenzie, missionary. Infant.*'

PART II

MAY 1831 – A VISIT

The wind was in from the west, and life in Village Bay was still on the lee side. A group of children were playing on the thin strip of sandy beach exposed by the ebb tide. Their cries and laughter glittered in the clear spring morning. An eider sailed past the rocks in the shallows, proud of her clever chicks which were towed after her in an erratic, downy line. Further out in Village Bay gannets were dropping into the sea, their necks stretched like feathered arrows as they pierced the surface of the waves.

The adult men and mongrel dogs had all gone off fowling on the sheer cliffs on the north-east side of the island. Their new minister, who had been on the island for barely a year, had accompanied them on the expedition as he took a keen interest in watching the cragsmen catching the fulmar. May was the most important season of the year to the fowler as the fulmar and many other manners of seabirds were hatching all over the grassy ledges on the sea cliffs of Hirta.

In the manse the minister's young wife was busy with the spring cleaning. Every now and again she would sit down to rest between a bucket and a broom. Although the new baby was not due until the end of the summer, she was a lot heavier than during her pregnancy the previous spring.

After the premature birth and death of the boy Nathaniel, Mr and Mrs MacKenzie had not talked of him again. The memories of the child who had been too small to live were hidden in the shadowy corners of the manse, buried amongst the futile daily chores of its inhabitants. During the black months when the island had been unyielding and desolate, when all the birds were gone and the natives had retreated into their burrows, the MacKenzies, who were convinced that their separate griefs were insignificant, had pretended to each other that they had almost forgotten the death of their child. They had talked about practical matters and of their friends and family on the mainland, but for much of the time they had been quiet, smiling vaguely at each other in the dusty light from the fire. Winter followed autumn almost unnoticed, in the same way that dusk was merely a darkening of each gloomy day. The island was thus empty of life, and the fierce Atlantic gales that swept across the crags and glens week after week, month after month, increased the isolation of the couple in the manse. When their need for closeness and their longing to be loved was too great they would sneak around each other like cats around a plate of hot milk, snatching at tenderness. Their shared misery, which was too great to convey, made them shy and kept them apart until, at last, they were united again by truth and silence. It must have been around this time that their new child was conceived.

Just before Christmas, after a period of paralysis and dark moods, the minister had thrown himself into his work. He organised Bible classes at least once a week and often gave two or more sermons on the Sabbath. In addition, he started a day school for the children in order to teach them reading, writing and arithmetic. He would regularly visit their dwellings in the *clachan* to test the natives on the shorter catechism, and many of them had practised it at home throughout the winter. Hibernating half underground, the St Kildan men and women spun, weaved and made clothes from the wool of the Soay sheep. In the twilight, disguised by the smoke that escaped from the hearth and clung to the low ceiling, the reciting of the catechism was intermingled with the singing of the old songs.

As she swept the floor on this May morning Lizzie stirred up whiffs of grief and unexpressed emotion, of silent love and words not spoken. She swept them out of the open door into the spring air, into the smell of new life and secret decay which was blended into the sunlit space between the stunted lilac and the sea-struck hawthorn which grew on either side of the porch.

The unfortunate puppy had grown into an anxious young dog eager for Lizzie's love and friendship. It had no purpose and it still had no proper name. The letter which Lizzie had started to her sister had never been sent. She was still in bed – due to her injured leg and low spirits, it was generally agreed – when the taxman called a month later to collect the last of the rents. No ship had been sighted since.

Now, at the end of May, the supplies of flour, sugar, tea and tobacco were running low and the St Kildans craved news from the world outside their own. Over the winter months Lizzie had begun to think that the name *Dog* suited her animal just fine. Her own language, which she had taken for granted, had become precious and rare to her. As no one on the island, except for her husband, understood anything she said it was almost as if she spoke a secret language. *Dog* was therefore a highly appropriate name for the only other creature on the island that seemed to understand English.

Dog had been greatly alarmed by the return of the seabirds in early spring which so delighted his braver cousins. He had cowered under the desk in the study with his preposterous paws folded on top of his nose. For two days on end he stayed there, failing in his genetically ordained purpose, as the noise of the gathering birds grew stronger and stronger. Perhaps somewhere in his poor mind lingered a memory of the two great skuas he had roused the previous summer. Lizzie, on the other hand, had been pleased to see the birds returning.

54

Although she had found the seabirds hateful and frightening when she first arrived on the island, the silent winter had been equally unbearable. But spring was different – suddenly everything was alive again – man, bird and beast were so closely linked with the elements in this place that the very seasons seemed to depend on their fusion.

Spring also brought a dangerous glimmer of expectation. As the birds busied themselves making their nests and hatching amongst the forbidding rocks Lizzie refused to allow herself to hope for the birth of the child she knew by heart; the child inside her who was nearly the same age as the boy Nathaniel had been when he was brought forth to light and death – when she had let him slip away. She withdrew from this new mystery; she did not stroke her growing stomach, she did not whisper to it at night and she did not talk to it during the day, but she knew that the little heart which was beating stronger as spring progressed was communicating with her own.

Through the open door Lizzie heard excited cries from the children playing on the beach. She looked out to find them pointing towards the sea. She stepped on to the porch and turned to scan the horizon and there, far out on the waves, she could see a small sailing vessel tacking against the westerly. It looked almost comic, like a dimple in the great flesh of the Atlantic. The commotion on the beach was increasing as the children debated how to handle the situation. In the end the younger ones rushed up towards the cluster of houses to break the news to the women while a couple of the older boys set off towards the passage beyond the small glen to tell the cragsmen on the other side of the hill. The boat was making slow progress – it would be a good hour before it reached the wind shadow of Village Bay.

Lizzie could feel a new excitement rise in her as she watched the small vessel tossing on the waves. She wondered who it might be and prayed silently that whoever it was would speak her language. To hear English spoken would surely break her sense of seclusion. She went back inside, removed her apron and put the broom down behind the door.

She washed her hands and face in the bucket she had drawn from the spring and went into the bedroom to look in the mirror. Her complexion was fresh, her cheeks pink from the morning's activities and her eyes were swift and dark, but her hair was as unruly as ever. She lifted her arms to unfasten the coil at the nape of her neck and brushed the hair slowly until it shone, illuminated by the faceted light which was breaking in the salt crystals on the window panes. Then she arranged it again in the fashion that young ladies had worn in Paisley before she left the mainland. She put a thin lace shawl over the shoulders of her plain dress of navy cotton and fastened it with the silver and amethyst brooch which her husband had given her when he was courting her. She looked in her box of ribbons for a silk one to tie around the waist of her dress, choosing a broad purple one to go with the amethysts. She returned to the mirror, and this time she was not too displeased with her appearance in the dull glass.

Lizzie was still lingering there, dreamy with her own reflection and memories of other times when she had dressed up, for balls and dances, when the minister entered the manse a moment later, flushed from his walk across the hill. 'It looks like we will be getting visitors!' he called cheerfully. Looking at his wife from the doorway he realised that he may be bringing old news. He smiled at her and added quickly, 'And they are sure to be much impressed by the beauty of the minister's wife!' She blushed, feeling blood and life returning to her face as he kissed her briefly but softly on the forehead.

'Who do you think they are?' she asked, unable to hide the high-pitched excitement in her voice.

'I do not know,' he answered thoughtfully. 'The boys who brought the message thought it was the taxman, but John Gilles, who returned with me from the rocks, tells me the vessel is too small to belong to the laird's representative – our visitors seem to be independent travellers.'

'Surely we will need to host them in the manse,' she said pleadingly, almost desperately. 'We cannot let them stay in the hamlet amongst the filth of the natives!'

The minister looked slightly put off by this

remark. 'Our friends in the *clachan* may seem primitive to you, but they are most hospitable; they have been putting up strangers for thousands of years,' he said sharply, but added, 'but of course it is my duty as minister to invite any gentleman visitors to stay with us.'

Lizzie ignored his rebuke and looked anxiously around the room, which was fresh and pleasant after the spring cleaning. 'I will prepare a luncheon – we will have to roast a few of the puffins which the old widow gave you a couple of days ago,' she exclaimed agitatedly. 'What else can we offer these strangers?' she asked herself anxiously. 'Our supplies are so low there is hardly any fresh fare, except for the birds that the men caught this morning, and it would be too inhuman to serve them the *gibean*!'

'If the *gibean* is good enough for us it will be good enough for our guests,' said Mr MacKenzie sternly.

Lizzie gave no answer. *Gibean* was the most common meal on St Kilda and, to her, the least palatable – being comprised of the fat extracted from boiled fulmar mixed with that of the young gannet. This grey matter was eaten with rye bread and porridge and considered greatly nutritious by the natives. They were much attached to their concoction, and one of them who had taken ill while visiting Harris claimed that it was due to the absence of *gibean*.

How hateful to be the mistress of a manse where

she could not serve a proper meal, Lizzie thought bitterly. The manses on the mainland could serve both food and wine in abundance and they were filled with beautiful furniture, rich textiles and valuable books. She made a mental note to order a larger supply on the taxman's next visit and went out to search the outhouses for some of last year's apples or potatoes.

When she returned, the small ship was drawing up towards Dun and the crew started to take down the canvas and put out the oars. She could make out five people on board the open vessel. Two tall men in hats were standing idly by the bulwarks, looking towards the island.

'There seem to be two passengers,' said Mr MacKenzie importantly, needlessly confirming her own observation. 'Indeed I believe them to be gentlemen!' Lizzie could sense that her husband's excitement at the prospect of meeting the strangers was as great as her own, although in contrast to her he had made several friends amongst the natives. He was especially attached to Donald MacKinnon, who was the headman of the St Kildans. MacKinnon was still a young man, but he had earned the respect of his kinsmen and they had recently elected him to represent them in dealings with the taxman and to settle disputes. MacKenzie was also very fond of John Ferguson, who was unusually intelligent and who could read and write a little and helped out with the religious education. But even so

59

Lizzie knew that her husband missed the company of learned and civilised men. She had done her best to engage him in what she thought would be intellectual conversations, secretly reading old copies of the *Edinburgh Review*, trying to memorise some of the arguments presented by the authors, and then reproducing them in conversation. At such times the wish to please her husband was greater than the humiliation at her weakness being exposed. She knew that he craved the company of these gentlemen as much as she did, and she suddenly felt a hot surge of jealousy. As a man he could easily befriend the guests, but she would not have the opportunity to enjoy their company in the same way. Oh how unfair! Had she not suffered the isolation more than he had? Lizzie had never contemplated her home before coming here. The house of her parents had been a place to live: no more, no less. But it was not the place itself she missed. She longed for the familiar smells, tastes and sounds that had made her belong in that place which she could no longer clearly remember. Would she be able to feel at home in this place and yet be forever alien? She could already feel the strangers putting a wedge between her and her husband. Suddenly she dreaded their arrival. She could have cried for her own weakness – she was too desperate to see their faces and hear their voices.

By now, Mr MacKenzie had changed into his black coat and white cravat and looked every bit the Glasgow gentleman that he had once, if briefly, been. He was talking to her while he moved agitatedly about the house, telling her to draw the best chairs close to the fire and look in the storeroom at the back for the bottle of claret they had kept for a special occasion. Lizzie was not concentrating; through the window she could see the natives gathering on the landing rocks to greet the visitors. Men, women and children were milling around in a turmoil. Lizzie had never seen them so excitable and emotional. She had often watched them from the windows of the manse as they went about their business around the hamlet and she had been struck by their leisurely movements; the men especially seemed to be characterised by extreme laziness.

'Let's go down to the rocks to meet them – why don't we go now?' she enquired of her husband somewhat too languidly. 'Be still, dear.' He gave a short laugh and patted her on the shoulder. 'I will wait a moment yet – you wouldn't wish me to appear as easily excited as the natives, would you?'

'I suppose not, no.'

'And I will go on my own.'

'But . . .' Her voice faltered as he gave her another stern look.

He avoided her bewildered gaze and dragged his dark fringe out of his face with the fingers of both hands. 'You had better stay behind to tend to the luncheon. We do not want these gentlemen to think that the minister's wife does not do her duty, do we?' he said humorously, knowing that he was hurting her. She looked at him incredulously but said nothing. He came to stand next to her at the window, their shoulders not touching, and as the boat approached the landing rocks he said to her calmly, 'It is important that I exercise my authority as the spiritual guardian of the island in these situations.' He walked out of the manse then, and she, diminished now, watched him from the window as he strolled nonchalantly down the path past the store towards the rocks.

Donald MacKinnon and a couple of the other men were holding the boat steady as the two gentlemen and the three crewmen stepped ashore. The taller of the two passengers removed his hat and put out his hand to greet MacKinnon and the other men. He greeted them heartily in English and they answered as gaily and politely in Gaelic, quickly followed by a question which the newcomers did not understand. By this time Neil MacKenzie had reached the rocks. He extended his hand to the young man, saying, 'Welcome to St Kilda, sir. I am the resident minister by the name of Neil MacKenzie. To whom do I owe the pleasure?' MacKenzie studied the man in front of him; he was tall with thinning fair hair and a narrow nose that made his face look rather long. He was not exactly handsome, the minister noted, but he looked like a cheerful and agreeable man.

'I am pleased to meet you, sir,' the younger man

exclaimed. 'George Clayton Atkinson. I am a natu-ralist and artist from Newcastle and this is my brother Dick, who is also a true devotee of the beauties of nature!' He indicated the other gentleman, who was nearly as tall but darker and slightly heavier. 'I say, what is it that these kind people ask us?'

'The natives enquire whether there is any war raging in the Empire. This is always their first question to a visitor – we are rather isolated here.'

'Of course, I understand. You can reassure these peaceful souls that there is no war raging within our borders at present – apart from the usual domestic and political squabbles of course!'

Neil MacKenzie looked relieved and relayed the good news to the islanders before turning back to the young travellers. 'What is your business on the island?'

'We have come to make a study of the birds and wildlife.' Mr Atkinson's voice was somewhat slurred and the minister thought the two brothers looked a bit unsteady after their long journey. He shook hands with Richard Atkinson, who had kept in the background thus far, and addressed them both. 'From Newcastle, you say? Do you know of the artist and ornithologist Thomas Bewick? I have his book on British seabirds in the manse – it has been an invaluable source of information to me since I came here!'

'How uncanny!' cried George Atkinson. 'Bewick is my mentor – indeed it was he who suggested

63

that I should undertake this journey to the Hebrides!'

'Ah, my dear friends, I cannot say how pleased I am to welcome you to St Kilda. We will have a lot to talk about no doubt, but it can wait a while I am sure . . .' MacKenzie was interrupted by loud laughter from the St Kildans, who were welcoming the crew the Atkinson brothers had hired for the crossing. They seemed to be exceedingly well received and no wonder, for they were a merry group and they had brought a supply of whisky for the journey which they were willing to share.

Dick looked on with a slightly worried expression. 'I hope they will not keep serving these islanders whisky at the same pace as they served us.'

The native men and women were emptying the boat of its sails and movables and as soon as this was done they started hauling the small vessel on to the rocks under a particular cry from MacKinnon the headsman: '*Robh maht na gillean, Robh maht na gillean – shid I, shid I!* Well done, lads – there she goes!' There was much laughter and chatter.

One of the native men cried, '*Tha fios an fhithich' aige!*' and his friends laughed loudly but not unkindly.

'What did he say to make them laugh so?' Atkinson asked curiously. 'Oh,' MacKenzie replied with a smile, 'they say that you have got the Raven's intuition.'

'Whatever could they mean by that?' Atkinson looked greatly alarmed.

Now it was MacKenzie's turn to laugh. 'They use that expression for somebody who turns up unexpectedly, and I would dare say uninvited, to dinner. Which reminds me, you and your brother must be hungry – would you care to join me and my wife for luncheon. Mrs MacKenzie has put the kettle on and I believe she is preparing some roast fowl. Bird is all the food you will get while you are here, I am afraid, but the puffin is quite acceptable when roasted!'

The Atkinson brothers looked greatly relieved at this prospect. They had been sailing in an open boat with a few wisps of straw and a peat fire in an iron pot as their only comfort. In spite of this, the young men seemed to be in remarkably good spirits and MacKenzie suspected that the five or six bottles of whisky that they had brought along for the journey had helped to keep them warm.

As the three men entered the manse, Lizzie, still humiliated and rejected, busied herself at the fireplace. Her back was stiff with disapproval. 'Come, Mrs MacKenzie, and welcome these two gentlemen from Newcastle,' said her husband, taking no notice of her mood. Thank God, they are English! she thought almost triumphantly as she turned to smile at the guests. 'Welcome to St Kilda. I trust the crossing was not too hard?' she said enquiringly. Ah, she could not take her eyes off them; they were her people, they spoke her language! The two young men seemed a bit embarrassed under her intense gaze. They bowed their heads and greeted her awkwardly. George's boots suddenly felt too big and he wished that he had gone easy on the drink which had been served with the oatcakes that morning. He raised his eyes to hers for a moment and held her gaze. She was pregnant, he noticed, but her figure was still light and pleasing and her face open and pleasant. But it was her eyes that really caught his attention; they were of a dark steely blue that reminded him of gathering thunder – but without any of the malice. She looked remarkably fashionable for somebody living in this place, he thought, and her hair, which was softly gathered around her face, was arranged in the fashion of a lady.

'Thank you, madam,' he managed to answer at last, 'our journey was quite pleasant. We sailed through a white night from Rodel, and the evening was so fair! It was marvellous – even without a moon it was so bright that I could still consult my watch at midnight!'

At this point Dick, who was not convinced that his older brother had the situation under control, remembered his manners and said, 'It is indeed a great pleasure to meet such a fashionable lady in these barren parts of the Empire. We are much obliged to you for accepting us into your lovely home.' He looked quickly around the small drawing room and couldn't help noticing a damp patch on the wall.

'You are very kind, sir, I am sure,' said Lizzie, 'but let us leave such formalities; please make yourselves at home. Luncheon will be served shortly. I am sure my husband would like to show you to your room.' She was in charge for a moment and enjoyed being the mistress of the house, however insignificant.

The meal, when they finally sat down to enjoy it, was a cheerful event. The tension between the MacKenzies eased as they both drew pleasure from the presence of their guests.

The Atkinson brothers, who had been travelling around the Hebrides for some time, were quite threadbare of recent intelligence but they managed to convey some of the latest news from the mainland along with reports of the most spirited murders and accidents. The MacKenzies were much intrigued to hear about the suggestions of an abolition of the slave trade. George and Dick's brother Isaac, who was trading in Jamaica, had sent them word of societies of black men calling for their freedom. Amongst the other news, Mrs MacKenzie was particularly horrified to hear of the unfortunate statesman William Huskisson who had been killed by one of the new locomotives that transported people along the recently built railway line from Liverpool to Manchester. She had seen a picture of a locomotive the previous year and it had terrified her; but to think that it could kill a man, and a Member of Parliament at that!

The two brothers continued to ask the minister about the nature of the island and its people.

'I was struck,' said Mr George Atkinson, 'by the good looks of the inhabitants as they turned out to meet us on the landing rocks.'

'Yes,' agreed the minister enthusiastically, 'although they are rather short they present neat and compact specimens of the human form.'

'I have never seen teeth as white as theirs; did you not notice their teeth?' asked Mrs MacKenzie of no one in particular as if the thought had just occurred to her.

'Oh yes, I did indeed,' said the other Mr Atkinson. 'However, I was mainly impressed by the air of intelligence which they conveyed.'

Lizzie, who did not feel qualified to comment on the intelligence of the St Kildans, continued to remark on their looks. 'The women have the finest flowing locks and yet their hair has never known a comb and the only water that cleanses it is the mists and rains of the Atlantic!'

'Although I think,' Dick disagreed, 'that the women are not generally so good-looking as the men. The negligence in their dress is not becoming!' He seemed to be blushing.

'Is it possible then,' George, who was greatly interested in the nature of man, mused, 'that these natives have become quite sublime creatures by being bred in such an awe-inspiring environment?'

The minister laughed at this and remarked, 'You must not ennoble them with more excellent virtues than they deserve, for they are quite crude in many ways.'

'How so?' asked George eagerly.

'Well, for example, however much effort I put into teaching them the Scriptures, it is as if they will not take them to their hearts. They can repeat the catechism like a child repeats a nursery rhyme, but they do not seem to feel the weight of its truth on their souls. Nor do they let it influence their life and conversation. Indeed –' the minister was heated now by that missionary zeal – 'I have heard them swear in the most medieval manner!'

'Medieval, sir?' Dick, who was secretly fascinated by all forms of vice, looked suddenly interested.

'Oh yes. They use un-Protestant expressions such as "by the Book!", "by Mary!", "by the Sacred Name!" – and worse still! And some of the traditional songs which they are so fond of are frankly appalling! I do not think their manner of Christianity has changed since the Norsemen came to these islands.'

They were all quiet for a moment taking in this information while the minister calmed down.

'Would it be possible to visit them in their homes?' asked George.

'Of course. I will take you to the *clachan* this afternoon,' MacKenzie replied without hesitation.

'*Clachan*?' Dick was still keen to know more details about the native life.

'Oh, it is the local term for that miserable little hamlet of theirs,' the minister translated helpfully.

Dick pondered this for a moment before he asked, 'On our departure from Harris we were assured that we would imbibe a stench from living amongst the natives that will adhere to us for five or six weeks. Indeed some friends told us that our whole neighbourhood back in England would be able to smell our return to their society – is that true?' He was blushing violently now.

Mrs MacKenzie, who felt that she had something to contribute, started to speak at this point, but her husband interrupted her: 'The stench in those hovels is villainous enough! I dare say that you will bring a souvenir of a rare and delicate perfume when you leave Hirta, but I assure you that Mrs MacKenzie and I do whatever we can to keep the manse as free of foul smell as possible. You will be quite safe here!'

At this they all laughed and the brothers glanced at each other, confirming their relief at being housed in the manse.

After lunch the three men set off towards the *clachan*. George asked if Mrs MacKenzie was not going to join them, but the minister replied that she took little interest in the rest of the island and preferred to stay around the manse.

Lizzie did not let on that she had overheard the comment. She looked at her husband's back as he walked brashly across the glebe between the gentlemen brothers. *Is this the man for whom I left everything?*

White clouds were sailing the skies above the

island, carried swiftly on the strong westerly wind. Every now and again the sun came out to steam off the remains of the morning mist which had lingered in the shade. The men soon broke into a sweat as they climbed the short distance through the dewy grass towards the cluster of rude huts in the centre of the amphitheatre of enclosed land. The hamlet lay snugly under the peak of the mountain they called Conachair, or the Roarer, because the wind and the gales would often sound around its summit. As they walked, the minister often stopped to point out features in the landscape, and the two brothers marvelled at the beauty of their strange-sounding names – Cnoc na Gaoithe, or the Knoll of the Wind, Gob Chathaill, the Point of the Wailer, and Laimhrig nan Gall, the Landing Place of the Strangers. A peaceful-looking silver stream that dropped into Village Bay was called Abhainn Ilishgil – the Deep Stream of Evil.

George Atkinson looked around in wonder – the grandeur of the place far exceeded any expectations he had previously had. The rocks and cliffs around the bay were the most magnificent and sublime precipices that he had ever seen during his extensive travels in the British Isles.

The *clachan* of houses lay about a hundred yards from the sea. They were around thirty in number, and as the gentlemen approached the open yard in front of them George was for the first time met by the smell of fulmar oil, joined to the powerful odours of the profusion of putrid bird carcasses and unwashed men and dogs. Nothing could have prepared him for this stench. He pulled a hand-kerchief from the pocket of his waistcoat and held it over his nose. As they drew closer to the houses he could see that a great many bird carcasses were jammed into cracks in the stone walls by their bills, thus drying in the air. Dogs were chewing on discarded bones and offal. A group of children were playing with some fulmar heads, feeding them to the dogs. George was appalled to see a girl of about four or five years old trying to pull the neck of a gannet over her foot as a stocking. The minister followed his gaze and explained. 'They often make shoes out of the necks of gannets – they cut the head off at the eyes, and the part where the skull was serves as the heel of the shoe and the feathers on the throat offer warmth and waterproofing. They generally only last a couple of days, but at times there are so many birds that they can wear these disposable socks almost daily.'

The three men could hear voices, and the minister led them towards a house which was slightly larger than the others and lay in the centre of the hamlet. A group of men were sitting on a ledge formed by a wall protruding from the low roof of the building. They looked comfortable enough as they leaned their backs against the straw roof and chatted cheerfully in their strange language. The man who had greeted them on the rocks, a handsome man of about forty years old, with a stripy woollen vest, was talking purposefully and pointing at different men in turn.

'What are they doing?' asked Dick breathlessly.

'This is the mòd, the assembly where they decide on the activities of the day,' answered the minister. 'They normally meet in the morning, but their routines have been altered by your arrival. Donald MacKinnon, the *maor*, or the headman, who is the man over there –' he pointed towards the handsome man with the striped vest – 'will portion out the rock amongst the cragsmen and enquire into the state of the equipment. He will also settle any minor disputes which may have occurred during the previous day. At the moment I should think they are also dividing the responsibility for housing the three sailors whom you brought from Rodel.'

'It is much like a parliament then?' George suggested. 'A parliament which serves the same democratic principles as that of any free state or nation.'

'Yes, it is true that they are largely used to governing their own affairs,' agreed the minister.

'My word! These men are not just living in primitive simplicity – they are as free as most enlightened people can ever dream to be! If St Kilda is not the Utopia we have sought so long, where will it be found?'

'You forget that their morality is much underdeveloped.' The minister was slightly alarmed by George's suggestion. 'I face a laborious task and it will take some time before I can raise these men in the echelons of humanity – they will need much instruction in all matters which concern the nature of their husbandry as well as the salvation of their souls!'

'Forgive me, sir, but do you not think that we have something to learn from them?' George insisted.

'I believe that we must all strive towards a society based on advanced moral integrity as the foundation for happiness. The society which you and I come from, Mr Atkinson, has evolved quite a lot further in this respect, and so I feel it is my obligation in this case to impart rather than to receive knowledge.'

'But these people live so close to God's creation – this world is still pure and unspoilt by industry and commerce. Their principles of community and democracy may provide a useful reminder to some in our society who are driven by ambition and self-advancement.' George could not be stopped. Maybe this was the answer he had been looking for – perhaps the St Kildans held the solution for humankind. 'The St Kildans prove that we can survive in a society without money, arms, care, politics or taxes!'

Dick, sensing that their host was getting much annoyed, broke in to bring the conversation on to safer ground. 'You said we might be able to visit one of their dwellings, Reverend?'

'Yes, yes, of course. I will speak to MacKinnon,' he answered absent-mindedly.

George and Dick looked around the yard as MacKenzie went to talk to the natives. The men were all idly leaning against walls or squatting on boulders while their womanfolk were busy with a variety of chores. Dick nudged George and hinted towards a group of young women who were plucking the breast feathers of some puffins. A number of other live puffins were tied together by their feet and hanging from a protruding roof beam, noiselessly awaiting their fate. Feathers were whirling through the air. The young women were talking and giggling and glaring at the two *Sassenachs* from under the shade of their cotton headscarves. Their gowns were hitched up by the cord around their waists so that their skirts did not reach further than their knees. Their bare legs were tanned by the May sun, and downy feathers were sticking to their feet and ankles. George, who was quite taken by the scene, thought that he had never seen such a picturesque sight in his life. He glanced at the girls again and almost at once looked away. He was much troubled by a sudden physical discomfort, and although he tried to convince himself that he was superior to such baseness he was forced to button his coat to cover up his shame.

Dick, who had been so eager to point out the girls to his brother, had suddenly coloured and could not concentrate enough on a feather he was twirling between his fingers. George stretched his back with a somewhat tortured look on his face and cleared his throat: 'Right,' he said failing to affirm himself. 'Right, Dick, perhaps we should get going?' His gaze swivelled back towards the girls and he could not resist commenting: 'Have you ever seen such fine legs, Dick?' Dick's voice sounded thick and distant. 'Legs?' he echoed. 'Oh yes, legs, of course. No I hadn't noticed, but you are right, they are certainly most excellent specimens of their kind.' At that moment the two brothers were saved from their exposed shortcomings and further awkwardness by the minister, who called out to them to join him.

'Rhoderick MacLeod has offered to show us his house.' The minister did not seem too keen on the prospect of the visit himself. 'I suggest you leave your good coats outside,' he added.

MacLeod was a stout man in his early fifties with dirty blond hair sticking out under a cap of coarse tweed. Although the day was turning out quite warm, he wore a muffler of soiled red cotton wound, roll upon roll, around his neck.

MacLeod vanished into a nearby hut and MacKenzie stooped to follow him. Dick had already taken off his coat and thrown it on the straw roof of the dwelling. George turned to face the wall as he unbuttoned his coat and removed it as primly as if he had been quite naked underneath. He could feel the girls still watching his back and he stooped quickly to enter the doorway. Just inside the door he faced a dark passageway which led through the thickness of the wall, a passage so low that he had to get down on his hands and knees and crawl as through a tunnel. He was immediately revolted as he put his hand in what seemed to be the putrefied remains of a bird. He heard a cry of appalled warning from Dick who had come across something equally disgusting further inside. George tried to hold his breath against the stink but ended up gulping in the air that he had tried to avoid. The passage ended in the byre, the narrow diameter of which could only just be made out in the faint light. All the manure had not yet been cleared out, and George felt his boots sink into the dung as he waded blindly towards the low *tallan* which separated the byre from the living area. Dick grabbed hold of his brother's waistcoat and helped him across the low passage wall. At last George could straighten up. The room in which he found himself was close and airless. A lamp was burning fulmar oil in a corner, and a turf fire was flickering in the fire pit in the middle of the floor. MacLeod grinned proudly as he indicated his few possessions: a couple of tin plates, a wooden chest and a large coil of horsehair rope which hung on the wall. There was no window but for a narrow chimney-gap at one end where the straw thatch met the massive wall. The smoke had impregnated the walls and ceiling, and every now and again a drop of soot fell from the thatch, which still held some humidity from the last rainstorm. Dick was aghast – 'Does an entire family live here? Where do they sleep?' The minister turned to MacLeod and exchanged a few sentences in Gaelic. 'Rhoderick says that his first wife died of the strangers' cold last year, but he is happily remarried to Effie Morrison and they are expecting. His daughter from the first marriage, Kirsty, who is thirteen this year, also lives here and sometimes the child's grandmother. This is one of the smaller families on the island,' he explained.

Rhoderick had retreated to the far end of the room and was beckoning the brothers to follow him. As they approached they saw a strange hollow which had been dug into the wall about three inches above the floor. George sat down to look inside, and to his amazement he saw that bracken had been spread across the floor of the hollow to form a bed. 'Is this where they sleep?' He could not believe it. 'Yes,' answered the minister, 'I have tried to persuade them to sleep in more sanitary conditions but I have yet to succeed.' He sighed. 'Perhaps now you understand better what I am up against, Mr Atkinson.' George did not reply; he was still staring into the chilly dugout.

'These dwellings are standing so close together that they can sometimes speak with their neighbours through the earth in the bed hollows,' explained MacKenzie. 'In a few cases they have dug out the partition altogether to form a communal sleeping area. These huts are commonly used for the young during the white nights in the spring, when they stay up late to play their courting games.'

'You mean that the young all sleep together — unmarried boys and girls?' Dick, who had been quiet for a while, could not disguise the fascination in his voice.

'I am afraid it has been known to happen, but I am quite committed to stamping out such un-Christian behaviour,' the minister answered ardently.

The two brothers thanked Rhoderick in English for the visit. It was slightly easier to find their way out as the light from the tunnel indicated the direction, but the abominations through which they had to crawl were still as threatening, and the smell was vicious enough to make George gag and swallow hard.

It was a great relief to get back out into the fresh air. As they brushed the worst of the muck from their knees and elbows, collected their coats and turned to walk back towards the manse, the minister told them that the natives had offered to take them to Boreray the following morning to see the nesting gannets.

Back at the manse, Lizzie had prepared a light meal of local cheese and bread. The Atkinsons had little appetite but agreed that the local cheese was good enough for any market on the mainland. The brothers chatted gaily to Mrs MacKenzie about their day and everyone seemed contented. After the meal the men brought their chairs out into the glebe to smoke their pipes and watch the bay. The evening was as light as midday. The wind had died down and the clouds were gone. The salt air was mingled with a scent of hawthorn. A flock of starlings was swinging high above the bay, mirroring the shoal of herring flickering in wave upon wave in the depths below. The men watched in silence for a while, each drawn to his own memories of beauty and perfection to equal the moment. Their emotions at that instance were so exposed that a stranger would have read them in any of their faces.

It was George who broke the silence. 'How far man in the civilised world has moved from God's creation!' he exclaimed with feeling. 'Life on this island must be as God intended it.'

The starlings ascended like the stroke of a brush through the high summer skies.

'Ah, but the beauty of this evening has made you forget your feelings as you visited Mr MacLeod's house this afternoon,' replied the minister, who felt uncomfortable when the young man issued judgement on the people he was supposed to know best.

'Not at all! I admit that the hygiene in this place wants for improvement, but what I saw today of the community of men was most encouraging.'

'How so?'

'Here is a web of rights, powers and obligations that protects the citizens. Men exist in harmony with nature and keep the peace amongst each other through a simple system of governing and loyalty.' George leaned back in his chair and spread his legs. Born to relative wealth, sharp-witted and the protégé of Mr Bewick, he could afford to be confident.

'Yes, but would you not agree that it is a bit unfashionable? We must move with the times and do what we can to improve before God.'

'Unless I am misinformed, this was the argument adopted by many ministers to justify the Clearances. Did you know that over ten thousand people were evicted from the Sutherland estate while ministers and lairds stood by and did nothing to save the communities they were supposed to care for?' George was beginning to sound quite heated now.

'Yes, as a matter of fact I am well aware of the Sutherland Clearances; my own family were amongst those who left for Canada! But the old way of life was not sustainable – you know that as well as I do, Mr Atkinson.' The minister had raised his voice and seemed agitated; he brushed his hair out of his eyes. He could not believe that this privileged young man was implying that the Highland ministers had deceived their congregations.

'With all respect, sir, I am not sure that I agree.'

'Oh?' There was a note of sarcasm in the minister's voice.

'Well, how can it be in the interest of any state to diminish the lives of its most loyal and moral people? Why expatriate those who support the nation in war and provide for it, in the most economical and contented way, in peace?'

'You have always been a man of means, Mr Atkinson. I was born into the years of starvation, after a series of failed crops in the Highlands towards the end of the last century. I know that agricultural improvement, hard work and an unfailing belief in God are the only things that can save communities like this one from disaster!' He was surprised at his own confession.

'Have the lairds and politicians nothing to learn from the experience of a community that has survived on this island for a thousand years?'

'Believe me, Mr Atkinson, when I say that I know these islanders better than you do. What they need is sophisticated guidance from men with experience of the greater world. And they need to ask God's forgiveness so that He may listen to their prayers.'

'You want them to fear God? Have they not got enough to fear in this place?'

'George!' Dick said warningly, but was ignored.

'My purpose here is to improve these people and bring them closer to God.' The minister was desperate; he knew that he had lost the upper hand but could not think how.

'These people are, as you noted yourself, politically primitive. They are used to having no leader. Do you not understand that as you take authority of their souls and minds they will turn to you as to a God? Do you not fear the consequences of your tuition?'

'George, please! Mind your words and your temper!' Dick said, as he would always lean a little in either direction to balance a situation. 'I am sure our generous host has no taste for your adolescent arguments!'

George, reminded of his position as a guest, cooled down and said in an even voice, 'I beg your pardon, Reverend. I get carried away in discussions. It is my nature, I am afraid, and it is most deplorable. We will perhaps differ on this topic as I, an artist and a scientist, will remain morally much inferior to you, a man of God.'

The minister, quite shaken now, mumbled a conciliatory answer. George's words had disturbed him deeply. At the same time he could not help but admire the young man's engagement. In fact, as he looked at George's flushed face he remembered the vigorous youth he himself had once been, before that fatal storm off Arran. William's death and his own survival had been the most defining factor of his life. If he had not survived for a purpose, William's departure would have been in vain. Or had there been more of an act involved in his survival? Had he saved himself and left William to drown? *I will not be held responsible – there was nothing I could do.*

The night was still light although it was ten o'clock. The flock of starlings was swirling closer above the manse and the lively chirruping and shrill whistles which rang through the air were suddenly irritating to the uneasy minds of the men.

Dick sensed that it was time to break up. 'We are much exhausted from our travels and from all the impressions of the day, and as I understand we can expect an early start tomorrow we must bid you goodnight, minister,' he said, nudging George with his boot.

'Yes, my brother is right, we are much fatigued,' George said, feeling it too. 'Goodnight, minister, and thank you for a most fascinating day.'

'Goodnight, gentlemen,' MacKenzie answered from some distance.

As the brothers retreated to their beds the minister remained in the garden, deep in thought. Lizzie, who had been sewing by the window after their tea, had been a silent witness to the heated discussion. She watched her husband's face, which was as pale as water in the white night. He made a melancholy figure in his black coat, but she found him almost unbearably handsome. The discussion had revealed to her some of her husband's inner conflict that would otherwise never have come to her knowledge. She sensed for the first time that he carried an enormous guilt: a guilt on which she could not quite put her finger. It was related, she was sure, to the reason for his joining the Church and leaving behind his old way of life with his kin in Arran. Her heart was dark with pity and she wanted to reach out to him and soothe the pain which she could not fathom.

She stepped out into the ghostly light and walked up to stand behind him. 'It is getting late. Will you come to bed, my love?' she said softly. The palm of her open hand touched his cheek before resting on his shoulder.

He started as he heard her voice but did not rise. As he continued to look out to sea he was aware that her gentle devotion threatened to embrace him. Despising himself, he felt a need to deflect his sense of failure and shield himself from her love. At that moment he resented her decency as much as his own weakness. 'Our guests did not seem to enjoy their meal very much; perhaps you will be able to improve on the fare tomorrow?' he said, hoping that the cruelty would relieve his frustration and knowing that the hurt it caused could not be repaired.

She stood back and lifted her hand from his shoulder as if it had touched hot iron. The unfairness of the remark struck her with full force. It must be a misunderstanding, she thought. She was determined not to let dejection overcome her; she held it tight in her throat and went back inside.

George and Dick woke to a most glorious morning. The gold that tinged the island was shining through the muslin curtains of their small bedroom window. They could hear Mrs MacKenzie moving about next door, preparing their breakfast of porridge and a most agreeable cup of tea.

George watched Mr MacKenzie closely as he sat down to join them at the breakfast table. He seemed himself again, George noted with relief, and, if not quite the gentleman that they had first taken him for, at least his eyes were honest and intelligent.

'I should advise you,' said the minister as he poured milk on his porridge, 'that you should give the natives some of your tobacco in payment for the troubles involved in bringing you to Boreray.'

'Oh yes, of course!' said Dick, who was always anxious to do the right thing. 'I would be more than happy to offer them a liberal pecuniary compensation for their labours!'

'Their idea of the value of money is so vague that I think they would be more pleased if you were to give them about half of what is in your tobacco pouch,' answered the minister, who enjoyed brokering a deal on behalf of his subjects, and so the business was settled.

The natives were already busy preparing their boat when the three gentlemen arrived on the landing rocks. The vessel, which belonged to the community, was a heavy, awkward ship's boat given to them by the laird. It weighed two tons and was rowed with three pairs of oars. The sail was a curiosity in itself. It seemed to be constructed like a patchwork quilt where each square was made up of a woollen fabric of various colours. Like everything else on the island, the task of making the sail had been divided in equal parts between the families.

Twelve of the St Kildans had turned out for the excursion. They were as jolly as ever and although their work at preparing the boat was frequently interrupted by the telling of a story or the lighting of a pipe the group eventually set off for Boreray. The island, situated five miles north of Hirta, had no natural landing place and the St Kildans would therefore normally let those who would catch the birds and eggs on the island jump from the boat on to the sheer rocks with a rope fastened around their waist. The rest of the crew would then return to Hirta until it was time to pick up their comrades or, if the day was fair and the sea calm, they might let the boat drift off the island while they smoked and talked. However, on this occasion, the return crew would wait for the fowlers and their guests in the calmer waters just off the island. A trip like this one could only be attempted in fair weather, as even the slightest swell made it very difficult for the men to land.

The boat was making slow progress through Village Bay, and George soon remarked to the minister, 'I say, minister, these islanders are truly wretched mariners!'

'Yes, their naval tactics are very poor indeed. I think they must be the most uncomfortable, anxious sailors I have ever encountered,' said the latter, and laughed.

'How is that?' Dick chipped in. 'Islanders are generally very good sailors.'

'Well, I believe it stems from an unusual fear of and respect for the sea. They do not swim, and many of their kin have died at sea, either from falling into it when climbing the crags and stacks or from boating accidents.'

The natives were pulling six oars at a time: in threes, with two men sitting on the same bench. But although they were all singing to keep the rhythm and urge each other on, none of the pairs managed to dip their heavy oars into the water at the same time. Instead they splashed in at irregular intervals, spraying the passengers with cold sea water. Moreover, the anxious rowers seemed inclined to stick close to land for as long as possible and the boat was thus coasting every little bay and headland on Hirta before setting off, splashing more furiously than ever, across the open expanse of sea between the two islands. Somewhere halfway between the islands the six oarsmen were relieved by their kinsmen. This change-over was carried out in the most casual manner and the St Kildans were gossiping and chatting away while, to George's frustration, the boat was carried back towards Hirta on the current.

'It is a miracle that they get any work done at all, judging from the amount of gossip that goes on,' said Dick grumpily, trailing his hand in the water over the gunwale.

'Hmm, that is a most intriguing point,' said the minister with scientific interest. 'You see, I have calculated that it takes them on average five times longer to carry out any task related to agriculture than it does the farmers on the mainland. They are naturally inclined to forget the task at hand as soon as they are distracted in their work.'

'Ah, they are just plain lazy. You will have to teach them some good Protestant work ethics, minister,' said George cheerfully.

Dick stiffened at his brother's impertinent remark, but relaxed when he heard the minister laughing behind him. Mr MacKenzie was enjoying the younger men's company. They reminded him of his time as a student. He had even begun secretly to admire George's impudence. The young man seemed to be driven by a confidence which he often lacked himself. Of course he would never admit this to anyone, sometimes overcompensating to hide his feelings of inadequacy as a man. In one area, however, he was very confident: his mission. He was convinced that even if he failed in every other way, at least he would not let himself fail in his mission. George's remarks the previous evening had hit him hard, as they had questioned the very core of his commitment. This mission was more than a vocation – it was the only way to make sense of his survival.

As the boat left Hirta behind, the numbers of gannets increased rapidly until the air seemed to be thick with them. George turned his head back and looked into the sky where the myriad of birds resembled the whirling of snow. Occasionally a bird would dive into the sea, resurfacing with a glistening herring partly hanging out of its beak. A couple of skuas were scanning the flock of gannets for a suitable target to harass. Suddenly one of the skuas caught sight of a well-fed gannet and closed in for the hunt, closely followed by his partner. The two brown birds bombarded the gannet from two directions. One of them managed to get close enough to pick at its white breast feathers while the other one pushed down hard from above in an effort to bring it down towards the sea. The gannet was caught by fear and as it realised that the battle was lost it vomited up the freshly caught fish into the waiting gapes of the thieving skuas. Such a display of the unfair cruelty of nature was of great interest to the three would-be naturalists. Each would create his own theology to explain it.

As the boat slowly approached the island the Atkinsons looked in awe at Stac an Armin, the Stack of the Warrior, which rose abruptly from the sea like a thorn – its sheer cliff-face looking like the topsail of a man-of-war, a shadowed threat on a bright day.

After much splashing and some rather fair singing the party eventually reached Boreray. The boat drew up with its broadside along the rock. Although it was an exceptionally calm day, the swell of the Atlantic kept the dinghy rising and falling fifteen feet by the side of the cliff. If the St Kildans were unusually disastrous oarsmen, they certainly excelled in landing on a rocky shore. As the Atkinsons watched from their seats at the rear, one man positioned himself in the prow and another one in the stern, each with a long pole which they used to steady the broadside against the rock. A third man, with a coiled rope on his arm, one end of which was attached to one of the seats, was balancing in the middle of the boat waiting for a high wave at the peak of which he leaped on to the rock. Once the first man had positioned himself safely on the rock another man performed the same trick, thus creating a rope bridge or gangway for the safety and benefit of the less experienced cragsmen and the guests.

After the minister, George and Dick had assembled safely on the rock with four of the St Kildans, the remaining eight natives pushed out from the rock and let out a drogue anchor made of a sheep's stomach filled with stone. Floating slowly on the great shapelessness of the Atlantic, they soon resumed their chattering and gossiping and seemed much content with the general situation.

The cragsmen indicated to the gentlemen to follow them and at once started to climb the most arduous cliff. It was about seven hundred feet high and they seemed to dance up the rock face completely oblivious of their heavy loads of ropes and gear. The minister, who felt a need to possess the gap between the cragsmen and the gentlemen, started to ascend the cliff in his shirtsleeves, and George and Dick realised that they had no alternative but to follow his example. While they were trying to find a foothold on the jagged rocks the minister told them between breaths that the St Kildan women often descended or ascended these same cliffs with a sheep or a lamb in their arms. This remark had the intended effect, and the two brothers, chafing the shiny leather of their fine boots against the rock, soon reached the grassy plateau at the summit.

The party crossed the island, following a ridge which spined from the east to the west. As they walked they could see the Atlantic on all sides. Its oily surface stretched and stretched in all directions until it poured over the horizon into another space. On the north-east side of the ridge was a grassy heath which went by the Norse name of Sunadal – a most appropriate name on this morning when the sun warmed the valley and lit up the sheep like lamps, one after the other, as it moved across the steep slopes. After some more walking the party stopped to examine a curious old structure on their left. If it had not been for the natives pointing it out to them, the guests would probably have missed it. It was an ancient dwelling, sunk into the ground and divided internally into a central oval-shaped chamber flanked by smaller compartments, like the petals around the pistil of a flower. The natives called the house *Taigh Stallar*, the Staller or taxman's house, and explained that this was where they would normally stay when they visited the island for longer periods. Supplies of dried food and fuel were stacked neatly in one of the compartments, and some dried bracken remained on the floor in one of the other hollows. The smell was stale as in a cave. No one knew how the dwelling had come into being, the natives claimed, but it was supposed to have housed a recluse at one point in the history of the island.

When they reached the north-west side of the island the men were faced with a most extraordinary view. Before them was a chasm in the rock at its most elevated point. The square gap formed an immense chimney, and George exclaimed that it was without exception the most sublime sight he had ever seen. He knew that he would never find the right words to explain its full splendour to anyone. The sea which sighed deep under the rocks would frequently sneeze and a puff of air would rise through the chimney. From this point they could watch the nesting gannets that covered the rocks and nearby stacks. Stac an Armin lay close and threatening to the north. From a distance it looked as if the cliffs were of a white mineral substance, but on closer examination you could make out that it was the gannets themselves which coloured the rock as they covered every square inch of the precipice. In some cases they seemed to be sitting on top of each other, and the noise that rose from their million throats was so loud that the fowling party had to shout to each other to make themselves understood.

At this point the two St Kildans who had first jumped ashore on Boreray started to uncoil a thick rope about eight fathoms long. Made of horsehair, the rope had been clad in many places in sheepskin to prevent it from wearing against the rock. One of the natives wound the rope around his waist just under his arms and another one took it over his shoulder and under his arm and positioned himself with his feet braced against a boulder in order to carry the weight of his comrade. His companion went to the edge and then walked backwards over the cliff, descending with his body extending horizontally from the vertical rock face and with his back towards the sea which was breaking far below. George and Dick both threw themselves flat on their stomachs and looked over the edge of the rock. The climber was jumping lightly between the grassy ledges on which the gannets nested, his feet seeming barely to touch the rock in a manner which made him resemble an insect skimming the still waters of a pond. As he landed on a new ledge the climber would chase some of the birds away and quickly reach out to secure their eggs, which he put in a straw basket that was tied to the rope. In this manner he managed to fill the basket in less than ten minutes. He then started his ascent, agile as an ape, and aided by his friend he soon was back at the top of the cliff.

The Atkinson brothers were much impressed by this competence. 'Why did he not catch some of the birds – they seemed to be within easy reach?' asked Dick.

'They are leaving the adult birds to hatch the remaining eggs in order to ensure the harvest of *gugas*, the young gannets which they consider to be a delicacy, in August and September. The adult birds are generally killed earlier in the season and dried or salted in barrels for the winter,' the minister explained.

'They tend to harvest the fulmar and guillemots in May,' he continued. 'We will probably be able to see this on our way back to Hirta this afternoon.'

George was busy taking notes of all that he observed. He was hoping that his experiences would result in him being asked to read a paper to the Natural History Society of Northumbria. Mr Bewick would probably be impressed by some of his ornithological observations. Perhaps in the future his writings would even lead to his being elected a fellow of the newly established Linnean Society of London. He wanted his family name to be linked with science and exploration. He greatly admired the men of science who had made their names abroad: Banks, Solander and others who had all been given land and titles as a result of their work.

'Come on, George, we are leaving.' Dick had to nudge his brother hard in the side to wake him from his daydreaming.

'What?'

'They are taking us to see a pair of nesting peregrine falcons!' Dick cried excitedly. He was still young, and some things would make him revert to being the boy who had often roamed the Northumbrian moors around the family estate.

George, who had been enjoying his ambitious dreams, was irritated and followed a few steps behind the others as they set off to find the nesting birds of prey.

However, when they reached the inland cliff where the falcons bred he was the first to display his enthusiasm over the pair of birds who were trying to conceal their four chicks in their nest.

The young cragsmen were as apt at raiding the falcons' nest as they were at collecting the gannets' eggs, and the Atkinsons were soon presented with a young bird each.

The chicks were still covered in white down, but the adult feathers of a steely blue-grey were starting to come through on their backs. They looked very vulnerable, with their disproportionately large feet and blinking eyes. The young St Kildans made a bed of their woollen scarves for them in one of the egg baskets and covered it with a basket lid.

'Are you sure it is necessary to remove them from the safety and comfort of their home?' asked the minister, who had not realised that the intention was to add the birds to the Atkinsons' collection of specimens.

'I am sure the parents will rear their two remaining young in a satisfactory manner,' said George, who was still too inexperienced to understand loss but was at least familiar with the nature of birds.

The minister, who had experience in both fields, could think of nothing to say.

As the party returned to the rocks where the boat had dropped them off, the St Kildans began waving and shouting to attract the attention of their kinsmen who were still drifting near Stac Lee. On hearing their calls the boatmen splashed up to the rock and received the party and the baskets of eggs. No one mentioned the two chicks, but their pathetic cries disturbed MacKenzie. He could not help but remember the slimy purple body that he himself had delivered from his unconscious wife just before the old crone who acted as midwife arrived to cut off its lifeline and smear the stump with fulmar oil.

Before returning to Village Bay the boat drew up at the base of Conachair. A couple of teenage boys were working away sixty feet above the surface of the sea. They were both standing on impossibly narrow ledges with long poles that looked much like strong fishing rods, twice the length of a man and with a horsehair noose at the end. George soon saw that they used the rods to fish for birds, pushing the noose over the heads of the unsuspecting, silly-looking guillemots. Sometimes the fowlers could catch two or more birds in one swoop. George could not help but laugh when the birds looked quite puzzled as their relatives disappeared around them, but few made any more active endeavour at escape than to move their head from side to side in order to avoid the pole, although some tried to push away the advancing noose with their bills. However, as their numbers dwindled, a few of them started to show signs of distrust and apprehension. Some of them took the trouble to shuffle away to the furthest extremity of the shelf and one or two even quit it altogether. The two boys had already gathered a large quantity of dead birds, which they had stuffed into nooks and crannies in the rock in anticipation of the boat. Now they started to throw the birds into the boat and the three passengers soon found themselves quite inundated by carcasses. The boat sat heavy in the sea as the six oarsmen started their laborious journey back towards Village Bay. The sun was still high in the west, but the light had changed and heralded the coming of another white night. One of the crew started to sing, his voice high and clear. He chanted a verse and the other men would answer in unison, thus establishing the rhythm of the oars.

'What are they singing?' asked Dick, who liked the sound.

'It's an *iorram*,' answered the minister. 'It's a

rowing song but I have also heard the women sing it while waulking the tweed.' He was quiet for a while and listened, then translated for the benefit of the two brothers:

My love, the hunter of the birds,
Earliest home across the wild channel;
And O, the ocean chant-man;
And O, the beautiful;
And O, the ocean chant-man.
I'd make white tweed for you,
Woollen thread as thick as rope;
My love, the mariner of the deep.

They were all quiet now and listened as the *iorram* brought the boat into harbour, the oars dipping miraculously in unison.

Lizzie heard the song of the returning boat. She had already set the table. She had picked sorrel to flavour the bird meat and had put some wild flowers in a vase on the table. They had no more wine, but she had blended some dandelion and primrose in the cold water that she had just drawn from the well. She prayed they would notice that she had made an effort. She hoped they would notice.

As they sat down to tea the men were exhausted and slightly bleached by the sun, the sea and the wind. They did not talk much but answered politely as Lizzie asked about the nature of their day. She would have liked to say something amusing or clever even, if only to bring the conversation out of the men and into the room, but she could not think of anything, and the meal, she had to admit, was rather dull.

As the Atkinsons lay in bed an hour later they *did* grumble confidentially to each other regarding the somewhat indifferent fare and fell asleep while the peregrine chicks died in their cage by the window.

The following morning a deputation of natives visited the manse to say that in return for more tobacco they would be happy to take the two *Sassenachs* to the Thumb Rock to see their climbing skills. It was also made clear that the gift of tobacco the previous day had been deemed too small and that the St Kildans were quite dissatisfied. George and Dick, determined to make it understood how much they intended to give, showed their remaining tobacco supply. The natives shook their heads and said it was too little, thinking perhaps that there was a hidden store in the gentlemen's bags. The bartering went on for a little while until George produced a bottle of whisky and served a glass apiece. This immediately changed the situation, and the natives became most obedient and generous for the rest of the day.

The rock that they called Stac Biorach, or the Thumb Rock, was the most awe-inspiring and

100

inaccessible stack in the archipelago. It was the ultimate test for any cragsman, and those who had managed to climb it were held in reverence within the community. It had taken its name from the fact that at no point would the climber find a grip larger than a thumb. Situated in the narrow sound between Hirta and Soay, the island in the north-west, it was flanked by a most impressive archway. Stac Biorach and the nearby cliffs of Soay could easily have been mistaken for the clashing rocks through which the bravest heroes of antiquity had once sailed.

As the boat drew near, the Atkinsons could tell that the cragsmen were losing heart. The minister felt it too, but he assured his friends that the St Kildans might be cunning and tricky barterers but they always kept their word. For a while the boat drifted at the base of the pinnacle as the natives folded their arms and chafed their bare feet against the deck boards. One man attempted to light his pipe. Dick had almost started to hope that nobody would risk the dangerous ascent when a fine, strong lad jumped up and said that it should never be said by strangers that they were inferior to their fathers in skill and courage, and that if anyone would accompany him he would lead the way. Another lad joined him. The minister named the boys as the cousins Donald and Finlay MacDonald. Donald quickly tied a rope around his waist and managed to jump on to the rock. Twice he lost his foothold and fell into the sea, but he was quickly hauled into the boat only to try to establish himself on the rock again. As soon as he was secure he called for Finlay to attach himself to the other end of the rope and helped him on to the rock. The two boys then started the ascent in the most remarkable way. Their bare hands and feet frisked the granite as their agile young bodies snaked their way towards the summit. Every now and again they would get hold of a guillemot in their way, break its neck and throw it down into the boat to the cheering of the crew. When they reached the top the boys were flushed with adrenalin and their broad smiles betrayed their pride. Finlay shouted down to his kinsmen to leave them up there on the stack for a couple of hours to kill some guillemots – Donald was courting a girl called Marion and he wanted to bring her the fattest rock-bird from Stac Biorach as a love token.

The group in the boat was getting weary in the swell and was only too happy to set off for nearby Soay. They soon landed on the south-east side, facing Hirta. Soay was not as steep as the other islands in the archipelago and hundreds of archaic-looking sheep grazed its grassy slopes. The three gentlemen set off on their own to explore the island, while the natives lit their pipes with the new supply of tobacco. They seemed hugely content and the two brothers could not help but suspect that the men were overly pleased with their bartering. On the east side of the island MacKenzie and the Atkinsons found a large colony of puffins which had burrowed themselves into the grassy slope or the occasional natural holes and crannies in the rock.

MacKenzie explained that each couple laid one egg in the depths of its burrow. If the egg was taken from them they produced one more and if this was taken they produced yet another one. But the puffins were hunted mainly for their fine feathers. The women would pluck the feathers of the dead puffin and either roast it for food or throw the carcass in a pit where it would putrefy and later be used to manure the barley fields. Sometimes the women would pluck a live puffin, and they swore that the feathers would grow back as white as snow – though MacKenzie had yet to see evidence of this miracle.

It was no wonder then that the puffins' calls which filled the air sounded so melancholy. 'Oh! Oh! Oh! Oh!' they called mournfully to anyone who was prepared to listen. They looked pitiful and sometimes rather comical, thought Dick, like a great assembly of drunken churchmen swaying back and forth on their webbed red feet, unable to decide where to put their weight. He mentioned this analogy to the minister, who laughed and said that in the current climate within the Church of Scotland the birds may well pass unnoticed.

George, in the meantime, had begun to throw

stones at the puffins. He cheered as he managed to knock three off balance at the same time. The birds around looked slightly disconcerted as their friends tumbled down the slopes like skittles, but at the last minute before they fell into the sea the fat little creatures took wing and skimmed easily away over the waves. Soon they were swarming the air like midges, and George, who had tired of his boyish game, suggested to his companions that they sit down to eat their lunch of cold mutton and hard-boiled birds' eggs. They passed the rest of the afternoon in a peaceful and agreeable manner, looking for the nests of stormy petrels.

On their return to Hirta they stopped to pick up the two brave cragsmen on Stac Biorach. As the boat drew up to the rock the boys started flinging great bundles of tied-up dead birds down into the sea for the boatmen to collect. The huge bundles bounced off the surface of the water in clouds of blood before settling and crimsoning the sea. Donald was beaming. He had found a most voluptuous bird, which he would pluck and present to Marion as an *Eun-creige* – a rock-fowl love token. There is sure to be a wedding soon, the natives joked with the minister. The latter explained the custom to the two brothers. 'I wish it was as easy as that to find a good wife,' said George. 'I was just about to say that they go to an awful lot of trouble to secure their partners,' said Dick, who suffered slightly from vertigo. 'None but the brave deserves the fair,' the minister remarked with a wink to George.

George, who was beginning to find that the slow rowing and splashing were grating on his nerves, let his mind trail off. He was thinking of the skills of the cragsmen. He had become conscious of his own insignificance and littleness as he had watched the two young men suspended and crawling amongst the cliffs. At times it had been difficult to make them out amongst the chaos of rock and sea, as if they were truly part of the elements. He knew that he could never be one of them.

As they reached the beach in Village Bay George was met by the captain of the crew he had hired in Rodel. 'We must be off tomorrow, sir,' said the sailor. 'Why so?' asked George. 'Why, sir, if the wind was to change direction, we might be kept here for months.' George, sensing that the crew may not have had a particularly sumptuous time living amongst the natives, tried to convince the captain to stay on a few days longer, but he could see the sense of the plan as none of them wanted to get caught on the island. After a short discussion it was decided that they would leave the same evening after tea, while the westerly breeze was still fair.

After they had eaten and carefully packed all their specimens in crates and baskets, George, who fancied himself to be a man of words and who had been humbled by his time on the island, sat down to write in his notebook:

> *Nothing can be more interesting, or more instructive and ennobling, to the mind of man, than the contemplation of the works of his Maker, which are daily before us, but when scenes of such immensity and grandeur present themselves, that even imagination has not pictured them, the soul must indeed be unsubdued which does not bow with admiration and awe.*

The MacKenzies followed the brothers to the landing rocks. The evening was mild and the westerly was dying slowly. George noted that Mrs MacKenzie seemed downcast. Perhaps we should have made more of an effort to talk to her, he thought. It must be awfully lonely for her without anyone but her husband to speak to. She came alongside him and smiled. 'Would you do me the favour of posting this letter when you get to the mainland? It would mean a great deal to me,' she said intensely. 'It is for my sister Annie in Paisley,' she added flatly as if she was reading the address out loud.

'Of course, madam, it would be an honour.' He looked at her and was surprised that he had not seen her beauty before. Perhaps he had not seen her at all, he realised. 'I wish you good fortune with the birth of your child,' he said, and added lightly, 'Perhaps it will provide nice company.'

'Company, sir?'

'It must be lonely here at times?' he suggested.

Now that he was leaving she could admit it. 'Yes,' she said. 'Yes, at times it is.' She glanced quickly at her husband, who was out of earshot.

They left then, as they had to, and as George called his farewells in Gaelic like the minister had instructed him there was much emotion amongst the islanders as one after the other they shook the hands of the naturalist brothers.

As the little ship set off on the failing wind George looked back for a long time towards the landing rocks where Mr and Mrs MacKenzie remained, standing a little apart.

About half a mile south of the manse, at the base of Oiseval, was the Point of Coll. No particular feature marked this place, but it was relatively sheltered from the prevailing winds and, of all the promontories on Hirta, it was the one closest to the Long Isle. From the manse a faint path, trampled by conformist sheep rather than humans, led past the barn where the natives stored the feathers for the taxman's visits. The path then joined the head dyke, which separated the enclosed land from the outlying lands, and once the dyke stopped abruptly at the end of the headland the path hesitated and meandered for a while until it gained confidence and struggled across the traverse of the steep slope. At this point the path gave access to the sea. It was said that the point had got its name from Colla MacLeod, one of the laird's men, who, sometime in the distant past, had fought with a MacDonald from Uist over the lordship of St Kilda. The two men agreed that the one who got to the island first would gain possession of it. They set out in their *currachs* and raced the sixty miles across the Atlantic from the Sound of Harris. The race was well matched, but once the two boats got in sight of the island the Uist oarsmen were a few strokes ahead. Threatened with defeat, Colla MacLeod drew his sword and promptly cut off his hand and threw it on to the island. It landed on the point of Coll, and the MacLeods, who claimed that they were the first to lay a hand on the island, have been the rightful owners of the island ever since. Another, and perhaps more likely, story was that a man named Coll had once died at the point. It was generally agreed that living at the point was impossible, whereas losing your life there would be easy enough. You needed courage, rather than a strong rope, to clamber down towards the sharp rocks that emerged from the sea here to join the island.

Young boys would sometimes come here to fish, occasionally catching an unfortunate herring or a blue-ribboned mackerel surfacing too close to Village Bay. Mr MacKenzie, the minister, would often come here to be alone. He enjoyed practising his climbing skills on the boulders, imitating the young men of the island. But most of all he enjoyed being out of sight of the hamlet and the manse. He would sit with his back against the sheltering rock and read, scribble notes for his sermons or just think about the nature of things. This is where he found himself on a particular morning a few weeks after the Atkinsons had left the island. Across the bay on the island of Dùn he could just make out some of the men, women and dogs catching puffins. The men would place a snare with multiple nooses on the ground and wait until enough birds had stepped into the trap before pulling the rope and snaring as many as ten or fifteen at a time. In the meantime the women and the dogs would coordinate their efforts to extract the puffins from their burrows. MacKenzie had seen the women reaching into the holes to grab a bird which was retreating as far into his burrow as he could while uttering the most heartbreaking sound. The women would always win, and as soon as the bird had been retrieved they would snap its neck and tuck the carcass into their belt.

The tide was low and the smell of seaweed and barnacles drying in the warm July sun was comforting to this man who had been born by the sea. He felt at ease, perhaps even peaceful. He thought about his child about to be born and about his wife, whose kind face was well worn and familiar by now, yet still beautiful at times. His congregation was increasingly attentive. He had also noticed that the islanders would often turn to him to settle their disputes and affairs. He remembered George Atkinson's warning about getting too involved in the souls of his parishioners. But authority was part of his duty. He had been chosen to serve as a father to these primitive but cheerful beings. He shuddered, not altogether from discomfort, at the task that lay ahead of him.

A dead black-backed gull was floating close to the shore. Its gas-filled body bobbed lightly on the choppy waves. At a closer look it seemed to lack wings. Neil MacKenzie sat up. Had this bird flown too close to the sun? He let out a short laugh at the symmetry of his thoughts. Slowly easing his way forward, clambering on his hands and feet like a crab, the minister balanced towards the floating gull. When he had reached the rock closest to the carcass he stretched out his leg and caught the bird by the heel of his boot. The stench was no worse than he was used to from the *clachan*, but as he prodded the bird with his pen he withdrew in horror. It seemed obvious, although unlikely, that the huge gull had been tortured to death; its eyes had been gouged out and its wings had been tied to its body with a strip of sheep leather before it had been thrown into the sea to drown. This was most certainly the result of one of their pagan superstitions, thought the minister, as a shiver ran down his back. He had often eavesdropped on the folk tales and ancient songs that reflected the superstitions and rituals of the natives' mythology. The minister was suddenly cold. He feared that there was a layer of existence on the island that he could not get to: a dimension that was deliberately hidden from him. He had charted all the place names and translated them into English in an effort to rob them of their threatening magic. He had tried to stamp out the St Kildans' vernacular way of explaining the world and replace it with the Gospel. Ah, was this tortured bird a sign of his failure? His distressed mind invested the omen with unhealthy significance. Could it be that the Devil was at work amongst his congregation? His responsibility towards them was greater than ever. It was his duty to eliminate all witchcraft and secure the island for the Almighty. Disgusted and terrified, he lifted the dead gull by its still-powerful bill and started to climb the rocks back up to the path. His mind was racing and sweat dripped down his back between his shoulder blades as he hurried towards the manse. There was no time to lose; he was carrying barbarism in his hands. He had never been so close to pagan sorcery before and could feel a stir of excitement in his bones; at last he could confront the natives with evidence of their own black magic!

Lizzie looked up from her sewing as her husband stormed into the manse with the terrible bird in his hands. She gasped, and the dog they called Dog winced and retreated into a corner. 'Ha!'

cried the minister. 'Even the dog of the manse recoils at such unholy conjuring! He has got more Christian spirit than the natives of this island.'

'Calm down, my love. You will upset the baby inside me with such wild talk,' said his wife, who had reclaimed her equilibrium after the departure of the gentlemen brothers.

'This,' cried the minister, 'is the result of demonology!' The bird shook in his grip. 'I will find out what it means. They will not keep this kind of secret from me. I will call an extra service tonight when the fowlers return.'

'Yes, yes,' she said soothingly while rising heavily from her chair. She had to steady herself against the windowsill as she was really quite large at the end of her second pregnancy. 'I will bring you a cup of tea,' she said to his back as he stormed into his study, bird in hand.

Lizzie had never seen her husband like this before. It worried her slightly, but at the same time she felt strangely suspended. This huge body was no longer her own, and the last couple of weeks she had had a sensation that she perceived her life from a distance, calmly and objectively. So she brought her husband his cup of tea with a steady hand, and when evening fell and the fowlers returned she wore her best bonnet to church in an act of support and loyalty to his cause.

As the St Kildans assembled in the cool kirk the summer evening reigned outside. A bumblebee buzzed and bounced against a lancet window and the tide was swelling in the bay. The sweet peas that Mrs MacKenzie had planted in the garden scented the kirk air like incense from the east, mingling with the wild honeysuckle which spurted silently from cracks and crevices. Soon, however, a smell of fulmar oil and sweet sweat like bad carnations filled the room as the natives gathered in their summer best. The women had undone their waistbands and wore their gowns loose, flowing to the ground. The married women wore their *mutchs*, the frilly white muslin caps that indicated their status, under their tartan shawls. The men had cleaned their hands and faces, and their hair, which had been released from under their filthy caps, had been forced into submission with the aid of some unknown concoction, whose origin Lizzie did not want to contemplate. She was sitting at the head of the church next to the pulpit, watching the faces of her strange neighbours. She recognised them and knew all their names by now, but she still could not communicate with them. They in turn looked at her with unveiled curiosity. Lizzie felt awkward and clumsy and she was no longer pleased about her bonnet; she worried that the cluster of velvet pansies attached to the hatband might be slightly too garish. Her gaze fell on Marion Gilles, whose daughter Catherine had died of the eight-day illness at the end of March. The young woman looked pale and drawn. A small bouquet of

St John's wort was fastened to her shawl by a crude brooch. The flowers were past their prime and a few yellow petals had fallen and littered the woman's dress. Next to Mrs Gilles, tightly holding her hand, sat Ann MacCrimmon, who was expecting her first child at the age of forty. Lizzie could feel the older woman searching her face and reluctantly she raised her head to meet her eyes. She regretted it immediately. Her own eyes told too much. Exposed, and unable to withdraw her gaze, she felt a sudden affinity that went beyond sympathy and gender. And as she looked into Ann MacCrimmon's eyes she knew that the bird's death had been necessary. She did not understand how or why, but the act itself was not threatening or alien. Lizzie felt now that of course she had known all along. This sacrifice could only be matched by the fear and foreboding that colour a woman's dreams and thoughts as a new soul is about to break out of her body.

At that moment the minister, who had been interrogating the *maor*, Donald MacKinnon, about the bird incident, entered the kirk from the passage behind the pulpit. His face was tired and saddened as he looked out over the congregation that he had begun to love. Silence fell over the rough timber pews and naked feet came to rest on the earthen floor. Some thought they heard their minister sigh.

The Rev. Neil MacKenzie turned the pages of

114

his Gaelic bible on the pulpit and read, his voice dry and intense:

> *Thou shalt not make unto thee any graven image, or any likeness of any thing that is in heaven above, or that is in the earth beneath, or that is in the water under the earth: thou shalt not bow down thyself to them, nor serve them: for I the Lord thy God am a jealous God, visiting the iniquity of the fathers upon the children unto the third and fourth generation of them that hate Me; and showing mercy unto thousands of them that love Me and keep My commandments.*

He looked up and his eyes rested briefly on Ann MacCrimmon and Marion Gilles, who sat huddled together, before he resumed his sermon:

> *You will recognise the second commandment from Exodus. It has come to my knowledge that there are people in your midst who believe that superstition may save your newborn children from the convulsive fits which often take their lives within eight days of their coming into this world. This plague, which haunts our island, does indeed seem to be a cruel trick of nature.*
>
> *But I tell you now that if you want to change your providence you must take heed of the heresy of superstition and image-worship. Our*

human nature is as prone to this sin as a river to run to the sea. It concerns us, therefore, to resist this sin. The plague of heresy is very infectious and it is my advice to you to avoid all occasions of this sin.

You must avoid superstition, which is a bridge that leads over to Rome – to popery and idolatry. Superstition is bringing any ceremony, fancy, or innovation into God's worship which He never appointed. It is provoking God, because it reflects much upon His honour, as if He were not wise enough to appoint the manner of His own worship. Superstition is Devil-worship!

A sharp intake of breath was heard from the congregation, and Lizzie wondered what her husband had said.

There are evil forces in existence that seek to destroy our souls and sanity. I see how you suffer from the childlessness that afflicts this island. You are isolated amid a hostile ocean, and your very existence in this place increases the spiritual vulnerability of your Christian lives. God holds His hand over those who suffer – His grip never fails – but do you honestly think that God will care for you in this secluded spot when you turn from Him to superstition and witchcraft?

Hear what Paul saith to the Corinthians:

'The natural person does not accept the things of the Spirit of God, for they are folly to him, and he is not able to understand them because they are spiritually discerned.'

You must not be like these heathens who do not understand the glory of God. You must follow the righteous path. You must work hard and pray sincerely from the depths of your hearts. You must strive for purity and adhere to cleanliness – not just of the soul but of the body – for uncleanness is an evil that brings disease and pain.

He ended the sermon with a short prayer. The parishioners clenched their hands tightly and bowed their heads in embarrassed submission to the Lord they were only just beginning to understand.

Later that evening Mr and Mrs MacKenzie sat by the table in the manse. A bruised sky had crept in over the island and a soft rain was falling on the mustard plant that stretched below the open window. Mrs MacKenzie was sewing a new waist-coat for her husband, who was reading from Adam Smith's *Moral Sentiments*. A couple of candles were burning on the mantelpiece, spreading a thin carpet of slow light across the floor. He put the book down and listened to the rain.

'The dread of pain makes us selfish. It is a natur-ally directed instinct to care first of all for ourselves and those we love. But those instincts do not foster a peaceful society. Do they not understand that it is the business of God, not man, to ensure universal happiness?'

Lizzie assumed he was talking to her. 'Eight out of ten children born on this island die of the cramps within eight days of their birth – as long as we are at ease we cannot begin to understand the hardships of these mothers!' She had drawn strength from his weakness, but realised too late that he had not wanted her to answer his question.

He looked at her in surprise. Perhaps he did not know his wife; the thought had not crossed his mind before.

'It might be good to be able to suffer along with my subjects,' he agreed, but remained unconvinced of the benefit of identifying with the emotions of others. At least he was magnanimous, a guider of spirits and soother of souls. 'Do they understand that I have compassion for their misery?'

'I am sure they will understand,' she answered, as no one else could ease his mind, 'but you must give them time. Your sermon will have made them ashamed of their actions – I could not understand its meaning, of course, but judging from your tone it was very harsh.' She hesitated but as he did not object she continued, 'They are impressionable and they seemed greatly upset by your reprimands. Perhaps next time you should focus more on the blessings of the Gospel?' She did not want him to worry, but she felt a certain loyalty to Mrs MacCrimmon, whose eyes had shared their secrets with hers. She wished she could hold her husband's head between her palms and stroke his temples, but the act would have been too large for the small room on this evening. Instead she continued stitching her love into his waistcoat. She made an effort to make every stitch equally perfect, although the light was poor.

After a while she yawned and said she was going to bed. He nodded and smiled. Everything was all right then, although he wished that he could have remained a while longer looking at his wife sewing in the blue night.

Two weeks later Mrs MacKenzie gave birth to twin girls. It all happened as it should. The old crone from the village was called to cut the umbilical cords from the tiny bodies and smear the stumps with bird grease. The first to be born was called Margaret. She seemed to be the stronger of the two. Jane slithered out of her mother in close succession, much to the surprise of the minister, who assisted at the birth. The old woman wrapped the girls in linen towels, but rather poorly as there was only enough linen for one baby. Lizzie was concerned that the girls were not washed before being wrapped but was too exhausted to do anything about it just then. She lay back on the pillows with a silent daughter in each arm.

She could not help worrying about them, but soon they started feeding and she laughed with relief at their swollen lips and tiny hands that fumbled blindly at her breasts. The minister watched the scene of nativity as the gay sun fell through the window on to the blue-veined heads of his daughters. Their vulnerability was too great for him and he drew the curtains to shield them from the intruding light. But his wife smiled at him and said that the light was good for them, it would make them stronger. MacKenzie felt too large, his hand as it held a tiny foot seemed grotesque and he wondered how he was going to be able to keep his family safe.

In the end, of course he could not. On the fourth day Jane gave up suckling, and after another day Margaret followed suit. They did not cry much but lay breathing with their eyes closed, head to foot in the pretty cot with the sprig of juniper carved by the workmen from Dunvegan. Lizzie tried to pour warm cow's milk blended with a little whisky into their mouths, but after another day their gums were clenched together and it was impossible to get anything down their throats. Soon their bodies were ridden by convulsive fits. Wave upon wave of cramps would toss the girls as if they were riding out a great storm at sea. The little bodies seemed to struggle against excessive torments until, on the eighth day, their strength was exhausted. Jane, who was the weaker, died first, in one breath, one moment, one life.

Margaret struggled on for another three hours before she too gave up and joined her sister, just after midday on the sixth day of August.

Perhaps now I will be able to pray, Lizzie thought, and maybe they will be saved.

The minister went to the Point of Coll. He shouted soundlessly into the waves, and his knees were bloodied on the rocks as he bit at his prayers: 'Lord, why did you have to take Margaret and Jane? Why did you take their brother, Nathaniel? I continually ask You forgiveness for my sins. I serve You as faithfully as I can. My children were innocent, Lord. Do not let them suffer for the sins of their parents. I am weak and unworthy, I know, and the children were the fruits of my lust. But their souls were white and pure. Did You not see their beauty? What suffering do I need to endure in order to redeem myself for William's death? Would not one death have been enough?'

He realised this was not the way to speak to the God he had chosen to serve, and he slumped wretchedly on the rocks. He wanted the world to make sense, and as he lay there, with the waves sighing miserably around him, it occurred to him that God wanted him to suffer with the islanders and become their equal. Had he not told Lizzie only a few weeks ago, after the incident with the tortured bird, that it might be good to suffer with his subjects? He shuddered in admiration of God's omnipotence. He had been too proud, that must be it! He had not been humble enough, and God had exercised justice. It was cruelly perfect, and the minister thanked his Lord for revealing this mystery to him.

A group of women had gathered outside the manse as the minister returned. They looked at his trousers, which were torn and bloodied at the knees, and the shirt which was ruffled and dirty, but MacKenzie had known the lowest depth and could not be ashamed.

Mrs MacKenzie was sitting impassively by the cradle. Somebody had covered the girls so that their faces, frozen and deformed in the last, monstrous cramps of the eight-day illness, could not be seen. Marion Gilles was standing by Lizzie's side stroking her hair, but the latter did not seem to notice. She looked up as her husband entered the room. 'I want them to have a proper burial,' she said factually. 'With a coffin each,' she added. He looked at her with greater compassion than his heart could afford to waste. 'Of course I would like that too, but you know there is no wood on the island,' he answered carefully. 'I don't care – I will find some myself if I have to!' Lizzie cried, and stood up. Marion Gilles looked questioningly at the minister, who said a few words to her in Gaelic. She nodded sadly and left the room. Mr MacKenzie put his arms around his struggling wife to calm her. 'Why?' she cried softly now against his shoulder. 'I don't know, my love,' he said, because he could not tell her the truth, 'but God will answer our prayers.' He knew that sounded weak but could not yet admit to her that the children had died because of his shortcomings. 'I want the coffins,' she demanded childishly. 'Yes, yes,' he soothed her, 'but our loss is not greater than the loss of the other parents on the island, and there just isn't any timber that can be spared for coffins.' Then, as if it would somehow make a difference to her grief, he added, 'I will ask the taxman to bring some when we see him next.' She knew of course that he was right. She also knew that her grief could not be important – that she was insignificant in all this.

A couple of the local women, including Marion Gilles, came back that evening to wash and shroud the twins. Lizzie managed to smile gratefully at them and wondered if she would have found the right words to express her feelings if she had known their language. The women served her tea brewed with St John's wort and she slept exhausted through the night. As she got up to fetch some water from the well the following morning the door struck something as she tried to open it. She pushed carefully and stepped on to the porch. There on the stone step in front of her lay two small wooden coffins. She knelt down to examine them. They were quite crude and of varying dimensions and they had been put together from odd bits of wood; the sides were partly constructed from a barrel and the lids contained fragments of washed-out driftwood whitened by salt. One of the coffins contained the wooden sole of a fisherman's boot, and the other one part of a wooden plate.

Lizzie remained on her knees. She recognised this generous gesture by the St Kildans whom she had tried so hard to avoid getting to know. A group of children were peeping around the corner of the manse, shuffling and hushing. 'Did you make these?' she asked with tears in her eyes. 'Thank you, oh, thank you so much – they are truly beautiful!'

The funeral service was brief. All the St Kildans – except for Mrs MacCrimmon, whose labours had started – turned up to the unmarked grave site as the makeshift coffins which sheltered the tiny bodies of Margaret and Jane were lowered into the ground. As her husband offered the souls of their daughters to God Lizzie thought of the tortured gull. Her husband had told her that the women on the island hated the black-backed gull as they somehow connected it with the death of their children. The women would often take a gull's egg and suck out its contents, only to replace it so that the gull would roost on an empty shell for the rest of the summer. Lizzie, still struggling to believe in the God who had taken her girls away, wished that she too could free her mind and create a mythology of her own like the St Kildan women had done. She wished that she could find some sense to her situation.

The morning after the burial she rose early and

dressed in her plain blue dress and straw bonnet. She packed a basket with some bread and a few apples. MacKenzie was astounded. 'Where are you going?' He needed her close and unchanged.

'I am going to visit Mrs MacCrimmon – she must have had her child by now,' she answered determinedly.

'But you don't know where she lives.' He was dumbfounded. 'I will take you there if you like.'

'Thank you, dear, I would rather go on my own.' She was out the door before he could say anything more. The sea mist was rolling in over the island like the smoke of a spent battle. Soon it closed around her until she walked in a void. The fog muffled all sound and she was completely on her own. There was only one single element and she had entered it as if it were a liminal place, a place of transition from one world to another. She knew that she was tempting fate, but she was not frightened; she could still make out the path to the village under her feet. This is where I belong, she thought. My heart broke and split in two equal parts for my girls. Nothing will ever be the same again; I will never be what I was. I have shed a layer of my soul like a snake and I must be naked until I find new life – until I can bring new birth. This island is my home now, and I must enter its cycle where everything comes again, light and dark, storm and stillness, life and death, again and forever. Shapes were moving in the fog; cold, damp hands were stroking her cheeks and her brow. As she looked up she saw the forms of her death children walking beside her. They had grown up, and she was grateful to them for showing themselves as they would have become.

When she reached the *clachan* she put out her free hand to follow a wall until she heard voices and walked in their direction. A dog which did not recognise her barked, catching the attention of two men a couple of yards ahead of her whose features she could only just make out. 'MacCrimmon?' she asked softly so as not to break the spell of the mist. The two men, their fair hair curled into pelt by the moisture in the air, looked at her in astonishment. 'Ann MacCrimmon?' she asked again, and showed the basket in her hand. One of the men indicated to her to follow him and led her to the wooden door of a nearby dwelling. Mrs MacKenzie stopped for a moment to gather herself. She nervously tucked some staying hair under the bonnet and knocked on the door. She could hear no answer from within so she opened the door on to the dark passage. The stench was more than she could bear and she took a step back. However, she had not come unprepared and she pulled out a handkerchief dabbed in lavender water which she had kept up the sleeve of her dress. With the handkerchief pressed over her nose and mouth and with the basket held out in front of her like a shield, she stooped to enter the house. When she reached the dark byre at the end of the passage somebody caught her arm and helped her across the *tallan* into the room where a weak fire was burning in the pit on the floor, casting strange shadows around the rough stone walls. Mrs MacKenzie pulled the handkerchief from her face and tucked it under the neckline of her dress where she could still smell it. It was hard to say who was more shocked by the situation, the guest who had never been in one of the native houses before or the hosts who had never before received a lady in their midst. Mr MacCrimmon, who was the person who had helped Lizzie into the room, was the first to come to terms with the unusual situation. He greeted her formally in Gaelic, and Lizzie, who could think of no other way to reply, bowed gently. 'I have come with a gift for the mother and child,' she said, and showed the basket. A number of people were seated on the floor of the house; Lizzie recognised Catriona and Niall, two of the children of Mr MacCrimmon's first wife, who had died in childbirth ten years previously. Marion Gilles was there, along with a few other young married women. Ann MacCrimmon was sitting close to the fire with a baby in her arms. The baby was so new to the world that it could barely open its eyes. Lizzie was suddenly shy and blushed, but Mrs MacCrimmon smiled at her and somebody pulled a chest up to the fire for Lizzie to sit on. She sat down, grateful not to have to squat on the floor which was covered in all sorts of horrors. Mrs MacCrimmon showed her the baby, a little boy, and said his name, Iain. She shook her head sadly and made a gesture to indicate that he was not feeding properly. Lizzie did not reply as there was nothing for her to say, but she sat quietly listening to the soot dripping from the damp ceiling. More than anything else she wanted this boy to survive, and she could feel that the women who had assembled in the room had all forgotten their separate griefs and pains; they were all praying wordlessly to their own gods and spirits for the survival of this golden boy. For every baby who survived was a gift to the community; every child who lived ensured the continuation of the way of life as they knew it; and every mortality – although often accepted as providence – was a threat to their future and a manifestation of the curse that seemed to be endemic to their island.

It was late afternoon when Lizzie left the vigil for the boy who was to die at dawn. She could not bear to see the cramps and convulsions again. The mist had cleared, and as she got home she could see that her husband had been waiting for her. He was sitting at the table in his shirtsleeves with his head in his hands but rose quickly as she came through the door. He stood looking at her, at the tired face which was familiar and kind. 'What?' she said, exhausted and irritated by his muteness, but he could not put words to his feeling – how could he ever find the right words for those feelings? – he could only hold her, which he did; in one step, one movement, he held her hard against his chest, but he was soft and so was she as she felt his heart against her own. They stood together for a long time, swaying slowly from side to side, as their bodies slotted together and they were able to comfort each other in spite of their separate pains.

Iain was buried three days later. A sheep was slaughtered, barley was ground and bread was baked while women came and went, watching and keening over the body of the dead boy. As evening fell a few young men went into the burial ground to dig the grave while some others were sent off to find a broad turf to cover it. There was no wood for this coffin so the baby was shrouded and carried high along the course of the sun around the *clachan*. Three times did the procession encircle the houses and gardens before they entered the graveyard. Mrs MacKenzie was standing by her husband's side. It was not the custom to read the funerary sermon by the open grave; the service would take place in the kirk on the following Sabbath. Lizzie looked into the dark hole in the ground and saw that the bottom of the grave had been lined with something white. She took a couple of steps forward to see better and saw that somebody had put a single wing of a white swan in the grave. She gasped and looked up at her husband. He looked her straight in the eyes; it is all right, he seemed to say, let it happen in this way. She was relieved. The baby was lowered on to the wing. It was one of the most beautiful things she had ever seen, Lizzie thought. The tiny bundle looked like a perfect angel, and as the men started filling the grave Lizzie had to look away, it seemed so brutal that such whiteness should be soiled. Her husband had told her that because of the frequency of infant deaths, the St Kildans saw their island plague as providence, as an inevitable part of life. But as she glanced quickly back into the filling grave she knew that these ghost children, who would never be kissed and cared for, were mourned and loved just as hopelessly in spite of their fate. Their spirits were forever there, in the lap of a wing or the ripple of water.

Once the grave was filled and the turf placed on top, everyone sat down on the grass or on nearby stones and shared a meal of mutton and bread as the sun set in the west and the warm August night lowered its blue shadow over Village Bay.

Back in the manse MacKenzie said to his wife, 'I have been thinking that perhaps we should get a maid, a young woman who speaks English so that you can have some company – what do you think?'

Mrs MacKenzie had got used to coping on her own and did not think their small household needed a maid. 'I am not sure . . .' she replied hesitantly.

'Well, I will ask the taxman if he can recommend some suitable young woman from the

130

mainland.' He was quite set on the idea now and pleased by his own generosity.

Later Lizzie was lying sleepless in bed. Her husband was breathing heavily; she watched his upper lip slacken and shudder like a sail driven by a trade wind. She liked to watch him sleep – he seemed more vulnerable then and she could believe that she belonged to him. Her eyes scanned his face and his strong shoulders, which were white as snow below the line where his shirt cut off the tan. It was very hot in the room and she could not lie still. There was a great restlessness inside her. The night was soft as fur outside the window, and the darkness seemed to pull at her. She got out of bed and threw a woollen shawl around her shoulders. She stood for a while looking out the window before she left the room, her bare feet silent on the carpet. Outside the thick night was starry, but the barley moon was still hiding behind the massive bulk of Conachair. Lizzie breathed in all the heavy scents of the night. She walked dreamily through the dewy grass; the fresh clover and buttery cowslips washed her feet and shed their last petals between her toes as she descended towards the beach. The white sand there would soon be sieved away by the autumn storms, but for now it was cool and soft under her feet. Lizzie looked out across the blank disc of the bay. There was something strange about its deep darkness. She looked harder until her gaze floated on the surface where a faint sparkling like a million tiny diamonds seemed to reflect the firmament. It was as if the Pleiades had sunk into the sea and were looking back up at the sky. She picked up a pebble and dropped it into the shallows – an explosion of fluorescent brilliance expanded and flickered through the ripples. 'Oh!' she exhaled and stepped back. She looked around and listened – the village was quiet and dark; she was all alone with this miracle. Carefully she hitched up her white nightgown and stepped into the water. Her feet lit up like St Peter's – she proceeded further out. A jellyfish glided past, shining like a green corn moon or a drowned meteor. Lizzie stared at its suspended glowing sphere in awe. Suddenly she knew what she had to do – she needed to be washed in this light – she needed to be enlightened by the life force that illuminated it. Quickly she pulled off her shawl and nightgown and bundled them safely on to a rock. Naked, with her loose hair flowing down her back, she stepped further into the cold water, carefully avoiding sharp rocks and stones with barnacles. She stretched her arms on the surface and dragged them like wands through the white-green glare. Her whole body was outlined by the starry light; she spread her limbs like a giant starfish and floated on her back as if carried by the Milky Way.

Mr MacKenzie, who had woken up as his wife left their bed, was watching her from the dark shadows of the landing rock. He knew, of course, about the plankton which lit up the late summer seas, but the scene in front of him was still unworldly. He could not take his eyes off his wife as she swam calmly and quietly in a halo of bright light. He was not sure if he was witnessing vice or a mystery. Suddenly she stood, illuminated, and waded towards the beach with her back half turned to him. She lifted her arms to wring the saltwater out of her hair, and her husband watched with his fist pressed into his mouth as a few flakes of light clung to the glimmering pearls of her vertebrae. She turned to fetch her nightgown from the rock, her hard nipples standing out from her dark silhouette. She dried herself quickly on the shawl and slipped back into the white linen gown. Mr MacKenzie let out his breath. Was this his wife – this woman who glided like a bright angel over the dark sand? He stretched soundlessly and hurried back to the manse. His eyes were misty with shame and humiliation for this lurid desire which had overcome him – this passion for an unknown and otherworldly woman. A woman he had never known.

Lizzie felt clean and calm and she was once again convinced of her youth. She had reclaimed a place of her own, and by becoming individual she was once again human. Her teeth were chattering in the cold and she hurried back to the manse. As she slipped under the sheets her husband turned to her and kissed the salt from her freezing lips. His hands slipped under her damp nightgown and rubbed heat back into her body until she shivered from more than the cold. She clung to his lips and drank him down. As the August moon rose over the summit of Conachair the rekindled flare of love brought them together in sharp pain and hot, sweet beauty.

Later, as he slept, spent and fulfilled, Lizzie listened to the whispers of all the days of light and darkness that lay ahead of them on this island.

PART III

AUGUST 1834 – CHANGE

The little girl was turning slowly in a falling whiteness. She looked down at her feet, which were covered in a drift of light. All around her soft frost was lifting and falling, whirling and dancing in the breeze. This was very different from the world the child had known so far – a world of contrasts and seasons – light and dark, even and perpendicular, silent and roaring. Here was only one aspect but the girl was not afraid as feathers of snowy white settled on her dress and turned hot summer to winter. Wonder had only just awakened in her along with the recognition of beauty, the power of expression and the ability to move freely, to run down a hill through budding cowslips or climb the high back of her father's armchair. If there were sounds around her she did not hear them: the world was as silent as a storm in a fairy-tale snow globe. Only she understood that this was something important – that this was all at once and nothing at all.

There was a movement nearby and then there were arms around her as somebody stooped to pick her up. Noise came back to her as if she had surfaced from under water. There was light and joy as she went up through the air which was thick and white and made her want to sneeze. As she was carried away the child buried her face in the warm, musky smell of a girl who was turning into a young woman. She was perfectly happy.

It was the third week of August and the fulmar harvest was at its peak. Women and children were plucking tens of thousands of birds in order to salt them into barrels for the winter. Bundles of live birds, tied together and awaiting their fate, hung from hooks on the walls. Feathers covered the hamlet and made it look like a perfect water-colour of a wintery Alpine landscape.

'Betty, Betty, where are you, girl? Hurry. I will be late!' A woman's voice cut through the babble of birds.

'Yes, ma'am. Sorry, ma'am. I took Eliza to see all the feathers,' cried the young woman breath-lessly as she was still carrying the child in her arms.

'For pity's sake, Betty, don't call me ma'am – it makes me feel old!' cried the woman, who could not get used to having a servant.

'Yes, Mrs MacKenzie, I am sorry.' Betty managed to look rather downcast, but she was not sorry; she was a cheerful girl and rebuke ran off her like water off the wings of a solan goose.

Mrs MacKenzie laughed. 'I am sure you managed to see young Calum MacDonald while Eliza played with the feathers?'

Betty blushed and looked at her naked feet. 'Calum was trying to teach Dog to sniff for puffins.'

'Ah, was he now . . . ? Well, I am sure that was not very successful,' Mrs MacKenzie muttered mockingly, and looked down on the dog, which pricked up its ears on hearing the name which had not really been given to it. Dog looked slightly bewildered – seabirds frightened him, and he placed his paws delicately wherever he went.

'Oh, Mrs MacKenzie, everyone is so frightfully excited, what with the fulmar harvest and the ship and the gentlefolk and all!' Betty, it seemed, was most excited of all. She had never used any form of the word *frightful* before, but she thought it was appropriate under the circumstances.

Mrs MacKenzie smiled at the maid and kissed her daughter Eliza, who was nearly two years old. Eliza's younger brother, James Bannatyne, had been born in December the previous year. He was sitting like a tiny Buddha on a blanket in the manse garden, pulling the petals of a meadowsweet in clumsy tufts. His chubby hands continued to tear at the soft flowers. The boy had been entrusted with a name which demanded something of him; it suggested that greatness was expected of him. He was the firstborn boy in the family, but throughout his life, as his many brothers and sisters were born and grew into single beings, he would have the feeling that there had been one before him against whom he was constantly measured.

He listened carefully for hints that might reveal the secret to his origin and purpose, and as he grew and matured he searched for his lost brother in the lines around his mother's mouth and behind the grief that would sometimes show in the dark depths of his father's eyes.

Both children were remarkably healthy, and life in the manse was busy and noisy where only a few years back it had been still and silent. Lizzie would often stand over the children's beds at night and listen to their breathing – Eliza's was barely audible, whereas James Bannatyne's came in little staccato sighs. Soft and untroubled dreams would pass over their sleeping faces like the midday breeze across the sea. At such times she would occasionally be overcome by the familiar terror which had possessed her throughout the pregnancies – the fear that the fate of the island had somehow marked the growing life in her womb. While carrying Eliza her nerves had been so raw that she could not sleep or eat for days and nights on end. Back then MacKenzie had had little patience with her. Once he'd said, 'The baby will live, Lizzie, you must have faith.' 'But how can you be so certain?' she had asked quickly, lacking the breath to amplify the words. 'Oh, I am redeemed, my dear. There is nothing to worry about. Just remember to pray.' He had laughed as if she was a child unable to take instructions, and stooped to kiss her on the forehead. But despite herself she had felt her body stiffen.

Blushing, she had wished him away, for he suddenly repulsed her.

The taxman had brought young Betty Scott from the laird's fishing station at Lochinver a couple of years previously. The fisheries had been established to accommodate the Highlanders who had been cleared from the lands of the Duchess of Sutherland. Those who refused to take up the new livelihood were forced to emigrate. But soon the fishing stations were overpopulated and there was poverty more miserable than ever before. The laird's factor tried to control the population increase by deciding who could marry whom, and when. It was the factor who had decided that Betty should go to St Kilda, and Betty's father had agreed. She had no future in Lochinver, and Betty was a practical girl – a job was a job, even though it meant that she would not see her family and friends for a long time. The girl, who spoke both Gaelic and English, was easy-going and strong, and Lizzie had grown very fond of her. Her features betrayed her Highland ancestry. Her soft ginger hair and chubby cheeks had been passed down generation after generation since her kinsmen first drove their cattle into the hills. She had inherited strong arms and an independent spirit. That she should now be a maidservant was only a twist of fate, and she knew in her heart that she would soon be mistress of her own home.

'I need you to help me look after the children for a few hours. Mr MacKenzie and I have been invited to dine with Sir Thomas and Lady Lydia aboard the schooner.' Mrs MacKenzie's cheeks wore the roses of a young girl's and her eyes were shining for the company that she would soon keep.

'Oh, Mrs MacKenzie!' There might have been tears in Betty's eyes if only she had been a little less practically inclined and a little more experienced in romance. 'How wonderful!'

The elegant schooner was anchored in Village Bay. It was the grandest ship the natives had ever seen, and their pride and amazement knew no boundaries when they were told that it had been named after their island and that it was written clearly in gold letters on the aft: the *Lady of St Kilda*. The schooner was the property of Sir Thomas Dyke Acland, a rich landowner from Devon and a Member of Parliament. Sixteen years previously, as a young, newly wed couple, Sir Thomas and his wife Lydia had visited St Kilda on a hired boat while they were travelling around the Highlands and Islands of Scotland in search of the sublime. Some of the natives remembered the gentleman's visit; he had drawn sketches of their dwellings and of the lofty, dark peaks around Village Bay. On acquiring the *Lady of St Kilda*, which was actually named after his wife, whom he assumed had been the first *real* Lady ever to set foot on St Kilda, Sir Thomas had decided that its maiden voyage should be to the island that had so impressed him in his youth. Lady Lydia, of whom it was said amongst the higher society of the West Country that she had an *interesting* and *adventurous* soul, had been only too pleased to accompany her husband on the journey. Audacious voyaging was not altogether agreeable, of course, but Lady Lydia was apt at putting certain things and events to one side in her mind. The episode with the rampant ram in Loch Awe was one such incident, which she had of course forgotten. She had got rid of the contemptuous dress she had worn that day and never thought of it again. She was convinced that her rare ability made her a superior traveller, and as travel was in itself an embodiment of the ideological apparatus of Empire, it was suitable for her class.

On perambulating the *clachan* the day before, tossing sweets and tobacco amongst the natives, Sir and Lady Acland had been absolutely appalled to see that nothing had improved since their previous visit. The natives still lived in the most miserable and un-Christian hovels. Not even the most wretched vagabond who squatted on Acland's lands in north Devon lived in such filth. The horror that they felt on seeing the *clachan* again was quite natural and right as it arose from love of the less fortunate and a genuine social affection. The well-being of the St Kildans was of great concern to Sir Thomas, who was a philanthropist as well as a politician, and he had decided to invite the good minister and his wife to dinner to discuss the matter.

Some of the natives had turned out on the

landing rock to watch as the boatswain of the *Lady of St Kilda* arrived to pick up Mr and Mrs MacKenzie in the dinghy. Mrs MacKenzie wore her best summer dress of white calico printed with small blue and purple pansies. It had been made shortly after her wedding five years previously, and Lizzie was relieved that she had spent some time last winter updating it. Her sister Annie had sent her recent images and drawings of young ladies in Glasgow. Lizzie had lowered the neckline so that it rested on her bare shoulders and she had puffed the sleeves using material from an old blue dress which she had torn on the rocks. She had no crinoline, of course, but in order to achieve the right width of the skirts she was wearing three petticoats starched with sugar. The underskirt had been lined at the bottom with a willow band which had been shaped around a large barrel. She had been quite pleased with the result at the time, but now she worried that her creation would look hopelessly out of fashion. The tight corset made her sit very upright in the rickety boat as they rowed towards the schooner. Betty had helped her to fasten pretty blue ribbons in her dismal hair and she had formed ringlets at her temples with a hot iron spike. The coarse hands of the servant girl had worked slowly and methodically. The result was surprisingly good, and now Lizzie hoped that her coiffure was not getting squashed beneath her bonnet. There was a little seawater in the hull of the boat and Lizzie lifted her feet under the petticoats in order to save her best boots from the salt. Her husband, on the other hand, looked completely at ease in his black coat with the velvet collar. His white cravat had gone slightly yellow from disuse. To the natives who were watching from the shore the scene was utterly alien. They had grown used to the minister and his wife, and it worried them that the couple should look so different on this evening. Even the myriad of puffins, returning overhead from their missions at sea, seemed to take a curious interest in the colourful spectacle as it crossed Village Bay.

When they reached the schooner the MacKenzies were helped on board by strong deckhands and greeted by the steward, who ushered them down a flight of stairs below the poop deck. As they entered the master's cabin Lizzie removed her bonnet and looked anxiously for her own reflection in the polished brass. Her cheeks were badly flushed and her hair had curled above her temples. She could feel her throat contracting above her beating heart and her voice was pitched rather too high as she greeted their host and hostess.

Sir Thomas Dyke Acland looked exceedingly elegant in a blue velvet coat and slim cream trousers, but Mrs MacKenzie only had eyes for Lady Acland, whose vast gown of light green silk taffeta, strewn with tiny silk roses, like the satin sheet of a bridal bed, seemed to fill the best part of the salon. Lizzie lowered her eyes and blushed

145

as she thought of the ugly contraption of starched petticoats hidden underneath her own crushed skirts. She was sweating in the hot cabin, and as she sat down she could feel the melting sugar sticking to her thighs.

A valet served the dinner. Venison trimmed with greens had been brought from the Long Isle, and as the claret was poured into the crystal glasses it sent shadows of blood on to the white tablecloth. The candlelight was reflected in the brass and mahogany of the cabin and framed the diners in a warm, becoming glow. MacKenzie observed his wife as she bit delicately into a perfect potato, a spit of gravy clinging to her lower lip. She was well tutored, he saw, and recognised some of his own efforts in her manners. But there was something else too – something quite individual which he could not put his finger on. Perhaps he had underestimated her. His eyes rested on her golden features for a moment longer and he suddenly wished that he had been able to give her more.

Lady Acland watched her guests closely as her husband was talking. She saw that the minister was a handsome, dark man although, judging from his bronzed complexion, it was all too obvious that he often went without a hat. He had been to university in Glasgow, she understood, but it was not clear if he had ever graduated, nor if he had achieved a distinction in any of his subjects. Two of her own sons were at Oxford at the moment, but they were quite a different class of gentlemen, of course, and it would be unfair to the minister to make a comparison. As for Mrs MacKenzie, she had beauty, that was clear, although of the natural rather than the sophisticated kind. There was something disturbingly youthful about her, Lady Acland realised. It would be altogether more appropriate if her fresh spirit could mature into something less *gleaming*. A decent soul, Lady Acland thought, as she smiled graciously at the younger woman across the table, though not a lady by any means.

'So what brings you to St Kilda this second time, Sir Thomas? I thought politics would keep you in the south.' The minister accepted another slice of venison from the valet.

'My dear Reverend, a gentleman must never cease searching for adventure. Lydia and I needed a drama. It is as simple as that,' answered Acland cheerfully, and raised his glass to the churchman.

Mr MacKenzie raised his glass and inclined his head in response.

'You see, I'm afraid I cannot bear the idle life of my class –' the older man did not realise that this sounded somewhat pompous – 'so when politics doesn't keep me busy I travel.'

'And what, if I may ask, do you hope to find on your travels?'

'Oh anything really, anything that can catch my interest, or my pity for that matter.' He was naturally restless and needed impressions that would serve as a contrast to the life he had been born into.

147

'Well, I am sorry if you are disappointed because there is not much to cause excitement on St Kilda at the moment – we are in the middle of the harvesting of the fulmar and stormy petrel.'

'Ah, but you are mistaken, my friend; St Kilda is as sublimely beautiful and as darkly terrifying as I remember her. You see, as a politician and a man of the humanities I am interested in exploring how sensation, impression and imagination are interrelated with our experience of art.' Sir Thomas considered himself to be a fair artist and he had, when a student at Christ Church, composed verses which reflected his inner pain and the wonder of nature.

The minister had taken to the older gentleman, but he would not be patronised. 'I agree that the place is utterly unique, but for those who dwell here throughout the year the concern lies in survival rather than in art, as I am sure you are aware.'

Sir Thomas looked surprised; he was not used to being contradicted outside Parliament, and deep down he was terrified of the rise of the middling ranks. But he hated mediocrity and admired this young minister who was anything but tame. So after a brief hesitation he swiftly composed himself and answered with a smile, 'You must excuse me, Reverend, I am old enough to indulge myself in the dream of the Golden Age. I am sure your main concern, which inevitably lies in the *improvement* of the lives of the

St Kildans, is a deal nobler than mere ramblings in search of *beauty*.'

'I honestly believe,' Lady Acland interrupted importantly while the bright feathers of some exotic bird vibrated at the peak of her lofty coiffure, 'that you are the best thing that could have happened to these simple beings, these ultimate savages, Reverend!' She almost spat her contempt for the St Kildans but continued in a seductive voice, her head beautifully tilted as she smiled at him. 'Why, you can even speak that primitive language of theirs!' He was arrogant and handsome and she wanted him to admire her.

'It is my husband's language too.' Lizzie regretted her indiscretion as soon as she had spoken, but was rewarded by a single smile from her husband.

Lady Acland did not quite understand, but saw that the younger woman's dress was really dreadfully plain.

'As a matter of fact I have been trying to persuade the islanders to build a new village and create a better field system, which would improve their yields of barley and make their houses more hygienic.' The minister's voice was suddenly serious, and he looked intently at Sir Thomas.

'New houses – how perfectly romantic! It would be like a little hamlet of goblins and gnomes!' Lady Acland had exceeded herself, but did not know it.

Sir Thomas looked at her incredulously before

turning to the minister. 'What a splendid idea, my dear fellow. Land reform might be just the thing to bring the natives into the modern world.'

'Yes, that is precisely my ambition, Sir Thomas.' The minister could not hide his excitement. 'They hold the land in common, and at the moment each family farms small plots, using fermented offal and bird carcasses along with the soot-impregnated straw from their roofs as manure. I have studied Smith's ideas of the division of labour and come to the conclusion that what we need on Hirta is something like an Act of Inclosure. I would have them enclose the fields and build a high wall which separates the infields from the outfields and protects the crops from the salt spray off the sea.'

'I can see that your mission goes far beyond the spiritual, minister.'

'Ah, but it is all linked – the spiritual well-being of a community cannot be separated from the elements of its physical livelihood. We have a duty to God to improve our situation on earth and make the most of the gifts of nature which He has provided for His people. Only in this place that is harder than in many other . . .' MacKenzie's voice trailed off.

The gentleman was not slow to pick up the note of despair in the minister's voice. 'I quite agree, but I can sense from your tone that there is a catch – what is it?'

'Well, they say that they are happy where they

are and their current dwellings have been good enough for their ancestors for a thousand years – they believe their ancestors to have been heroes of gigantic strength who could lift the huge boulders and built the houses and dykes with their bare hands.' The minister sighed and raised his eyebrows in exasperation.

'Hmm, I can see that they need an incentive.' Sir Thomas thought for a moment while twirling the stem of the wine glass between his well-manicured fingers. 'I will issue a bounty – a reward of twenty guineas to the first man who builds a new house for his family!' He was delighted at the thought that this community might finally be transformed by his material expression of sympathy.

'Twenty guineas!' Lizzie was thrilled by so much potential. She thought of the poky dwelling of her friend Ann MacCrimmon. 'Oh, but it will never work.' She was immediately saddened by the realisation.

'Whatever do you mean, Mrs MacKenzie?' Sir Thomas asked in an avuncular manner. He saw that she was pretty.

'I beg your pardon, sir –' Lizzie looked to her husband for support – 'but the islanders will never accept a bounty which would make them compete against each other, nor would any of them accept a gift that was not also granted to the others.'

'My wife is right,' said the minister thoughtfully. 'The St Kildans are all equal, and fierce in their solidarity.'

'Surely they will be persuaded by twenty guineas!' Lady Acland had an undying belief in money.

Sir Thomas ignored his wife and rested his eyes on the minister. 'Well, I will let you decide how to make best use of the money.'

'I would like to thank you on behalf of the whole community and I am sure they will be very touched by this most generous gift,' said Mr MacKenzie. Sir Thomas, who was at once pleasantly rewarded by the good-heartedness of his own generosity, puffed his cheeks and brushed aside the expected admiration with his hand.

'At last, minister, you can move them out of their beastly hovels and into the world of human beings – they can leave their savage customs behind forever!' Lady Acland, who credited herself with the knack of finding the right remark for every situation, believed that she expressed what everybody must be thinking at that moment.

Only a few years previously Lizzie would not have reacted, but now her eyes were wide with disbelief. 'You speak of them as if they were no better than animals! It is precisely because they revere the past of their community and recount its stories and myths that they are human. How else would they survive?' She wanted to weep. She knew she was ordinary, mediocre even, but she could not let this woman whose jewels glittered in the light from the candelabras slander the people that she had observed closely over the last few years, since the twins died, and even begun to admire. Losing the children, and sharing her grief with the other St Kildan mothers who had experienced the same misfortune, had created an affinity that went far deeper than any social conventions. She wanted to protect her sisters from the outside world. How could anyone know about humanity who had not lived? How could Sir and Lady Acland, who had to sail this far to perceive the thrill of beauty, understand that the human soul is at times closer to nature than it is to God. Lizzie felt sullen and childish and wished that somebody would save her from this unpleasant situation.

It was Sir Thomas, rather than her husband, who came to her rescue. 'I think, Mrs MacKenzie, that your wisdom exceeds your years. I'm only sorry that I will not have enough time to speak to you on these subjects.' He looked at her with regret. 'It is late, and my steward must bring you back before it gets too dark.'

As the boat glided through the black water of the August night the minister remembered another such night of light and dark when he had failed to stand fast in his loyalty to God and been drawn into a myth where his own burning desires were as primal as those of a beast of nature. He could feel the warm arm of his wife against his own as they rocked gently with the strokes of the oars. She smelled faintly of burnt sugar. He suddenly broke into a cold sweat as he thought of her as she had been on that night three years previously, when the glowing algae had outlined her body in such beauty that he had not been able to tell whether she was an angel of God or a temptress sent by the Devil to taunt him. He realised that there were times when he did not know her at all, and that frightened him. She seemed to be continually changing: whether with the seasons or with the age of man he could not tell.

Lizzie felt foolish and uncomfortable – she wished she had never accepted the invitation to the dinner. But what choice did she have? There was no alternative on this island, no tea-party that would keep her occupied, no evening lecture or charity ball. The dinner had rocked her hard-won equilibrium. She felt ugly and coarse: not a lady at all but a simple minister's wife living amongst savages – at least according to that peacock Lady Acland. Is that how she should think of herself? Oh no, she did not think like that at all, not any more! She felt closer to the St Kildans than to the gentry on the schooner. She had learned to be happy on the island, but now she felt miserable again as she remembered her youth in Paisley, her friends and family. She tore the blue ribbons out of her silly hair and crushed them tightly in her hand.

As the boat drew up towards the landing rock a flock of kittiwakes lifted from the still water of the bay, their flight as silent and soft as a silk slip pulled from the warm skin of a naked woman.

★ ★ ★

Neil MacKenzie broke the good news to the St Kildans the next morning at the *mòd*. As expected, they would not accept the gift unless it was granted to the community as a whole. There was much discussion amongst the men who made up the parliament. MacKenzie explained with great patience, over and over again, what the virtue of the new *clachan* would be. A couple of hours later he could feel his endurance waver as the men were still chafing their backs against the stone walls of the houses without having got any closer to a conclusion. As they smoked and spat and chatted they would often be carried away by another topic and the minister found it very difficult to keep them on track. 'Our ancestors were much stronger than us. They built these houses with their bare hands. How are we going to be able to build a whole new village with no building material?' asked MacKinnon, the *maor*. 'We will use the material from the existing houses and import some timber for the fittings of the doors and windows,' answered MacKenzie. There was a surprised murmur at the mention of windows. 'Where will we live while the new houses are being constructed?' asked another. 'We will build one house at a time, and we will share the work between us,' came the answer. 'What if the spirits of our ancestors get angry if we abandon the houses they built for us?' asked John Gilles, who was not as clever as some. 'What have I told you about spirits, John? You had better come and see me in the manse tomorrow after your work is done,' answered the minister, who really was running out of patience. 'But if we reuse the building material from our old houses, what then would we need the gentleman's money for?' asked one who was better equipped. 'I thought you could buy furniture and household equipment such as bedsteads, windows and chairs,' suggested the minister languidly. There was renewed muttering and spitting, itching and shuffling. 'Och, minister, we are not sure about this. It would be nice to have a window, that is for sure, but these new houses may not be able to stand the seasons. And to move an entire field system . . . We need some more time to think it over,' said MacKinnon after another interlude which seemed to have passed with agonising slowness.

MacKenzie left them to it. He had had as much of the St Kilda parliament as he could take for one day and he had a project of his own to get on with.

A little way above the landing rocks and close to the manse was a rough piece of land which could not be used for grazing or cutting hay. MacKenzie had decided that he should put it to good use and build a saw pit where all driftwood could be cut up and stored away from the weather. He had ordered the two-man saw blade the previous summer and it had arrived with the taxman a few weeks earlier. Unfortunately it was rare to find good pieces of driftwood on Hirta as the constant surf around the rocky shores would grind most wood to kindling before any of the islanders could save it. However, there were times after a winter storm when a proud and solid ship would perish at Rockall. If fortune was on their side the crew might save themselves in a dinghy and be carried on the current to Glen Bay on the north-western side of Hirta. But more often than not the St Kildans would encounter no survivors and their only notion of the wreck would be the broken timber floating in the bay in the wake of the storm. These remains of vessels which were once sturdy and home to men were great bounty, and were collected without much concern or sentimentality for those unknown sailors who had lost their lives to the roaring sea.

While the St Kildan men and women went to the rocks for the fulmar, MacKenzie started to clear the ground for the saw pit, which was to be the first of many improvements. He had realised that it was hard to work the land in the glebe, as it was strewn with boulders and small rocks eroded from the face of Oiseval during many winter storms. Nearby was a low, grassy mound and he reckoned that if he dug the foundations of the saw pit into the mound he could build a structure shaped like the prow of a boat and with walls about two meters high, so that one man could stand on the ground and another at the same level as the timber log they were cutting. It was a very simple design, which he had seen in use in Glen Sannox as a boy.

He started by stripping the mound of its turf, as that could be dried and used for fuel in the winter. To his surprise the soil under the turf was rather soft, and unlike the area around the mound there were no boulders or large stones. The earth was dark and rich, and field mice had burrowed deep into it, thus disturbing the topsoil and making it quite porous. This puzzled the minister and it suddenly occurred to him that the mound might be man-made rather than natural. He stood up to straighten his back. A light rain had begun to fall and his hand left a muddy streak across his brow as he wiped a lock of wet hair out of his eyes. He could feel his heart quickening as a notion dawned on him. He looked into the dark soil and realised that he might be looking into the past. His legs trembled slightly as if he stood on the threshold of another world, knowing that if he entered it the world that he had left would never be quite the same again. If he had believed in the concept of fate, this would perhaps have been where he tempted it. But fate was an abstraction, a superstition to a Presbyterian Christian. Yet it was not fear, nor anticipation of the unknown, that occupied him as he started digging again, kneeling now and feeling the earth carefully with the spade and his bare hands. On the contrary he felt as powerful as when he explored the souls of his congregation; when the fear of God made them lay themselves bare, exposing their inner selves as raw as flesh newly stripped of its skin. Slowly and methodically he continued to dig, to unveil this great unknown, this secret, layer by layer, to the core of its mystery. Then, as he knew it would, his spade struck metal, and he was at last rewarded with a glimpse of eternity. He was looking into the grave of a warrior who was as ancient as the hills that guarded him. These hills that had once erupted from the sea were the only witnesses to this breach of a tomb which had been sealed since antiquity. Neil MacKenzie used his hands to carefully unearth an iron spearhead and then a sword – heavy and terrible – followed by a number of irregularly shaped iron objects, the use of which he could not determine. He turned them over in his hands, gently brushing the sods of soil from the rusted metal. His heart raced as he thought about the hand that had forged these tools of war. A long and narrow whetstone accompanied the metal objects. He could see no bones in the grave, but the artefacts were laid out in such a way as to outline the shadow of a man who had once been tall and strong.

Neil MacKenzie had been so engaged in his excavation that he had not noticed a couple of men had joined him and were looking into the pit. They were both too old to take part in the fulmar harvest and had come to the manse for a chat with the minister. He looked up at them now from the edge of the grave, caked with dark mud, his hair pasted to his skull by the drizzling rain, and the two men looked back at their minister in

159

astonishment. They could not decide whether or not this was all proper, and the excited, crazed look in his eyes frightened them.

'What you see here are the remains of a Norseman,' the minister almost whispered, so as not to dampen the importance of the moment.

'A Norseman?' The two men looked still more perplexed.

'One of your ancestors from the Golden Age when the Norse ruled our shores.' The minister suddenly wanted them to understand the significance of his finding. More than anything, he wanted them to live up to their own past.

'Was he a big man – big enough to build our stone houses?' one of them asked. The reconstruction of the *clachan* was still on their minds.

'He was a large man all right, but not so unlike yourselves, I should imagine.' He was disappointed by their lack of enthusiasm.

'There was a fisherman from the Long Isle who said he found a pot of silver coins on the beach once – said they had Norse inscriptions, he did,' said one of the old men and spat into the mud. 'Perhaps this man here was a rich man.'

'Perhaps it is the son of the King of Norway, the one they say floated ashore once and was killed by our ancestors, who took him for a selkie,' suggested his friend.

'Aye, he must have been a rich man with such a big sword.' The old man sounded impressed.

160

'Perhaps we can sell this here sword to the taxman and buy some more tobacco,' the first man added hopefully.

'Aye, and a dram or two to clear the smoke from the throat.' The other smacked his lips and broke into a toothless grin.

'For pity's sake!' the minister cried in exasperation. 'Does this not make you wonder about yourselves? Does not this dead warrior make you think about your own lives and achievements? He may have laid the foundations to one of the houses that you live in. He may have raised his family here much like you have done. For all I know he may have been the first man to oppose this howling wilderness and rock and sea!'

The look of pleasure died on the two men's faces and they seemed suddenly overcome by age. They were no longer allowed the luxury of dreams. Perhaps they felt that they were closer to the shadow of the ancestor in the grave than they were to the bright lives of their sons and daughters out catching the fulmar. The knowledge that their day was done weighed heavily on them, bending their backs and rounding their shoulders. Their whole lives these men had struggled to reclaim a piece of land from nature, to carve their existence out of the rock and till the shallow, salt-encrusted soil. What would they leave behind for eternity? Their efforts would last for the age of man, no longer. And at the end of their day they would be buried

161

by this young minister who stood dark and dirty in front of them, this stern man who did not approve of folly and who claimed that he had just disinterred one of their revered ancestors. Their shadows would stain the earth in the graveyard where the rough stones that marked their graves would fall and sink into the broom.

One day the community would fail to remember their ancestry and be forced to leave as all the knowledge and the old ways were forgotten.

MacKenzie at once regretted his insensitivity. He realised that death was already walking beside these men and that his duty was to provide them with an idea of the potentials of the afterlife, not to make them reflect on the end of their life on earth. At that moment there was nothing he could say to soothe their souls. As they turned to leave, embarrassed and uncomfortable, he could see that they had aged, and he hated himself for failing in his vocation. Ridden by self-contempt he wrapped the metal objects in a sack, and as the rain kept falling he continued digging furiously into the ground where his saw pit would stand and where timber would be cut to make the coffins for his congregation.

The mound of the Viking warrior was forgotten and the dust of his bones indistinguishable in the mud. The great swordsman had bled into the earth and now the rain carried him away and trickled into a nearby stream which was lined by a lush growth of irises. As the stream reached the sea the last of the Norseman was dissolved and freed by water – an end, and a beginning.

The St Kildans eventually agreed to build the new village. They wanted to divide the land into individual plots. Their minister was only too pleased with this suggestion, as evolution to his mind was dependent on individual ownership and responsibility. He took it upon himself to contact the laird and introduce him to the plans. The proprietor at once consented to the changes and sent his kinsman Donald MacDonald of Tanera to draw up the plan for the divisions of the crofts, but the plan that was presented to the islanders was not to their liking and created some bad blood amongst them. They were headstrong and close-knit and were not as biddable as the laird's subjects on the mainland. For days they grumbled and shuffled, until the minister persuaded them to try and work out a structure of their own and then cast lots for the individual plots. This idea was accepted, though it would take many months before the final layout was agreed. But that did not bother MacKenzie. He felt pleased to have reached the moment when the St Kildans, who had thought themselves complete and self-sufficient, had been made to realise that they were not and, moreover, that he was the one who had led their minds to this conclusion. He secretly congratulated himself on winning a small victory for civilisation and decided to write to the Society for the

Propagation of Christian Knowledge before the boats returned the following summer.

In the meantime he charged the islanders with the task of building a head dyke, to separate the new arable land from the pasture, and a wall by the sea to keep the salt from spraying into the fields.

As soon as the fowling season was over the project started. The summer had been a wet one and the ground was heavy and smelled of decay, but the St Kildans seemed excited about their new work. MacKenzie presided over them and guided them in their labour. His authority was complete, but he soon discovered that the men needed much incentive to keep at their work for extended periods of time. Frustrated by the slow progress, he started working alongside them as they drained the arable land and canalised the streams. He worked in his shirtsleeves, the fine dark hair on his strong arms turning a coppery gold in the late-autumn sun. He felt able and energised, more so than he had in a very long time. He took pleasure in working alongside the other men and he enjoyed the influence he had gained over them. At last his vocation seemed close to realisation.

Every day at lunchtime Betty Scott and little Eliza would bring a basket of food and drink for the minister. Neil MacKenzie loved his daughter with an intense passion. The feelings terrified him, and he felt utterly helpless at the thought that he might lose her. He prayed secretly and in silence every day, grateful that she had been allowed to live. As the little girl came towards him across the glebe the minister would stop his work and watch as she struggled through the tall grass. Her dark curls showed under her bonnet and his heart brimmed with tenderness as her arms and legs wobbled uncontrollably up the slope, her little face straining with concentration and pride at the importance of her task. Once she got closer and recognised her father amongst the men a smile would light up her face for she loved him equally and would do anything to please him. She would skip faster through the dock leaves and scurvy grass. She resembled a brittle butterfly as she stretched out her arms to keep her balance. He turned and closed his eyes hard against the light as he recognised in her living face the gruesome death masks of Margaret and Jane. And he remembered them as he had first seen them, lying in ephemeral beauty in their mother's arms as a cruel ray of sunlight found its way through the window and marked them for death. Would his daughter's innocent face always remind him of his own sins?

Betty would plod patiently behind, lifting Eliza to her feet as she fell and brushing dirt and grass off her dress of green tweed. Betty was all smiles and white teeth in those days, but her greeting and ruddy beauty were for one man alone, and as the child and the maid reached the work party young Calum MacDonald would blush and turn to his friends and laugh coarsely, his ears burning and his heart quickening as he felt the gaze of the forward Betty upon him. He would kick the turf with his bare feet and spit as far as he could. He would not leave the safety of his group of friends, nor would he talk to her, but once or twice he could not help but look at her from under his dirty blond hair. He knew by the thickness in his throat and by the way her presence burned white like magnesium inside him that he wanted to marry her.

Once the girl and the maid were gone the work could resume. The minister was soon aware that the men would only work as long as he worked himself. As soon as he left them to go and see to his ministerial duties they would quickly lose interest in the task at hand and throw themselves on the grass and smoke their pipes and laugh and chat. One by one they would drift off and no more work would be carried out that day. So during that autumn the minister's theology turned pastoral. He found that his influence over his congregation would weaken if he did not plan and design the work himself so that he had always the upper hand in the execution of the labour. Once he wanted them to lift a large stone into the wall of the head dyke and the men said that it was impossible – only a giant or one of their powerful ancestors could move such a megalith. They laughed at their minister and accused him of being unreasonable. The minister laughed along with his men but was secretly annoyed that they should doubt his abilities.

The following morning MacKenzie rose early, before dawn. In the ashy twilight he levered the great granite slab, little by little, into position with the help of his spit iron and a bank of earth. It took him three hours and he bruised his thumb badly in the process, but as he cleared away his tools and stood back to look at the standing stone he felt strong and powerful, and he smiled with satisfaction as he thought of the reaction the stone would bring.

As he returned to the manse Lizzie received him into their bed and held him with warm arms. He touched her face lightly and drew his fingers through her curls. She liked him the way he was at that time, strong and exhausted and smelling of musk and earth. She laughed at his story of how he had tricked the men and kissed first his bruised thumb and then his chest and his face until she could feel him taut and proud through her nightgown. When they were spent and satisfied she thought of telling him that she was again with child, but decided against it as the knowledge of new life budding inside her was her own luxury; her own well of light from which she drew comfort and delight – and which would sometimes darken with fear. She liked it on mornings like this, rare as they were, when her husband was in a good mood and they were united, when she was allowed to be one with him. She wondered if he too was thinking about how close they were and was just about to ask something to this effect when he said, 'Lizzie, I feel so happy.' 'Yes?' She kissed his shoulder. 'The natives, my parishioners –' he pronounced the last bit in a mock-aristocratic drawl – 'I believe they are beginning to listen to me!' He gave a loud laugh. 'Just you wait, Lizzie, I will be their master yet!' Lizzie looked at a red spot on his cheek where the stubble had started to grow inward and could think of nothing to say. After a moment she withdrew from his arms and got out of bed to get dressed.

A couple of hours later the MacKenzies stood watching from behind the gable of the kirk as the men gathered around the standing stone. Soon Lizzie and Neil were giggling like children at the reaction of the St Kildans, who were scratching their beards and talking excitedly between themselves – a couple of the older men crossed themselves and removed their caps in awe. Lizzie urged her husband to go forward; she wanted to see their reaction when it dawned on them who had raised the stone – she wanted to see the men admiring her husband as much as she did. She wanted him to feel good about himself.

He strolled slowly, hands in his pockets, towards the men. Their faces were long and dark as they realised what their minister had achieved single-handed. 'But how?' they asked, and stood chewing their gums. 'Och, it is simple enough if you know how to,' he answered indifferently, and hid his bandaged thumb behind his back. At that moment he won them over completely. If they had ever doubted the authority of this thin man with his fine talk of improvement and redemption, that was now forever in the past. How they loved him then. From now on they would all follow his word. He was indeed a great man with God on his side; he held their fate in his strong hands. His was the hand whose grip would never fail! He commanded the winds, and the waves of the sea.

The digging and the construction of the dykes carried on well into November, when the birds left the rocky shores of the island and went to the ocean. The rocks without their inhabitants seemed black and dead. The St Kildans retreated with the livestock into their hovels and hibernation began. Nothing living seemed to move in the landscape. In late November MacKinnon the *maor* came to the manse with the finished plan for the new village. The community had decided on the plan, and each man supporting a family had drawn a lot for his toft and croft. It seemed that everyone was pleased with the map of their new village.

Around the same time Betty Scott announced that Calum MacDonald had asked her to marry him. It happened on an evening when Mrs MacKenzie and Betty were alone with the children in the kitchen. A westerly gale was raging over the north Atlantic, and St Kilda was isolated amidst the hostile ocean. The minister had shut himself into his study. The gale inspired him; he saw it as a metaphor for the spiritual vulnerability of the Christian lives of his congregation. Gusts of wind were beating against the glass of his study window, threatening to shatter it at every violent blow. Waves as high as thirty feet were crashing with unreasonable fury against Dùn, breaking over its rugged peaks and rocky battlements and sending great showers of sea spray over the eastern slopes of Ruiaval and over the huddled dwellings in the *clachan*. Village Bay was a boiling cauldron; tufts of yellow sea foam lifted from its strange and secret brew and flew over the island, only to settle in shuddering sods between the houses, behind the ridges and in the furrows. The howling sound of the sea and the storm was everywhere; it roared down the slopes of Conachair, boomed in the sea cliffs at Mullach Bi and screamed through the arch at Toll sa Duin.

Lizzie was uneasy; it seemed as if the island was going to break in half and sink back into the mother ocean. The children were crying with fear as doors rattled and sparks flew from the chimney. Because she needed reassurance, Lizzie told Betty about Stevenson, who had drawn the plans for the manse and had built the great lighthouse at Bell Rock which would stand against the elements until the end of time. But Betty was calm and steady. She rocked James Bannatyne on her knee and sang all the songs and shanties she knew. The soft sound of the words in the old language and the clear tone of her young woman's voice soothed her mistress. The singing told of a people who had weathered fury like this for thousands of years.

On this evening Betty was strengthened by the love that lived in her heart. Nothing could touch her now that Calum had finally revealed his feelings to her. She could not keep it inside her any longer; the wonder of it was too enormous. She had finally escaped her fate; she would be her own at last. 'Calum MacDonald has asked me to marry him, ma'am,' she blurted out almost aggressively. 'What!' If Lizzie had grasped the full meaning of the statement, she was already hiding from it. 'As I have no relatives here, I suppose Calum will have to ask for the minister's consent.' The maid was glowing now and added quickly as if to crush any doubt about her intentions, 'He must give it, mustn't he? He has no reason not to.' Lizzie was pale; she felt very tired. The girl had become indispensable to her. On this night she felt it more strongly than ever. Betty had served as an intermediary, an interpreter between Lizzie's solitary world and the world of the island. Lizzie could not bear to be shut out of it again. She could not bear it if her language was to die again.

'Ma'am? Are you feeling unwell?'

'No, my dear, not at all. I was just saddened by the thought of losing you.' She hugged Eliza, who had fallen asleep in her arms.

'Oh, Mrs MacKenzie, ma'am, don't speak like that. I will come and help you during the days for a while until I have little ones of my own.' Betty seemed moved.

'No, Betty, you must have your own life. I will be

fine. I am sure there is a girl in the village who would be willing to come and help me. Perhaps somebody who would be willing to learn some English.'

The mistress and the maid looked at each other and smiled shyly at the first hint of the unlikely friendship which was to grow between them. The rest of the evening was passed in warm confidentiality, discussing the wedding and the nature of men and what made them so attractive – so soft and so hard. When Neil MacKenzie entered the kitchen just before bedtime he was surprised to see the two women giggling intimately, and he felt himself blush for no good reason at all as they stopped their whispering abruptly and looked up at him from the glowing dust by the fireplace.

The storm lasted for three days. On the third day, as the wind settled and minds eased, the *rèiteach*, or betrothal party, for Calum MacDonald and Betty Scott was celebrated. It was the custom to hold the *rèiteach* in the house of the bride's father, but as Betty was alone on the island it was decided that it should be held at Calum's father's house. Mr and Mrs MacKenzie were invited to the party, which was normally a family affair. The minister acted as the girl's representative and had to state the intentions of the betrothal before he was let over the threshold and into the house. As the MacKenzies entered the house on their hands and knees they found all the men reclining on the floor close to the walls on either side so that their feet met in the middle. The MacKenzies found it difficult to pass as they had to step over the outstretched legs of the guests. Calum's female relatives were in an adjoining hut with the bride, and Lizzie soon understood that she was intended to join them. Mr MacKenzie, in the meantime, was offered a seat on a chest and sat down to drink a toast of spirits which was passed around by the groom's father. The reason for coming together was not mentioned, and as soon as all the spirits had been drunk the party separated without much further ado. Lizzie stayed on for a while longer with the women. They did not drink any whisky, but in spite of this their gathering was less solemn; Lizzie enjoyed listening to the songs and stories and, although she did not understand the language, the feelings communicated filled her heart. One song in particular caught her attention. It had few words but the vocals which the women produced seemed to imitate the cheerful chirps of seabirds during the mating season. Betty laughed at the lyrics and explained to Mrs MacKenzie that the song described a young woman who makes fun of her admirer as he does not have the courage to climb even the smallest stack. But Lizzie liked the chorus best and laughed as the women sang the bird-like noises:

Inn ala oro i, o inn al ala;
Inn ala oro i, uru ru-i uru ru-i;
Inn ala oro i, o inn al ala.

The following Sabbath the betrothal between the couple was announced, and when it had been proclaimed on three successive Sabbath-days the wedding date was set, after careful planning and consultation of the omens.

When the day arrived it was wrapped in hoar-frost. One of the rare Soay sheep was slaughtered and two elderly men were appointed to boil the mutton. Young girls were given barley to grind and bake. Others who had no chores did no work at all but hung about in the houses, chatting and getting ready for the feast. One of the old men produced a fiddle which had not been seen for a while and expectations were high. It was as if everyone was set on defying the dark season and welcoming this stranger into their midst. It had been some time since an outsider had married into the community.

As the bride was being dressed by her future female relatives a story was told of an unlucky girl who once came with the factor to the island as a servant and married a local man. The St Kildans soon found out that the girl was giving information to her former master, about goods which were hidden from the factor when he visited.

Not long after, the girl's husband volunteered to go to Dùn to bring back a sheep which had strayed there. The St Kildan women then lured the girl down to the shore at low tide. When they got to the low-water mark all the men descended on the foreign girl and tied their ropes around her thin neck. They then pulled in each direction until she was dead. In this way everyone was equally guilty of the murder and no one had to carry the guilt on their own. As the tide returned it washed away not only the signs of the struggle but also the guilt. When the factor returned the following spring, each and every St Kildan could give him the same story – the girl had tragically fallen into the water from the landing rocks and been carried out to sea. The body was never found.

Betty felt slightly uncomfortable as she was told this story. She realised that her new kin were trying to tell her that from now on she had to be loyal to the St Kildan community and no one else, not even to her former masters in the manse.

Once the bride and groom were dressed in their finery, mostly in odd garments borrowed from family and friends, they went with a group of close relatives to the manse. It was a fine day in early December. The ground was covered in crunchy frost and the dying sun was too weak to rise above the summit of Conachair; it would soon be dark again.

Lizzie made a peephole in the frost-flowers on the window and watched as the little wedding party approached over the frozen glebe. They left deep footprints in the white grass and now and again a straying ray of winter sun would find its way down the slopes of the hill to send glittering diamonds in their wake. The couple looked very happy as they strolled hand in hand over the thin sheath of frost, the two of them only eighteen, with the rest of their lives ahead of them. Calum was young and proud in a fresh white shirt and a fine striped woollen vest. The red muffler around his neck had been washed and stood out in the dark landscape. Betty looked prettier than ever. Her clothes were rather dull, but her cheeks glowed and her copper hair had been curled with a hot iron. There was love and passion in their eyes as they smiled at each other, the youth gripping the hand of the girl harder as a low sparkle of winter light illuminated a straying strand of her hair. For a moment a queer sadness gripped Lizzie's heart as she remembered her own wedding day, which had been a very formal affair. She had hardly known her husband then, and the ceremony had felt more like a transaction than a celebration. Many of the guests had been alien to her and she had felt very out of place. How long ago it seemed now; how different she was. She would never again know the girl who had embroidered monograms on the wedding sheets on long Sunday afternoons, and for a moment she grieved for the innocence of her younger self. How flattered she had been by the idea of love!

The minister and his wife received the young couple in the kitchen before they all entered the kirk. Mrs MacKenzie had made Betty a beautifully worked lace *mutch* – the cap she would wear from now on to signify her married status. Betty received the gift straight and serious, but as Lizzie handed her one of her best silk ribbons Betty thanked her mistress with a thick voice. The former maid had never known the luxury of vanity, and as she tied the blue ribbon around her waist she blushed. Mr MacKenzie gave the couple a bible in Gaelic.

When it was time to go into the kirk the minister walked ahead through the passage by the pantry, closely followed by the young couple. His wife and the children followed last. Lizzie stopped for a moment by the kitchen door and watched the departing backs of the young couple. They were leaning into each other, sharing a lovers' secret, with their hands and fingers linked as tightly as all the days and nights to come. 'Goodbye, Betty Scott,' Lizzie whispered after the girl who stepped so lightly into her new life.

Most of the village had gathered in the church. Lamps on the window sills were burning fulmar oil, and the breath rose from the islanders in white puffs. But as soon as the little kirk warmed up, their woollen garments started steaming, releasing some rather unpleasant odours.

Lizzie was surprised to see that her husband had marked the words of Isaiah as a starting point to the wedding sermon; 'A man shall be as a hiding place from the wind, and a covert from the tempest,' he read in a low voice with an intensity that filled the high room. 'Each one of you must look inside yourself for comfort in this harsh world. The Lord Jesus lives inside those who believe and as you stand before me in this house, in this place where there is reason to hope, and where His Gospel is preached, know that you are married to Jesus first and to man second.' Lizzie listened to the sound of her husband's voice as he continued to tell the congregation in their own tongue of their vulnerability and of the sacrament of marriage, and of how two are one and yet must be single; without understanding the words she was drawn back into the eye of the storm that sometimes lived inside her. She thought she heard him talk of duty but not of love and she wished that somebody had told her as she stood next to her love in front of the altar that she would one day perceive her husband from this distance – that she would be so alone.

As soon as the couple were married they were followed out of the kirk by a procession of their kin. The young people were chanting and cheering as they returned to the village in anticipation of the feast. The MacKenzies returned alone to the manse and put the children to bed. After some time, the governor of the feast, Calum's brother Aonghas, arrived to invite the manse-folk to the feast. He had sewn a patch of white cloth to each shoulder to signify epaulettes and a patch to the front of his cap. These insignia showed that he was to lead the feasting. As the MacKenzies entered the house of the feast they found most of the adult village men seated on the floor with a table of planks before them. The livestock had been moved out to make space for all the guests. One end of the table was raised higher and placed before a chest to which the minister and his wife were led. Next to them and opposite each other sat the newly married couple. Three plates had been placed on the boards in front of the minister and his wife. One contained the boiled mutton, another one the barley bread and the third some cheeses saved from the summer. Across the long table similar crude planks with food had been distributed, but there was no soup or drink to wash down the food. The minister said grace, after which everyone ate greedily without talking much. Once the men had finished their food there was a bit of conversation before they left the table to let the women and boys have their share. Lizzie suspected that the party would only liven up once the minister had left, so she whispered to her husband that they ought to leave. It was a cold starry night and the frost was thick on the roof thatch. A white moon was hanging silently over Village Bay, illuminating the blue frost. The first tickling notes of a fiddle escaped from the smoke hole of the wedding house.

The dark sea cliffs loomed threateningly around the *clachan*. This was a different world from the Hirta which was populated by birds in the summer. This black island did not belong to mankind, only to the ocean from which it had once sprung. It was bitterly cold. Lizzie blew into her bare hands and leaned against her husband

179

for warmth and comfort. He was thinking about something quite separate and found her closeness rather irritating. Since starting his big project he had been withdrawn and distant. Normally Lizzie didn't mind. She was used by now to his moods and the way he would forget about her and the children for long periods of time when something more pressing related to his calling occupied his mind. But this night she felt miserable and lonely and she wanted him to give her reassurance. As they walked towards the manse she lifted his arm to put it around her shoulders, but he shook himself free and looked at her with cold eyes. 'What?' he said in a voice that made her shrink away.

'Nothing,' she answered, and sank 'I was a bit cold, that's all, and I thought you could warm me up.'

'Wind your shawl closer around you, why don't you?' His voice offered no comfort.

'I will miss Betty,' she said then, and turned her face towards the sea to hide her eyes. A thin crust of ice had formed by the shore.

'Don't be silly – you will be able to see her whenever you want.' He was getting quite annoyed. He could not understand her loneliness. Could she not engage her mind in something useful rather than acting so forlornly? What did she want from him? Was he not the minister – and master – of this island? Did being his wife not offer her belonging and purpose enough?

'I am not so sure,' she replied, his coldness for once making her stronger. 'She belongs to the St Kildans now and her first loyalty must be to them. They still see us as foreigners and gentlefolk – we do not belong in their world.' She tried to explain her feelings in general terms. She realised that he did not understand that she sometimes felt her exile and alienation so strongly that she found it hard to breathe. Perhaps he had forgotten – or chosen to forget – that she had left her world and her youth behind to follow him here.

'Nonsense!' he said, and quickened his step. But he had no wish to belong; he wanted to command.

'Well, why do you think they wanted us to leave the party just now? It was quite clear that they did not want us there for the rest of the festivities.' Her voice quivered with emotion.

'Well, for my part, I have no wish to partake in their merriments. They are crude and vulgar.'

'How can you know when you have never been invited? Are you not at all curious?'

'No, not at all. I look forward to going back to my study to read about world affairs.'

'World affairs that are a year old – you do not live in reality,' she muttered flatly. He would get an annual supply of newspapers sent with the taxman once a year and had made a habit of reading each paper on the same date that it was published, but a year on.

He said nothing to this, but she knew he had

won as he was fulfilled by his pride and his mission, wrapped in his magic robes, and she remained empty and solitary. He had become increasingly withdrawn since the children were born. He seemed especially awkward around his son, she thought. She had caught him looking at James Bannatyne once or twice in a way that she could not quite interpret. It was as if he was bewildered by a mystery in the boy that he could not decipher. It struck her that perhaps he had hoped to recognise himself in their son's soul. She shook her head and realised that in this she was stronger – at least she had knowledge of the children. Still she needed him desperately. As they got back to the manse she tried to make friends with him again by making him a cup of tea and smiling seductively. She wanted to sit up and talk by the fire, but he was suddenly tired and wanted to go to bed. She got in after him and put her hand on his chest. She tried to kiss his lips, but he pulled away and turned over on his side with his back to her. 'Do you not want to give me a goodnight kiss?' she asked, humiliated and diminished, still wanting him to understand and to open himself to her.

'No, I just want to sleep, leave me alone,' came his answer cold and hard.

She turned to the wall and curled up to cradle the empty pain in her chest. She held it there along with her pride until she could hear that he had fallen asleep. Then she let her limbs fall apart and stretched her soul thinly across the bed until, at last, she could let her misery and loneliness dissolve into the coarse sheets.

Once her crying had subsided Lizzie lay for a long time watching the moon which glided slowly across the bay outside the window. Throughout the night she could hear scattered notes from the fiddle in the still, frosty darkness. The sound seemed to travel far on the thin air. At times the music was tender and intent, caressing the rafters and spilling into the flesh of the night, only to be suddenly let loose in quick leaps and turns, skipping across the fields and chasing up the hillsides. Lizzie wished that she could dance with the wedding guests. Oh how she wanted to feel the music through her limbs and lose herself in the rhythm of the dancing feet. Eventually she fell into the slack sleep that follows dark passion, dreaming that the warm tunes carried her back to the party and into the strong arms of a dancing young man.

Christmas came quickly as the days shrank into what seemed like a long, single midwinter night. One of Calum's cousins, a thin girl of about thirteen called Anna, came to help in the manse. She could say yes and no in English and seemed to understand a bit more. Her clothes were hand-me-downs and too big for her, which made her look odd and younger than her age, but she was used to caring for small children and liked playing with Eliza and James Bannatyne while Lizzie was working on the preparations for Christmas. Anna, who was still a child herself, had an easy way with the little ones. After a while, she communicated in simple English, and Lizzie was almost jealous of the girl's straightforward connection with them. 'Put your boots on,' she would say to Eliza before they went out, and the child would sit on the floor and pull on her boots. 'Don't pee outside the potty,' she would say to James Bannatyne, and help him to hold his tiny penis so that the pee trickled into the enamel container while he stood obligingly on chubby legs.

Anna was a serious girl, though something of a dreamer, and beauty mattered more than anything to her. Her soul was so disturbed by the coarseness and ugliness of the domestic world around her that it would turn to beauty like a sunflower turns to the sun. Sometimes she was surprised when others did not see the thin disc of silver resting on the tarns at night, or when no one else seemed to know that water from melted snow tastes deliciously of air. In a different world she might have been called an aesthete, but in her own there were no means for her to improve her condition. Working in the manse was more important to her than anyone could imagine. Whenever she was alone she would sneak into the master bedroom or the minister's study and look in astonishment at some of the things her master and mistress had brought from the mainland:

books bound in fragrant leather lettered in gold, a silver ink bottle, a seascape painted in oil and hung in a gilded frame (actually a cheap present from Lizzie's sister after a day out at the seaside in East Kilbride) and – further into the private quarters of her employers – a bundle of silk ribbons in a drawer where white linen underwear, fringed by the most delicate lace, lay folded neatly, and a little crystal box with jewellery – a brooch of silver and amethyst, a thin gold chain with a pearl pendant and a finger ring with a red stone. To Anna these were treasures of unimaginable beauty.

But amongst all the riches of the manse there was one thing Anna lusted after more than anything else. The minister had ordered a hearthrug from the mainland the previous year. It was quite thin but with a pronounced paisley pattern and bright colours. Anna found it the most beautiful thing she had ever seen. In a world where no colour was ever brighter than the sorrel in the fields, the grey in the rocks and the yellow of a gannet's neck, the hearthrug reminded Anna of all the colours of the Bible – it was the mantle of Mary, the robes of the magi and the gowns of Rahab, the whore of Jericho, all in one. She would often sneak away from her chores to look at the rug and touch it with gentle hands.

It was for this reason she could not understand how her mistress could let that halfwit of a dog sleep on the rug. Her face would twitch as she watched the dog shuffle around the precious thing before snorting contentedly and lying down to rest, his slack jaws half open, drooling on to the crimson and the cobalt and the emerald of the cloth. Anna really had no time for the beast – it was stupid and lazy, for a start, but above all it was ugly. How could it be that it was allowed to befoul the treasure that she yearned for yet could only touch in secret? It was not fair. It really was not fair at all. Why could she not have something beautiful? Some of the older girls had got scarlet headscarves from some townspeople who came on a ship once. But she was too young then so she did not get one. All her own clothes were plain and too big; she loathed them, and hated the way they made her look like a wren chick. How embarrassing! No, really she could not think of any good reason why she should not be allowed to use the hearthrug as a shawl. After all, it was far too nice a thing to waste on a floor and a daft dog.

On Christmas Eve, when the MacKenzies settled in the parlour after supper and the midwinter dark cloaked the manse, Mr MacKenzie asked his wife what she had done with the hearthrug. Lizzie looked at the empty space by the fireplace in surprise. Dog was not lying in his usual place but had retreated under the table with a distinctly grumpy look on his face. 'I cannot think where it might have gone,' said Lizzie, perplexed. 'Perhaps Anna has removed it to mend a tear.'

The following morning at the Christmas sermon the minister looked rather baffled as he raised his gaze from the pulpit and spotted the new maid on the bench next to his own children, neatly wrapped in his hearthrug. Indeed all eyes were turned on Anna that Christmas morning. The younger women glared at the bright colours in wide-eyed admiration and envy, whereas one or two of the older women looked around the room and met the eyes of other women, distracted, frowning. As the atmosphere in the candlelit church thickened you could almost hear them think, Who does she think she is? Anna seemed oblivious to these glances of admiration, contempt and protest. She looked contentedly at the minister as he delivered the sermon. There was no triumph or vanity in her smile. She looked neither proud nor modest, but somebody who knew her intimately might have detected a certain change in her: an elevation and an ennoblement of her station. Somebody who had never met her before might have said that, at that moment, she did not belong in this world. But to those who still did, this was altogether not acceptable.

On the first day after Christmas the minister called Anna to his study. It was a bright day. Some snow had fallen during the night and the weak sun was resting in the day. He could see the golden down on Anna's upper lip as she entered the room and stood quietly by the door.

'Is there anything you would like to tell me, child?' he asked, and put down his book.

She looked up at him quickly with a puzzled look and shook her head. 'No, sir,' she whispered.

'Would you not like to say sorry for taking something from me?'

Anna bit her lip and shook her head again. One of her thin plaits fell across her shoulder and settled on her budding breast.

The minister watched her opaque face with an irritated expression. 'Taking somebody else's possession on purpose is stealing,' he said patiently. 'Did you steal the hearthrug?'

'No,' she said earnestly, for she had no experience of theft and the sun was in her eyes.

'Come now, child, small lies are the most difficult to confess, but if we let them remain they may fester and infect an innocent mind.' Some moth holes showed in his dark coat, Anna noticed, but she remained silent.

'Oh, Anna, Anna,' sighed the minister, shaking his head, 'why can you not just admit your crime and ask my forgiveness? Tell me honestly that you are sorry and I will let you off this time.'

'But, sir, I am not sorry.' She looked at him frankly. 'It is the most beautiful thing I have ever seen, and you let your dog sleep on it.' She blurted it out.

The minister rose from his chair and slammed his fist on the desk.

'Please, sir, let me keep it,' she continued to plead through her fear in a thick, desperate voice. 'You let your dog sleep on it, but it makes me look prettier than I have ever been before. It gives me colour,' she tried to explain.

'That is it! I will have no more of it – the rug must be back in its place by nightfall!' cried the minister, and he pulled a wooden ruler from the drawer of his desk. 'Our Lord Jesus sees you as you sin but forgives you if you repent,' he stammered, as he hit her once and then again over the fingers with the ruler until her knuckles bled.

Anna's eyes filled with tears but she said nothing. What was there to say? She had tried to tell the truth as prompted and she did not understand the reason for the blood on her hands. She was at the age of becoming: about to learn that life explains itself most clearly in challenge and failure.

Lizzie stepped away silently from behind the door where she had witnessed the scene. She felt upset and confused. This was a side of her husband she had not seen before. She could not comprehend his lack of compassion and compromise. Why was his world so black and white? He was being unreasonable – could he not see that Anna was only trying to tell the truth? The girl had not thieved; there was no malice or greed in her young heart – she was just a child, in love with beautiful things.

Overcome by a need to be alone with her thoughts for a moment, Lizzie slipped into the scullery and stood motionless in the cool, narrow passage. She held her breath for a moment or two and listened. The gloom hid her well and she relaxed a little, resting her back against the shelves. What was his mission? What did it signify? She thought of the pains he was taking to improve the life of the St Kildans. He studied their world with what sometimes seemed like detached scientific interest, but she knew that their welfare meant everything to him and he felt their tribulations as a personal agony. Surely only a good man would take such heed of those less fortunate? And yet there was a strange lack of imagination and empathy that kept him apart from the islanders. For the first time she felt a rush of pity for her husband – she sensed that his coldness and alienation were born out of a deep-rooted and lonely insecurity.

I am his wife and I admire him for his strength and conviction. I must not lose faith in him. I chose him, I am his wife and I need his warmth. Why is it not enough?

The year ended as it had begun, swathed in Atlantic mist. On the last day of the old year a certain tension rested over the *clachan* as the inhabitants prepared to celebrate *A'Callainn*, the old festival of Hogmanay. It was an unruly time, when worlds met and spirits travelled freely across liminal boundaries – the night when creatures emerged from the wrong side of the deep and the skies opened into space. The famous St Kildan hospitality was suddenly suspended and doors were locked against the gloomy day.

Betty Scott was grinding rye in a hand quern. The rhythmic sound as her strong arms turned stone against stone was calming to Calum, who snoozed in a recess in the wall of the hut that had been allocated to them until their own house was constructed in the new village. The sound brought back darker memories to Betty: the grinding of iron-shod hoofs as the laird's factor and his men rode into the glen, and the wheels of hand-drawn carts rasping against the loose gravel of the path as her kin left the mountains of Sutherland behind and travelled down to the sea.

She paused in her grinding and pushed a strand of hair behind her ear with the back of her hand. The fire in the hearth would flare up every now and again as an undetected draught found its way into the smoke hole. Calum stirred and studied his young wife as she started to bake the freshly ground meal into a bannock. From where he was, beyond the circle of light, it looked as if she was on fire. Her hair was in flames and the outline of her body glowed. 'You are so pretty, my lass, the queen of the village,' he whispered, surprising himself with such soft words. Betty, whose mind had been further afield than his eyes could see, twitched at the sound of his voice. 'And you are a very lazy man, Calum MacDonald.' She laughed and glowed brighter. 'Have you checked that there is enough whisky in the keg for the visitors tonight?' 'If we get any visitors,' he added quickly as one could not know what to expect from the *Gillean Calluinne*, the Hogmanay celebrants. He rose reluctantly and kissed the crown of her head

191

where she bent over the baking. Then he went outside, closing the door carefully behind him, to check on the stores in the *cleit* where they kept their food and drink. He felt uneasy in the grey daylight and wished that he had stayed in bed. He knew the stories. Oh yes, he had heard them told by the hearth of old Miss Ferguson, the *sean-chaidh*, who remembered all the tales of old and fed them into the individual memories of the St Kildans. He had heard of the dark forces at large on the night of *A'Callainn*. Once, not long ago, a father and his daughter had walked out on to the rocks to fetch some wood to keep their fire going into the New Year. It had been a misty day, like this one, and an old man who had met them on the path at the edge of the *clachan* had warned them not to go any further as the mist was thick and the rocks were slippery. The father and daughter were never seen again. Not so much as a piece of clothing ever floated ashore to remind the people that they had once lived on the island. The man's wife, the mother of the child, had gone mad from waiting for the two of them to return. For years she would set out into the mist as it rolled in from the sea. The villagers could hear the eerie sound of her voice as she called for her only child at the edge of the sea. But the man who had met the father and daughter on the path told his kin that there had been something strange about them, something that he could not quite explain. He swore that their gaze was distant and they had not looked at him as he spoke to them but walked passed him with their eyes far into the mist. Calum felt a shiver run down his spine and he quickened his step so that he was almost running when he reached the *cleit* where Betty had stacked their winter stores. Suddenly he wanted to be near her again. She always made him feel safe and strong – it was a strange thing to think about a lass who had been on the island for only a few years. He could not think of a single girl that he would rather have married, and he knew that many of his friends envied him and admired the beauty of his bride. He pulled out the keg of whisky and some dried meat and hurried back into the *clachan*. Dusk was falling, and in the long shadows he could make out some of the boys and youths who had begun to gather in the yards. He was no longer one of them, he had a wife to protect, and he hurried into his house and closed the door on all evil.

As the darkness of the old year settled over the *clachan* the voices of the young men became increasingly excited. Betty listened from inside the small house. She liked the excitement of the rituals and she could feel her heart beating faster as she heard a sound as of a muffled drumming. She stood on her toes to look out of the smoke hole. There in the yard of the houses the boys had built a small fire on which they lit some torches. They gathered around and suddenly she saw a beastly being rise from their midst. A horned creature with a hide like a winter cow's. The youths started to hit their sticks on the hide, which answered like a drum. The creature started running, leaping like a devil dancing in the flames of hell, and the youths followed, beating it hard with their sticks. 'Come over by the fire, Betty!' Calum called anxiously as the noise grew stronger. She went and sat by him with her hands pressed between her thighs as she continued to listen breathlessly. Suddenly they heard the din draw nearer. They began to shiver as they heard the horrible procession dance around their house; three times they went in the course of the sun, while drumming upon the hide of the screaming beast and on the walls of the house. The noise was terrifying, gruesome, as if all the evil spirits had been let loose. Calum moved closer to Betty as they heard the monster climb on to their roof and stamp his feet. Now they could hear the sticks beating at the door and somebody chanting the runes:

> We come here to you at A'Callainn
> Renewing the rites of Hogmanay;
> The rules are still the same, of course –
> The same since our ancestors' day.

Betty stirred towards the door, but Calum held her back as another voice picked up the chant:

> We will go southward round the house
> And we will descend through the door;

We'll pass through the home as we always do,
Round the man, as we've done before,

Another voice, recently broken by puberty, continued:

For the wife will get it, she that deserves it:
The giving hand of the Hogmanay.
Knowing the drought that is on the land
We don't expect any uisge beatha –

The banging on the door was louder as somebody sang the last verse:

Just a little drop of the summer produce
That we hope you'll put on some bread.
We have many houses to visit tonight, so arise now
And open the door – and please, let us be fed!

When the chant ended, there was a pause and then a deep voice said, 'Open up, let me enter,' and Calum, still shaking a bit, stood to open the door. Soon the horned beast was standing by the *tallan* and Calum bade him to step up to the fire. Betty thought she recognised the torn shoes of her brother-in-law, Aonghas, as the beast pulled out a piece of sheepskin from under the hide. He leaned towards the fire and singed the sheepskin until a thick smoke rose from it. Then he walked around the interior of the house once and held the skin under the noses of Betty and Calum.

Everybody was silent as this went on, but as the beast threw the skin back into the fire Betty handed over the bannock that she had baked earlier and opened the keg of whisky to pass it around the young men. Calum took one mouthful from the keg, and then another, before he passed it on to the youth beside him. Finally the spell was broken and he smiled, relieved and elated, as he saw the horned beast gather Betty in his arms and kiss her from under the hide. Everyone laughed and one boy, strengthened by the drink, cried at Calum that he was a lucky lad to have wed the prettiest queen on Hirta, and if he could bear to leave her side for a while he was welcome to join them as they went on their way.

The partying went on throughout the night, but as soon as all the young men had fallen into a deep sleep the New Year broke cruelly into another grey day.

Afterwards no one could remember that the first day of the year had begun in any particular manner. No one could remember seeing or hearing anything unusual as they went about their business that morning. But then most of them had slept in until after breakfast. One boy called Duncan, who was only nine at the time, had been out early to poke in the dying embers of the bonfire. Later on, when asked by the *maor* if he had heard or seen anything unusual, Duncan said he had not, but when the *maor* gave him a rare winter apple and asked him to think harder he said that there had perhaps been a noise as if a giant door had opened and closed far away. As his kin gathered around to hear about the noise, the boy seemed to remember more and more. Had he seen a light as of a great fire in the morning sky? asked one. Oh yes, he suddenly recalled that there had been a strange red light on the horizon. Had he heard a noise like the screaming of thousands and thousands of doomed souls? wondered another, and the boy furrowed his brows until his face lit up with the memory: yes, yes, there was a strange sound as if a lot of people were crying and wailing. So, at the end of the day, the St Kildans were convinced that some unearthly evil had once again settled on their island.

But that was later. What did happen on that New Year's Day was this: Anna and another young girl from the *clachan* called Rachel had set off over the hills to drink from the well they called *Tobar nam Buaidh*, or the Well of Virtues. It was generally thought that the water from this well could offer good health to anyone who drank from it. *Tobar nam Buaidh* was over on the north-western side of the island, on Gleann Mòr. The summer pastures of Gleann Mòr lay about a mile from the *clachan*, and the girls set off just before midday to make it back before the dark. The young friends had much to talk about, as one of the *Gillean Calluinne* had stolen a kiss from Rachel the previous night. It had been too dark to see who it was, and the girls were left to analyse the event over and over again. As they reached the ridge of Am Blaid they sat down for a while to catch their breath. They scanned the glen below them and one of the girls thought she saw a movement out of the corner of her eye, but when she looked again everything was still and quiet. They soon stood up again and skipped down the hillside into the glen, the thin braids which had escaped from under their woollen head scarves whipping around their necks. As they reached the well, hand in hand, they were flustered and breathless and they were giggling so hard that they could hardly stand. Rachel dropped into a hopeless heap by the side of the well, while Anna held on to her jaw, which was hurting madly from all the laughter. Suddenly Anna cried out and pointed at the ground. Strange footprints were scattered in the mud at the opening to the well. They looked fresh, but the shape was peculiar, as one foot seemed to be much larger than the other. In fact, one of the prints did not look like a human foot at all. This seemed odd as they had not seen anybody on their way to the glen. Nor had they spotted any animals on this side of the island. They looked around but could see nothing. Anna felt uneasy, but Rachel laughed and said she was silly and soon the two of them were drinking greedily from the cool clear water of the well. As they left their offerings to the spirit of the well, a couple of pretty shells which they had gathered by the head of Village Beach earlier in the day, Anna prayed earnestly for the spirits to keep her and her family and the manse-folk from illness throughout the year. Rachel, on the other hand, asked the well to make her pretty and make her breasts grow. 'You can't ask that of the spirits!' Anna gasped. 'They will get angry with you – the *Tobar nam Buaidh* offers health, not beauty!' 'Oh, Anna, don't be such a spoilsport. I can ask for whatever I want,' said the plain girl, whose chest was still flat and whose nose was rather too large for her face. 'Anything I want!'

'No, you can't!'

'I can!' she cried, and looked up at Anna with cool grey eyes. 'It is possible to change for the better. The minister says so.'

'The minister speaks of our souls.'

'I would much rather be pretty than soulful.'

'But if your soul is bad, there is no frippery in the world that can make you bonny.' Anna stroked her knuckles as she remembered only too well the impact of the minister's words.

'I'm sure there is a way around it,' muttered Rachel, who realised she had to rely on her wits.

'But you have got such pretty hair.' It was the best Anna could muster.

'Aye, well, I was born with it,' Rachel admitted. 'But your eyes are much nicer than mine. They are so blue.'

'They are only blue in certain lights,' Anna begged, afraid that the colour of her eyes would somehow stand in the way of their friendship.

Rachel did not say anything but dug a hole in the mud with her scruffy boot.

'Your hair really is very pretty,' said Anna again to make up, but it was too late. The good mood of a moment ago was destroyed. As they started the long journey back across the hill they walked separately, Rachel a couple of steps ahead of Anna, both girls' eyes fixed moodily on the ground. They walked on for a while until Anna tried again. 'Anyway, that boy, whoever he was, kissed you last night. Nobody kissed *me*.'

'It was probably so dark he didn't know who he was kissing,' came the furious answer.

Anna sighed. It was getting late and she wanted to get back to the *clachan* while they could still see their way. As they reached the top of the glen she turned to look back at the bay far below. Suddenly she froze and cried out.

Rachel turned around. 'What?' she said irritably. But Anna couldn't speak; she just pointed into the valley below, and as Rachel followed her finger and looked hard into the dark she saw a faint light flickering in and out of focus. 'What is it?' she whispered hoarsely and drew nearer to Anna. 'I don't know,' Anna breathed, 'but it seems to be coming from the Amazon's House.' At the mention of the Amazon's House the two girls looked at each other, their argument forgotten. No one had lived in the Amazon's House since the time of the ancestors. It was a strange round building which did not look anything like their own houses. Legend said that it had once been home to a female warrior, a *Bana-ghaisgeach*, who was feared by all the men in the Hebrides and who used to hunt deer on the great, storm-swept plain that connected Hirta to the Long Isle back in the Young Age. The girls suddenly remembered the strange footprints at the well. Anna was shivering hard, but Rachel grabbed her hand and started running towards the *clachan*.

As they entered the *clachan* there was great commotion and no one would stop to listen to what the girls had to say. A *cleit* had been broken into and robbed, it turned out. And no one had noticed anything, not even the dogs! Theft was almost unheard of amongst the St Kildans. Things did not get better when it was understood that the *cleit* belonged to the widow Mary MacCrimmon, whose husband had fallen over the cliffs on a winter's day many years previously. It was not just food that was missing but Mr MacCrimmon's old clothes, which Mary had kept just in case.

At last Anna and Rachel got to tell their tale. The girls were pale and shaken. Anna was sobbing lightly, but Rachel was cool and composed. On hearing what they had to tell, MacKinnon the *maor* ordered everybody to keep indoors and sprinkle water on their livestock and on the threshold of their houses. He said he would question anyone who had been out and about that day and asked them to ransack their minds for any

201

information that might cast light on the strange events of the day. It was once he had heard the tales of young Duncan that he decided to go to the minister.

'Nonsense!' cried Mr MacKenzie, and slammed his fist on his desk; a strand of dark hair fell into his eyes.

'But, sir . . .' MacKinnon stood miserably, his cap in his hands.

'No, man, I will have no more talk about spirits, whether good or evil, in this house!'

'But, minister, you do not understand.' MacKinnon tried again. 'The girls saw the light in the *Taigh na Bana-ghaisgeach* and old MacCrimmon's ghost has come back to claim his possessions.' The *maor* was sweating. 'Do you not see what it means?'

'No, MacKinnon, I do not *see what it means*!' The minister's face was alight with anger. 'You go back to the *clachan* and tell the people to pray to our Lord whenever they fear the dark, but I am tired of warning you not to provoke His anger with your pagan mischief!'

'But the boy Duncan said he heard a sound as like the opening of a great iron portal and the cries of wretched souls crying in pain.'

'Then I suggest you give the boy Duncan a good talking-to and explain what our Lord thinks of liars.' The minister's voice sounded dangerous as he stood up to face MacKinnon. 'You are a sound man, MacKinnon. Surely you do not believe in this primitive nonsense.'

MacKinnon looked at the floor and shook his head slowly.

'You are leading your kin into the new age.' The minister had placed a hand on the shorter man's shoulder and his voice was calmer now. 'We are building a new village, are we not? Well then, you know as well as I do that if there is a thief on the island it is one of us and we must pray to God to help us find the evil that is in our midst. Satan is not a beast who hobbles on one leg – he is an evil who finds his way into the souls of sinners.'

'Aye, minister,' the *maor* muttered almost inaudibly, but he was not convinced. He knew what he knew, and he could not turn away from this knowledge, not even to please God. He knew that his kin would not steal on the night of *A'Callainn*, and he knew that no one would light a fire in the *Taigh na Bana-ghaisgeach* unless they wanted to provoke the ancestors. This minister who preached of a different kind of good and evil, the approved kind, was trying to extract the old beliefs, to pull out the mythology of the island until it bled at the roots.

As he left the manse MacKinnon met Mrs MacKenzie in the doorway. She smiled at him and nodded as she started to remove her mittens and headscarf. He stopped for a second and looked her in the eye before hurrying on down the path to the *clachan*. Mrs MacKenzie glanced after him for a moment before going into her husband's study.

'I have been down to the *clachan* to see Betty, Neil.' She could tell by his back that he was angry.

'Yes?'

'Anna is in a terrible state; she and a friend saw some very frightening things on Gleann Mòr this afternoon.'

'Do you believe the hysterical tales of some young girls? Especially Anna, who lied to us so shamelessly after stealing the rug.' He turned quickly and stared at her. 'Perhaps you will be tearing the wings off birds next and gouging out their eyes!' She was close at hand so it was at her he vented his frustration.

Lizzie looked at her husband in disbelief, but when she answered her voice was strong and slow. 'But they are afraid, Neil, and we should take their word for it. They know this island – we do not.'

'I command this island!' The force and arrogance of his remark surprised him. He winced and was just about to make a joke to soften the stupid claim when she said in a tired voice, 'You have changed, Neil.'

He felt anger and frustration rise inside him again. What did she mean? The tone of her voice had hurt him more than the nature of her remark. How dare she!

She left the room before he could answer. Once she had put the children to bed she locked the front door. For a minute she stood by the windows, looking into the frosty darkness outside and wondering what treachery dwelt beyond the night and what, if anything, she could dare not to believe.

The island huddled under the signs of evil. Hail as big as fulmar eggs fell over the *clachan* and destroyed the winter thatch of a widow's roof; the water in the burns turned to blood at dusk; a child was born with a split lip and died a few days later, her face distorted and twisted like the Devil's. The nights rang with strange and terrible noises – dark airs that terrified and hurt. Many thought they recognised the haunting sound of the opening of a great gate and the screams of purgatory. Their dreams were of death by water and tides rising into great flood waves. They woke from their dreams crying.

Young and old prayed for salvation, each to their own God. But as the black month rolled on there was no sign that their prayers were answered.

On a cold morning in late January Neil MacKenzie strode darkly against the bright sky towards the summit of Oiseval. He climbed briskly past a headland where a sleek stream suddenly lost its foothold and fell, abandoned, into the sea in a thin, glittering waterfall. From above it looked like a string of saliva extending from the slack mouth of the huge, aged rock. Nothing could grow on the fell, which was exposed to the ruthless battering of the sea. The wind and the salt spray had made the ground as barren as a desert. When he reached the summit he stopped for a while and looked out to sea. He wore a dark tweed cloak that batted and flapped in the clear, wintery air, and there was no heat in the pale sunshine that fell on his bare head. The wind spoke to him and he answered back into the vast emptiness of the Atlantic. He could see no life; the sky was too immense, too blue, and the extravagance of it was almost perverse. 'I wonder . . .' he said into the space where his was the only existence. 'No, no, I do not have the answer.' And then, as if answering the call from the west, 'What? What did you say?' But it did not matter. He sighed and walked on because he knew he must blame his sins for his predicament. Things were not going his way any more. He was losing his grip. He had forced faith into the souls of the St Kildans, he was sure of it, and still they sank back into popery, lies and theft as soon as the elements were against them. Will they not be bettered by civilised association? Will they remain creatures beyond the pale of humanity? No, no, he must not despair! They suffer from a nervous disposition; their minds are weak, that is all, he told himself. Education will strengthen their minds like medicine strengthens the body. At once he felt better. And the truth was that, despite his brief spells of doubt, besides his feelings of guilt and all the setbacks and disappointments, he still believed that he was doing the right thing. Yes, he was convinced that he was doing good. God may well present him with repeated challenges, but the Lord had rewarded him with two children who lived and grew, and one more on the way. Yes, he was blessed. But there was that other concern. He had sensed it lately and could not master it. His Lizzie seemed to have grown distant. On several occasions she had turned away from him – his own wife refusing him, preventing him from doing his duty to God and procreation, preventing him from taking his pleasure. Not now, she had said; give me some peace. *Peace!* He spat the word at the wind. Ah, the humiliation! Did she expect him to swallow it just like that? Aye, let her be cold towards him, let her be as dry as a stick! He had another fire burning inside him now, he would put the wild waters in roar, he *would* succeed in his mission.

But as he turned to follow the path along the ridge of Oiseval he remembered the beauty of her temples and the delicate bones in her hands as she held them to his face, for how could he forget the only emotions that he had no way of expressing? How could he find words to describe the feeling of her living so vividly, so warmly, inside him? And from the far side of his secret grief he realised that he was partly to blame. They were no longer united through tenderness or intimacy but by the island itself – because there was nothing else. He had not allowed them to share anything else. He wanted to explain to her that the only words of love that he dared speak were the names of their children, but in order to be so brave – so honest – he would have to let his guard down. In the end it was because of his weakness that he chose to increase the distance between them.

As he reached *Bearradh na h-Eige* he stepped up to the edge of the cliff and looked down the vertical drop into the sea six hundred feet below. How different this place was now compared to in summer, when the fulmars would be skimming the rocks on stiff wings, crucified between the sea and the sky, or sailing the turbulence with breath-taking skill and elegance. He lay down flat on his stomach and looked over the edge into the clear sea. Far below, the swell sighed in and out of the caves. As he stared into the clear green waters he saw the dark shape of a killer whale. The silent predator was gliding towards a group of young grey seals, some of whom had not yet shed their snow-white puppy skins. They were oblivious to the threat as they played amongst the sea caves and underwater rocks. How amazing to be allowed to watch nature from above. Is this how God looks down upon us? he wondered. He watched with a dispassionate interest as the killer whale closed in on its young prey. They looked tiny from such a high distance; it was like a pike hunting a perch. He suddenly felt an overpow-ering urge to intervene and save the seals and cried out in a wordless 'Arghh!' His hands clawed at the rough ground about him until they found a small rock which he hurled over the edge of the cliff. It fell heavily while time stood still – life was suspended – and hit the surface with a distant splash just as the whale went in for the kill. Blood clouded the clear water as the seal was torn apart. He felt empty, and slumped with his face against the stone.

There was a strange sound which increased as he strained his ears against the wind. First the distant baying of a dog, and then he heard it again. A moaning song, eerie and sad on this clear day, it started like a whisper from far away but increased in strength into a faint, broken-hearted choir. The minister froze and made the sign of the cross; he remembered the boy Duncan's tale of the crying souls in purgatory. Was he going mad? Had God truly abandoned him? He crawled back to the edge of the cliff and braced himself for what he might see in the bloodied waters. At first he saw nothing; the killer whale was gone and the sea had cleared, but as he looked closer to the shore he suddenly saw them: hundreds of seals had appeared from the caves and were dotted over the sharp rocks by the steep shore. Stirred from their slumber by the struggle, they had all emerged to sing an elegy for one of their lost sons. Their song would sometimes resemble the strong high notes and airs of a single pipe; at other times the cacophony of voices would join in a strange harmony that echoed in the caves and see-sawed like a pibroch over the still Atlantic. More and more seals joined in the sad lament as the voices of their kin summoned them from caves all along the shore. And the minister, his broken heart longing for the sea and his face washed with tears, remembered the lone piper who had played as his own kin embarked on the ship to Canada, and he realised that humankind was indeed closer to nature than he had ever understood.

He must have fallen asleep, for when he came to it was already dusk. He was stiff and shivered violently as the cold had seeped from the ground into his bones. He could hardly walk and stamped his feet a few times to get his blood flowing again. Something, a sound or a change of light, made him turn around, and as he did he was sure he saw a furry creature with the face of a man crouching on a rocky outcrop some three hundred yards inland. He called out, but the creature slipped away, huge and mute, and merged into the twilight. The minister hobbled and limped as quickly as he could on his frozen legs to the place where he had seen the creature, but there was nothing there. He searched the ground closely, but there was no sign except for a slight impression in the short grass. He shook his head and realised that his mind was overwrought. He needed to sleep. More than anything else he needed to sleep.

There had been sightings. One man claimed to have seen a man with three legs step out of a seal-skin and slip into the sea at Glen Bay. Another *cleit* had been raided for food, and Anna told Lizzie in excited whispers that Rachel's cousin had told Rachel, who had told her – because they were friends again and Rachel had even given Anna a pin made out of an old coin – that one night when she went to fetch her dog, which had run off and was barking on the hill behind the *clachan*, somebody had grabbed her from behind and held her around the waist before the dog jumped on the man, for it was a man, with very large hands like flippers, and Rachel's cousin had managed to escape. And it was true, for Rachel had told Anna that her cousin had a bruise as black as night on her upper left arm, and Rachel had given Anna the pin and told her to swear not to tell anyone. And this was because her cousin had asked her not to tell anyone in the first place, but surely Anna did the right thing to tell Mrs MacKenzie, ma'am?

And then one night when her husband and the children were asleep Lizzie thought she heard a noise outside. She walked to the window and looked out. There was no moon and the night was pitch dark except, she saw, for a point of light somewhere in the direction of the feather store. This was the stone building on the path just below the manse. It had been built by the laird to house the feathers due to him as tax, but it was locked up and only used for storage. The keys were kept in the scullery between the manse and the kirk. Lizzie put her husband's coat over her nightgown and stepped into her winter boots.

She lit a lamp and fetched the keys from the galley. The smell of hoarfrost struck her as she opened the door and stepped on to the porch. She stood for a while and listened into the dark. There was no sound except for the familiar sighs and snores from the sleeping sea. When her eyes had got used to the dark she started walking towards the feather store. The light was still there. When she reached the door she fished out the large key and searched for the keyhole. The lock was broken. At once she was very frightened, but this did not stop her from pushing the door open and stepping into the room. A coarse candle burned low on an upturned barrel on the floor. But she could see no person. She hesitated briefly and looked around before taking another step into the store. Too late she sensed somebody step out of the shadows behind her. Her cry was muffled by a large hand that closed over her mouth. She could tell by his smell that the man was not a St Kildan. Of course she knew, she had known all along, that there was a foreigner on the island. It was the only rational explanation, but yet so unlikely that she had almost begun to believe the islanders' superstitions. He held her close with his arm across her chest and his hand over her mouth while his free hand searched her body. For what? For a weapon? She shivered as she felt his heavy breath against her cheek. She did not struggle, but his grip was surprisingly weak, and when it slackened a bit she seized the moment and broke free and turned to look at him.

A memory from her childhood came into her head – her father taking her to see Paisley Gaol, which he had built. Warm sunshine on the dusty street, blown roses and a tree heavy with plums in a garden. Whose garden? Was it the prison warden's? She gripped her father's hand. She had heard about prisoners, and the walls of the gaol cast a cool shadow which seemed to creep towards her as she stood under the plum tree. Plums and rose petals, red and pink. The light from the candle on the barrel fell over him. Red and pink, blood and flesh, wounds: pain. She looked up at him in helpless horror. Darkness was all around them but the candlelight lit up part of his broken body. He was awful, terrifying to look at, unearthly and beastly. His face was darkened by dirt and grime and his hair was matted and wild. He wore a jerkin made of seal-skin; the animal must have been recently butchered for the stench that came off the skin was unbearable and it seemed to be caked in blood. He was leaning heavily on a rough stick. She gasped as she looked down at his legs. One of them seemed to have been broken at a brutish angle, and she could see the shape of a crushed bone through the bandage rags which smelt sharply of decay. He stood quite still and did not make a move towards her. At last she dared to look into his face. His eyes were incensed with pain, she saw, and there was something else, something altogether more alien, which seemed to her to be a fear born out of hell.

It was as the darkest part of that long, dense night started to show its shadows that the men came to help carry him into the kitchen, where she made a rudimentary bed close to the hearth. The children were asleep, but Anna had been woken by the commotion and had been sent on sleepy legs for soapy water and towels. The stranger was moaning weakly as the men dumped him into the bed and stood staring in bewilderment. Lizzie, still wearing her husband's coat, blew on the embers to get the fire going. In the smoky glow the man on the bed looked barely alive; his monstrous body remained in the strange position it had taken when pushed into the bed, and there was no sign of breathing. One of the men walked closer and, with his face averted, put his hand towards the stranger's chest. At that moment the crippled torso heaved again and let out a few loud, erratic breaths.

'Thank you, MacKinnon, Ferguson. You may go back to your beds now,' she said, and nodded to her husband to accompany the men to the door.

MacKenzie too was confused, but his wife's new-found authority left him no choice.

'Yes, yes. Thank you, gentlemen. You would better go and catch some sleep. We will discuss this matter at the *mòd* in the morning.'

The two islanders made for the door, Ferguson wiping his hands on his already grimy trousers and MacKinnon gathering up the bloodied seal-skins they had stripped off the stranger. 'Phoo!' he exhaled as he carried them outside on stretched-out arms.

'Don't forget to sink them well with a stone,' the minister called after them. 'We don't want any of the children to find them, do we?'

When they were alone with the broken man MacKenzie said to his wife, 'And what do you think you will be doing with him?' He nodded towards the bed. 'You do realise that he is probably dangerous and he could hurt the children.'

'Dangerous!' She almost laughed. 'He cannot even walk on his own – he is barely alive!' The note of determined sarcasm in her voice was a surprise even to herself.

'You don't know anything about him! He could be one of those expelled pirates from the Barbary coast for all we know!' He had raised his voice and she shushed him, indicating with her head to the chamber where the children were sleeping.

MacKenzie shook his head in exasperation. His eyes gleamed black in the shadows.

'Yes, well, there is not much we can do about that now. He is an ill man and he needs care. It is our duty as Christians,' she added, and knew the stranger would stay.

At that moment Anna returned with water from the spring and the MacKenzies went silent.

As the women set about their work, MacKenzie was left to his own devices and was too obviously superfluous. Carefully and with studied precision he straightened his shirt and tucked it into the breeches. He felt threatened by the beast on the bed and shuddered. He did not understand why God had sent this man at such a volatile time. What was the purpose of these tribulations? It was as if some other level of the natural world had infringed upon this domain where he, MacKenzie, fought for civilisation and order. A lock of hair had fallen into his eyes – furiously he tugged it under control before striding noisily into his study.

In the kitchen the light from the fire had grown stronger and shaped the length of the stranger's damaged body. He seemed to have fallen asleep, but he was sweating heavily and his breathing was still irregular. He was very tall and must at one time have been quite impressively built. Lizzie sighed as she tried to remember any facts she might have known about nursing.

'Ma'am?' Anna was thin inside her nightgown and wide-eyed from having been woken up to this nightmare. One of her thin braids had come undone and hung in waffled creases.

'Yes, Anna, I'm sorry, I was just thinking . . .' She glanced towards the stranger again. 'We should remove those rags and burn them – but leave the loincloth.' There was purpose in her voice as she rolled up the sleeves of her nightgown.

Anna approached the bed and as she started

pulling at the few rags of linen fabric which still covered the body – the remains of garments that might have been worn for a lighter climate – the heat in the room increased the stench. The girl recoiled and looked pleadingly at Mrs MacKenzie.

'Go on, girl, decay is part of life,' Lizzie said in a matronly tone, although this was the first time this had occurred to her.

By now the water had heated on the hearth and the women carefully started to wipe the man's face and upper body. 'Wait.' Mrs MacKenzie held out a hand. 'I think we should shave him first.'

The face that emerged out of the shorn black beard was shrunken and of a strange beige colour which led Lizzie to believe that the man did not usually wear a beard but had recently been tanned all over. It was hard to determine his age, as the hollows under his eyes and cheeks had made the skin sag a bit. Long dark lashes fluttered in a restless dream. The women worked quietly and methodically, changing the soapy water as often as needed. Lizzie cut the man's hair, which was also black but with streaks of grey. Once she had got rid of the worst of it she lifted his head with one hand and rubbed the remaining tufts with soap, then rinsed it gently by squeezing water from the cloth. She could not help but run her fingers over his scalp. It seemed unbearably intimate to touch somebody's head like this. There were a few white marks on his skull – tiny scars as if his hair had been forcibly shorn at some stage. Anna, in the meantime, was cleaning the man's left leg, while anxiously staring at the right, with its terrible fracture poking out of the grimy bandages.

Lizzie looked up and felt a pang of regret when she saw the horror in the girl's eyes. She had forgotten that Anna was still merely a child. Leaning over, she stroked a damp strand of hair out of the maid's steamy face. 'You can go to bed now, Anna. You have been most helpful, but I can handle the rest myself.' Anna did not object. She put down her enamel container and the damp cloth and walked stiffly and without a word towards the children's bedchamber. Lizzie watched her leave the room and noticed with tenderness that her thin shoulder blades stuck out under the linen gown like the budding wings of an angel.

Left alone with the stranger, Lizzie felt incredibly calm. She could not determine the nature of her feelings at that moment; she was repulsed by the stench of the body but at the same time it evoked feelings of compassion and benevolence in her. She felt vaguely possessive of him. She was the one who had found him, and she invested her discovery with some significance; it was as if she had finally found a calling of her own. But, most importantly, there was a vague sense of kinship; this outsider was somebody more foreign than herself.

The body that emerged was still muscular, although it was clear that it had starved for some time – the ribs were starting to show, and the collarbones were too prominent. Illuminated by the flickering fire, the skin was surprisingly smooth, but dry and chapped in places. Lizzie stroked her cloth along his torso and arms. She had never been so close to a man's body before, not in this way. MacKenzie would never have allowed her to scrutinise his physique; nor would he explore hers beyond the necessary. She thought of his heavy body on top of her, pushing inside, probing, searching but never reaching quite far enough, never finding the secret, her secret, within. She blushed in sudden embarrassment; she must be truly disturbed to have such thoughts – and in the presence of another man.

There were no marks or scars on the body apart from a faint groove around each wrist. This puzzled her. She lifted a limp hand to get a closer look, but recoiled at the animal smell from a whiskery armpit. This distracted her and she had to soak the underarms several times in fresh water before she was content with the result. She could feel a great sense of satisfaction rising inside her as layer after layer of grime and dirt dissolved, revealing her patient's skin. It was the colour of dry leaves, a deep colour, different from the weathered rust of the St Kildans or the bronze of her husband's arms in the summer.

She stood back for a minute; the firelight briefly made her face look bruised, before the shadows settled in contrast to her flushed cheeks. Holding her breath she leaned over the man and removed the rag that had been left over his loins. She gasped and quickly put her hands to her mouth at the sight of another man's private parts. They looked different from her husband's, she noted, not without curiosity. Surprisingly hairless, the plum-coloured scrotum was sagging against one leg, and the other thing, shrunken and grey, was resting on top of it as if on a plush pillow. Lizzie touched it lightly with her cloth and immediately drew back. She was perspiring now and wiped her hairline with the back of her hand. She thought she heard a sound and looked up, but it was only the wind borne by the dawn and the sighs of the awakening sea. With an air of determination she wiped the area around, taking care not to touch anything. She looked into the stranger's face but he was still asleep, or unconscious, and then, averting her eyes, she moved the cloth to the soft parts, feeling them, light as hatchlings, through the fabric.

When she was satisfied that it was all clean she rested her hand lightly on his hip where a distinct line, like a geological stratum, revealed that the man had often worked without a shirt. Her trembling fingertips traced the length of the line from hip to hip and around towards the back. It made the strange body look more vulnerable, she thought. There was something so innocent – almost childlike – about the blue-veined white skin of the hips set off against the tanned abdomen.

Gently she covered his body with a clean sheet and stoked the fire.

She woke suddenly from the chair by the bedside where she must have fallen asleep. The stranger was moaning again, and the twisted sheet was soaked with sweat. 'O dear God, he is going to die.' She might have said it aloud. In two steps she reached the study door and flung it open. Her husband was asleep at his desk, his head on his arms framed in the hesitant light of the new day which was making a reluctant entry through the window.

'Neil, please, you have got to help me!' There was desperation and perhaps even tears in her voice.

MacKenzie leapt up at her call. 'Lizzie, darling, what's going on? Are you hurt?' There was fear in his drowsiness.

'No, no – it's him, you must save him,' she sobbed.

The minister, remembering of whom she was talking, answered wryly, 'I dare say he is beyond saving – he will be halfway to hell by now.' But as he spoke he rose and followed her into the kitchen.

The man on the bed was racked in a delirium of sweating shivers. 'Oh!' he moaned, his bloodless face drained further by pain.

MacKenzie looked at the stranger with disgust, only vaguely recognising the change in his appearance. 'His leg needs setting straight – tell Anna to keep the children in the bedroom and fetch the bottle of whisky the Atkinsons left,' he said, rolling up his shirtsleeves.

When Lizzie returned with the half-full bottle, MacKenzie was examining the broken tibia. 'I saw my father mend a horse's leg once. It needs to get back into position to stop the fracture from becoming further inflamed.' He bent over the stinking wound. 'Aw! It is too messy – I can't make out where the bone should be,' he said, agitated.

'Shall I give him some whisky?' Lizzie asked hoarsely.

'No, no. He is too far gone for that to be of any use. I want you to wash out the wound with it,' he said, and took hold of the stranger's shoulders, pinning them to the bed.

Lizzie swallowed hard and, holding on to the lower part of the leg with a cloth, poured some of the liquor over the wound.

The man gave a sharp cry and his body convulsed.

'He is suffering!'

'Yes, but it is the only way. Now, make sure you soak it properly.'

At least this time the liquid pain made the patient pass out.

'Now, you must try to hold him down, like this.' MacKenzie showed his wife how to push down on the patient's upper arms with all her weight, and she did as she was told.

MacKenzie took hold of the leg on either side of the wound and, after a moment of concentrated hesitation, he pulled sharply. There was a long scream and Lizzie struggled to hold on to her weakened patient.

'By God! I made a botch of it!' MacKenzie threw his hands in the air.

'You must try again!' Lizzie was blubbering now.

'No, no, I can't! It is too ghastly!' Lizzie could see that her husband's eyes were wild and frantic now and felt a new wave of desperation rise inside her.

'Oh, but, Neil, you must, or he will most certainly die!' She could hear the children crying in the other room and Anna's panicked voice trying to soothe them.

Fresh blood, mixed with thick yellow-green pus, was seeping from the distressed wound and dripping on to the floor. The stranger was breathing erratically and with obvious difficulty. For a moment man and wife stood watching in horror as life threatened to drain away. Then MacKenzie banged his fists on the mantelpiece before turning back to the patient.

'Arghhh!' This time the scream came from MacKenzie rather than from his patient as the bone was finally pulled back into position.

Fuelled by adrenalin and unable to think straight, MacKenzie smashed a chair against the floor several times until he had a couple of sturdy wooden splints. Lizzie looked on in shock at first, then she too sprang into action and tore strips from the damp sheet that had fallen to the floor.

Once the fracture was bound up and the patient had grown silent again the MacKenzies sat down, spent and exhausted, at the table. Lizzie spoke first, with new-found affection and admiration. 'That was extraordinary, what you did, I'm so proud of . . .' He held up his hand and interrupted her with a cold stare. The charge of a moment ago had subsided into anger and his head was throbbing. 'From now on he is your responsibility, do you hear me? Yours!'

'But, Neil, please! Steady yourself!' she began to protest.

'If he dies now it is not my fault – I did not kill him!' His eyes were livid.

'Shh, no one is suggesting it would be your fault,' she pleaded, dread rising in her throat.

'Don't use that tone at me – you were the one who got hysterical.' His face was red with frustration and indignity. Lizzie looked at him in incomprehension.

'I . . .' Her voice faltered as she did not know how to defend herself.

'You are always walking around with that self-pitying look, feeling lonely. But what about me – have you ever given me a thought?' He sobbed and was at once ashamed of this display of self-pity. His head was hurting with frustration and he shut his eyes. He did not know what he was saying; suddenly he did not understand the words – there was no clarity. Oh why was there no clarity – was he losing his mind? What evil had this man brought on to the island? He felt trapped and frightened, and now there was a bad sound in his ears. He held his fists against his head and wanted her to hold him. More than anything he wanted to lean against her and let her comfort him. He loved her – why could he never bring himself to tell her? He depended on her but he felt powerless around her – as if the love itself was taking away his strength. He wanted her to be happy, but sometimes he suspected that there was something dark at the core of him that prevented him from doing the right things and from feeling the right feelings. Over the years, as a vague sense of guilt had grown stronger he had started to shy away from emotional responsibility. It was not his fault – somebody else would have to take on some of the burden. Why must he always shoulder the blame?

He could feel her resentment filling the room, but there was something else too, some of that old insecurity. He would strike before receiving the blow. Did she not tempt him, sapping his power so that he could not get close enough to God? This was a new thought – why had he not realised it before? It was all terribly clear to him now. He opened his eyes again. She looked frightened and he smiled. 'It's all your fault.'

'Neil, you are rambling, I don't know what you are talking about. Let's not argue!' She tried to grab hold of him but he shrugged her off.

'Ha! When did you ever care for me? But now you have something to care about – you make sure your freak survives!' He stood up, and, pulling on his coat, broke out of the door and stumbled off, away from his wife and into the bleak day.

That February the sky was stretched so thinly over the island that it seemed ready to burst, and the evenings were murky and sad. The minister, however, had recovered from his bout of headaches and was busy working with the natives on the new enclosures. Anna, whose spirit was of the island, grew increasingly restless inside and would often dress the children in their woollens and bring them down to the beach, where the native children were looking for flotsam and jetsam or competing to spot the returning birds. Once they found a wooden box with lettering in a foreign language. Mr MacKenzie examined it closely and said it was most likely from the cargo of an Iberian privateer. Anna thought of the Iberian coast, where there would be lemons and apes and ladies in colourful dresses. Later, she found a piece of green glass in the shallows and fished it out of the icy water with numb fingers. Still wet from the sea, the glass looked to Anna like a gem that had fallen out of a foreign jewel, perhaps a ring or a tiara. She realised that she must hide it in her secret cache in the manse wall – the village boys must not see it or they would laugh at her vanity. She closed the glass in her hand and started running towards the manse. Almost at once she felt a jab as she had pressed the shard too tightly in her fist. She let out a short cry of pain and let the glass fall to the ground. Her palm was already coloured by the blood seeping quickly out of a large gash in her skin, which was dry and tight from the cold. She cupped her hand and tried to hide the blood as she ran on, sobbing and red with shame for the futility of her dream.

For long stretches of time Lizzie would be alone in the manse with the stranger. His bed had been moved into one of the chambers so the children would not have to come near him. Sometimes Lizzie would also venture outside to get some fresh air and stare at the melancholy sky. But she would never stray far from the manse, and she often would run back to her patient, suddenly fearful that something might have happened to him. He was still very sick, weakened by the fever that would not leave him alone, unable to keep any solids, but, miraculously, the leg seemed to be healing and the fluids which stained the bandages were becoming clear and less malodorous.

Fuel was scarce on the island at this time of the year, but Lizzie insisted on keeping the fire going in the grate to banish the insistent damp from the manse. She made soup from anything she found that was nutritious enough, and she would feed it to the stranger three times a day. He could not sit up, but she would hold his head in the crook of her arm and spoon-feed him with great patience; but in spite of this some of the soup would still trickle down his chin and on to his shirt.

Lizzie was less fearful of his body now that she had got to know it as well as her own, but this familiarity did not lessen its mystery – nor its beauty. Over the last few days he had occasionally opened his eyes and once, as she bent over him to wipe some sweat from his forehead with her hand, he had looked up at her with a sudden clarity, and although the eyes that met hers were the colour of peat she knew that they were not from this part of the world. She looked back into his eyes hoping to find a way out.

In his sleep he would sometimes murmur and stammer in a language she did not understand, but when he was awake he would not speak a word. His silences were like wet sand: cold and compact. In contrast, she could not stop talking to him, the kind of standard nonsense a nurse would offer a patient. Occasionally, in the afternoon, when dusk approached and shapes grew tender, she would call him by the name she had given him. Hesitantly trying it out and hearing it said out loud again. 'Nathaniel,' she would say, and stroke his hair.

As he grew stronger he would sometimes sit up and look at her through the open door to the kitchen. She could feel his gaze sweeping over her as she went about her business, and it would sometimes make her shiver. Once or twice as she turned to catch his eye she was shocked to see something rough and hardened in his smile, and a hunger in his eyes.

As March brought the first hopes of spring his face would often turn to the light. Once, on a bright morning as she entered the room after a brisk walk along the cliffs, her eyes brimming with the aquamarine of the sea and her face radiant with reclaimed youth, he looked up and froze at the sight of her. Lizzie, too, stopped in her tracks, and the sun that followed her through the open door seemed to stand still. She smiled at his eyes, which were suddenly soft and hopeless and, at once, and for the very first time, it dawned on her that this brutish man had finally found beauty in her. As he held her gaze she felt it reaching straight inside her and touching a moist softness in her very heart.

There was nothing strange about her caring for her patient. Had not her own husband told her to devote herself to the sickbed? And so there came a time when the nurse did not want her patient to get any better. He was fit enough to sit up on his own now, but his legs were still too weak to carry him. Every now and again Lizzie would urge the stranger to lean his elbows on her shoulders and stand up next to the bed. The physical effort would make him sweat as they swayed together in concentration. Locked in this strange dance, Lizzie would forget about her predicament,

229

about the fact that this man was in the intimacy of her family home, and as she listened for the possibility of music to guide her feet, her body seemed to belong to somebody else.

One morning, gently perfect up until that moment, Mr MacKenzie happened to enter the manse while Lizzie and the stranger were doing this exercise. She did not notice her husband at first, as her eyes were closed, but she felt the stranger tighten his grip on her shoulders and she looked up to find her husband staring at her with an expression that conveyed both anger and repulsion. Lizzie dropped the man back on to the bed. As she stood to face her husband she felt her neck flush in shame. She waited for him to say something while a dry fear stalled in her chest. He was quiet for a moment longer and then he cleared his throat. 'I see that your savage is doing much better,' he said.

She hesitated. 'Yes, I'm trying to get him to stand up.'

'Good, good. Although your efforts may be in vain – brutes like him are doomed to crawl in the dust.'

She could hear that he was furious, but could not stop herself. 'Don't speak of him like that. He is a human being just like you and me, and his circumstances are no fault of his own!'

'Well, if he is such a gentleman, why don't we let Anna look after him from now on?'

'But . . .' Humiliation made her weak.

'Yes?'

'He has got used to me. I am the one who should be nursing him.' She realised her mistake but it was too late.

'Have you no shame? Letting another man touch you in my own home! I will have no more of it!'

'But, Neil . . . he was only leaning on me for . . . for support.' She stammered for the injustice of it.

'Get out of this room immediately!'

She turned to the man in the bed and saw that he was looking at her. There were specks of green in his brown eyes and something else which she dared to interpret as compassion. Softly, almost invisibly, he inclined his head to her and held her gaze. She looked into his eyes to find some strength.

'Mrs MacKenzie, remember your place!' Her husband grabbed her wrist and pulled her out of the room, slamming the door shut behind them.

Mr MacKenzie remained true to his word and did not let her near the stranger again. Two women from the village would come in to feed him and change his dressings. Lizzie would see them walk in and out of the room with fresh linens, chamber pots and bandages. Secretly she thought she could interpret signs in the discarded bowls of half-eaten stew or damp rags – surely he preferred her ministrations to theirs?

Gradually, while she had been nursing the man,

Lizzie had come to hear about the remains of the shipwreck that had washed up around the island. A couple of bodies had been found in Gleann Bay. They must have been in the water for some weeks, but the natives who found them could still make out that they were not wearing uniform, nor did they have the appearance of fishermen, and one of them still had a pistol strapped to his belt.

At night Lizzie would lie in bed and listen to the noises of the house. Knowing that the stranger was in the room right next to her was almost unbearable. She pressed her ear and then her face against the cold wall where patches of damp darkened the wallpaper. Once she was brave enough to get up when her husband was asleep and listen at the door of the chamber. She could not hear anything, and she was too frightened to open the door.

Instead, she dreamed of him. She closed her eyes and they walked together through a forest where the foliage sieved the warming rays of the sun; brambles caught her skirts, and the scents of rich earth and crushed leaves rose from the ground. They sat down amongst violets, and the ever-inquisitive sun sought them through the canopy of trees. Once or twice, when she thought she had lost him, she stopped and turned around and he was just behind her, just there, and the peat in his eyes came alive as the fresh bark of a beech or the moss on a stone in a brook.

Another time they walked through golden

cornfields, vast as the sea and punctuated by islands of cheerful daisies and delicate poppies with petals ready to fall. And at such fragility and threat, unable to hold on, she would fall, fall, fall . . . fall to where she was once again alone.

Who was she? She had been deprived of passion for so long, during which time she had let practical matters rule. But now, when she was allowed to dream of the silent man who spoke to her so clearly, she knew she had forgotten how to love. If she opened her eyes the adventure would be gone and she would be back in the manse, facing the wall and its peeling paper, with damp smoke in her throat.

During the day she would turn to her children for comfort. As the sun fell through the window, competing for their love, she would hold them too hard while she read to them from the book with coloured drawings. For a moment she would forget to read as she bent her head to fill her nostrils with the scent of their hair – the salty blue and green smells of the island intermingled with the pure, slightly moist smell of the child. 'Go on, mother, read more, please,' they cried while they struggled against her hot embrace.

Anna noticed her mistress's mood but did not understand. She found it strange and embarrassing. It would be many years yet until she herself would grow into a young woman, years till she understood the pain and anguish her mistress had suffered in those few weeks: how that heart had woken again to romance and adventure and had been finally crushed.

This was the period of the spring storms, and one night, at the end of March, a south-easterly gale forced a Prussian ship on to the rocks of Boreray. Amazingly, the crew saved themselves on to the island and could be rescued by the St Kildans the following morning when the storm had died down. Their ship, however, was dashed to splinters. During the commotion caused by the rescue operation Lizzie saw her chance, at last, to return to her foreign sailor.

Making sure no one was in the house, she walked up to the closed door of the sickroom. For a minute she stood there, trying to control her breathing. There was still a wind around the eaves, and she could hear yesterday's sea through the walls of the manse, as if the waves were secretly conspiring. Then she opened the door and, closing it gently behind her, stepped into the room, which was surprisingly light and still. The man was lying on his side with his face to the window. He was asleep, but he looked better than before. She watched him quietly from the other end of the room. His dark hair had grown a bit, and was curling on the pillow. The shadows under his eyes and around the jaw were nearly gone and he looked much younger. She felt her heart tighten at such tender beauty. Under the blankets he seemed to be wearing a loose linen shirt. She frowned as she thought of the two village women dressing him in this way. Quietly, so as not to waken him, she moved over the floor and sat down at the bedside. Her skirts settled awkwardly around the low stool and, for an instant, the rustle of the dove-grey muslin filled the room. His left hand was resting on the rough covers, and softly she lifted it with her own to find his pulse. She was surprised at how warm the hand was and, as she followed the pulse through his wrist, she let her fingers slide into his palm and immediately felt his fingers link through hers. His hand was alive and his grip welded them together. Lizzie closed her eyes but did not withdraw her hand. Suddenly he was sitting up next to her and his right hand was tracing her face. Still she did not pull away. They were alone in the forest as she had dreamed. She felt his hot breath in her ear and her own pulse quickened. Now his hands were a feathered touch on her body. She recognised the quickening of his breath as he pulled at her bodice. She could feel his body through his linen night-gown and knew that the heat that radiated from him was another kind of fever. She pressed her mouth against his and heard him moan as he pressed her closer to his chest. He said her name, which was the first word she had ever heard him say except for in his dreams, and she wanted more than anything else to be loved by this man, this stranger she had brought back to life. His hands were grappling with her dress again, but it would not give and suddenly it ripped near the shoulder as he pressed his hand in to cup her breast. Now Lizzie was beyond herself. 'Oh no, no, no . . .' she heard herself moan, but she kissed him again. She was split in two and would never again be one. He grabbed her hand and guided it down between his legs. 'No! I can't! I have a husband!' she cried, and pulled away from him. She was sobbing now and stared at him in agony as he took hold of himself while looking into her eyes. She could not tear her eyes away and stood there by his bedside as his body convulsed and he let out a great sigh and fell back on the pillows. Lizzie was crying hard now, but she could not leave. When she dared look at him again she saw that he was smiling at her – a kind, gentle smile. 'Shh,' he whispered, and just then she heard voices from the rocks outside. 'They are back. O God, I have to leave.' He smiled at her again and nodded. She hurried to the door while clawing at her torn dress, but then she heard his voice behind her. 'What?' she asked. 'Solano,' he said softly, and then again, 'Solano, not Nathaniel.'

PART IV

1835–1838 – ECLIPSE

The Manse, Hirta, 24th April, 1835

To John MacPherson MacLeod of Glendale
and St Kilda. Mysore, India

Sir,
By this letter I convey to you a foreign criminal who landed on the shores of St Kilda on
New Year's Day 1835. Although the man has
lived amongst us for four months I do not
know his name but believe him to be a pirate
of Portuguese or Spanish origin.

On my orders Captain Dankshof of 'Die
Griffe', a Prussian ship which foundered off
our shores a couple of months ago, will take
full responsibility for bringing the criminal to
the Long Isle and meeting up with the taxman
who will prosecute the said prisoner in your
absence.

I have done what I thought was right in
healing this wounded criminal and handing
over his mended body to your justice. I cannot,
however, vouch for his soul, which to my best
judgement seems to be lost. As I was not able
to communicate with the prisoner in his own

language I cannot say whether he wants salvation or whether his mouth, which speaks so coarsely in a foreign tongue, is still greedy for wrong. As far as I can tell, his character will take no goodness. I therefore recommend that, should this man be locked up for the remainder of his life, he be given access to the Scripture in his own tongue so that he can start from the beginning with the Word so that life might return to his soul. Remember that purification from sin is a fearful struggle and this sinner should be given all the support he can get in order to reach enlightenment and obliterate sin from his heart.

We do not know what crimes lie in his past, but I am quite sure your worldly court will discover them. However, I do know this: the sin that is ripest in his heart is the hardest to redeem; he abandoned his friends to the waves as their ship wrecked on Rockall, and I dare say that his own survival will rest heavily on his mind. It reflects the original sin of brother betraying brother and thus perpetuating the wickedness of man. It is therefore of utmost importance that this man be given the opportunity to repent and find God's mercy through His Word: 'Purge me with hysope, and I shall be clean: wash me, and I shall be whiter than snow. Make me to heare joy and gladnesse: that the bones which Thou hast broken may rejoyce.'

Let me continue now, sir, on a more cheerful note. I would like to take this opportunity to tell you that the plans for the new village are progressing. I expect to see the first construction of the new houses this summer and the common arable land is gradually being divided into strips.

Your subjects have generally been faring well this past year. It is true that many of the children continue to die within eight days of birth, but the adults have all been mainly healthy and we have had no casualties at sea or on the rocks. All of the children of schooling age and most of the able-minded adults can repeat the catechism by heart, and I have even begun to teach some of the brighter young people to read and write. I try to teach in English but it seems hard for the Gaelic mind in these parts to make sense of a language which does not concern the birds and the sea. There was a brief lapse into superstition during the winter but I am pleased to assure you that I stemmed this weakness and returned my congregation to sanity and purity.

Dare I suggest, sir, lord and patron of this island, that you and your lady pay us a visit on your return from India?

I remain your humble servant,
The Rev. Neil MacKenzie

The Manse, Hirta, 24th April, 1835

To Mr MacDonald of Tanera, rightful taxman of the island of Hirta

My dear Mr MacDonald,
Captain Dankshof who delivers this letter to you brings with him a criminal who should be interrogated and tried by the court at Dunvegan. I trust you to act according to your convictions and use your best conscience in the matter.

Moreover, I would hereby like to order a dozen scarlet headscarves, preferably with a 'paisley' pattern. The costs for these can be deducted from my allowance, if you wish.

Sincerely yours,
MacKenzie

That day when he left . . . Lizzie could still feel the wound deepening inside herself when she thought about it. She had been away up the glen on the slopes of Oiseval with Betty and the children to look at the new lambs, which were struggling against their vertical world in woolly bewilderment. Eliza had been dreadfully upset to see a stillborn lamb hanging halfway out of its bleating mother. The ewe was scuffling back and forth on the slope, half-demented and with panic in her dreary eyes, as she tried to get rid of the terrible offspring – that slimy blue chimera of tendons and bones that would not leave her alone. Turning back down the slope with the crying child in her arms, Lizzie looked ahead over the sweeping valley and the sea beneath only to see a group of men assembled by the landing rock and the village boat being pushed out. She stopped in her tracks and put Eliza, who was getting too heavy now to carry any distance, back on the ground. The skies were racing over the island, busily tidying up for spring. A cloud sailed over the sun and blackened the water in the bay, and at the same time a strange foreshadowing settled like dusk in Lizzie's eyes.

'What does this mean, Betty?' she asked her friend, who had followed close behind, James Bannatyne on her steady hip.

'I couldn't say,' Betty answered slowly, 'but it looks as if them *Sassenachs* are leaving at last.' It was clear from her tone that she for one would not miss them. She frowned at the thought of the rowdy, near-sunken sailors who used up precious food and spoke like coils of anchor chain, short and sharp.

Lizzie at once recognised the crew of eleven sailors who had been saved from the Prussian vessel. That was almost three months ago now and the burden on the vulnerable community was apparent – supplies were already running so low that children and old people were beginning to weaken. There was just no way they would be able to support the extra mouths until the taxman's ship turned up with relief once the weather had settled for the summer.

Lizzie searched the crowd on the rocks until at last she saw him standing there, tightly guarded by two of the foreign mariners. Although he was physically locked in their grip he looked quite separate; his head was bent as if he was trying to read something on the ground, a secret message in the dumb rock. Just then the men started pushing him towards the boat, and as he shook off their hands she saw that his own were tied behind his back. Expertly and without the aid of the others he jumped into the wrestling dinghy and sat down by the stern. This is my element, he seemed to say as he looked back on his guards with a steady gaze.

'Stay with Betty, sweetheart,' Lizzie called to Eliza as she started scampering down the steep hill.

'Mrs MacKenzie, don't!' Betty cried behind her. But Lizzie took no heed – the blood in her veins was like a storm in her ears, and the brown bells of last year's heather rang out as her skirts brushed past. In spite of her efforts the boat had already pushed out into the bay when she reached her husband on the rocks.

'Where are they taking him?' she demanded between breaths.

'To Dunvegan.' Her husband, all cool and calm, continued to look out to sea.

'To Dunvegan? Have you gone clear daft?' She

tried to steady her voice; her fists hung like lead balls at the end of her rigid arms. 'But they will lock him up!'

'Precisely.' He still would not look at her. *Surely we cannot have grown this far apart*, cried his heart.

'What is Dunvegan to him? He is of the sea – do you not hear me, of the sea. We know of no crime he has committed!' She looked desperately towards the dinghy, which was riding tall against the swell in the shallows. Just then she saw the prisoner looking back at her and her eyes smarted as their gaze locked and burned. He was no longer the monster she had found in the feather store that night; gone was the gargoyle – half-man, half-beast – and in his place was this human being whom she had grown to know so intimately through the heat of her hands, through her fingers melting frost.

'You know this is wrong. God must have spared him for a purpose,' she tried.

The minister made a sharp intake of breath but said nothing.

'Perhaps God favours some people quite randomly and decides they must survive for no particular reason at all. Or perhaps God is sometimes just absent, and nature rules, so that the strong survive and the weak die irrespective of the purity of their spirit . . .' She didn't think that she had anything to lose. How could she have known what was at stake? What possessed her? All she could think about was how she had nursed the stranger back to life and how gradually she had seen humanity return into his eyes. He had been closer to death than life, but it was not right for him to die – he was too young and too strong. Human beings want to live. *Why is it*, she thought, *that we are prepared to do almost anything to keep our loved ones alive and close – and yet we fail them?*

Her husband turned to look at her in a way that made her feel sick – she could not read his eyes, but he seemed to be advancing through a range of emotions the way a soldier pushes through a battle towards the front line.

'Only through sacrificing yourself and your cause to God can you redeem yourself for surviving such circumstances – for letting your fellow beings die by your side.' There was such contempt in his voice.

Her heart was beating too hard and the sweat was cold on her forehead. She felt suddenly nauseous and looked towards the open sea, but its hapless mass offered no cause for hope. She tried to steady herself but recognised a familiar darkness just before she fainted.

She had been carried back into the manse by Ferguson and MacKinnon, just as the man who was now a prisoner had once been carried into her care. Presently she was at the table drinking a strengthening cup of tea. The children, who had returned with Betty, had been sent off again, this time with Anna to the *clachan*. Mr MacKenzie was looking at her mutely, impassively, leaning casually with his back against the door. She turned to him defiantly and started to say something but fell quiet when she saw the blackening of his mind through his eyes. He began to stride back and forth in the dull room.

'Look at this place!' He threw out his hands. 'Just look at it.' He swept his fingers through the dust on the mantelpiece, his lips set in a disgusted snarl. A few treasures which the children had brought in from the beach were littering the table in front of her – a handful of shells and a dried starfish, one purple arm broken at the heart. MacKenzie slammed down his fist on top of the trophies and swept them on to the floor. 'You have neglected your duties.' He kicked at the broken shells but missed and hit the leg of the table. This seemed to enrage him further and suddenly, before she had time to react, he caught her by the arm and pulled her out of the chair. The gleam in his eyes frightened her.

'You are hurting me, Neil,' she whimpered, but he only tightened his grip.

'You wanted it from him, didn't you?' He had got hold of her other arm too and was shaking her. 'Well, didn't you?' There was something close to panic in his voice.

'I have nothing to hide.' It was a strange thing for her to insist, and it made it all too obvious that she had.

Her husband gave a short laugh. 'Be quiet – you

will take it from your husband now!' He started pulling her into the bedroom and she tried to resist. '*This* is your duty!' She did not recognise him – she was quite certain that the man who took her was not known to her.

Afterwards he rolled off her and faced the wall. She was still too rigid to move. Her head was not related to her limbs. She hoped he would not speak but he did. 'I am sorry, Lizzie. I don't know what came over me. You know I never wanted to hurt you. I am not a bad man, am I?'

Was he weeping? Somehow she managed to raise herself out of the bed. She pulled at her skirts. She wasn't too sore but she could feel the stickiness between her thighs and it disgusted her. On stiff legs she took a couple of steps towards the door. A slither of warm indignity was trickling down the inside of her left leg.

His shame forced him to curl up towards the wall. He realised that he had no right to look at her, that in the end he was the one who had forfeited the trust. 'Don't leave me, Lizzie, oh, sweet, darling Lizzie, please don't leave me,' his heart was crying out, but did he say it?

Lizzie thought she heard him whisper something and strained to catch the words. 'Leave me' – it was all he managed, in a sigh.

Released, she closed the door behind her.

'Save me! Please bring me back.' This time mortification amplified his words, but the door was already closed.

Once outside the manse Lizzie started running. The shadows were settling and she hoped the dark would hide her. Low clouds had got entangled in the hills and it had started to rain. It surprised her that she didn't feel hatred for her husband. All she could feel was a great sadness; it came upon her as silently as the mist from the sea. When she reached a small stream she squatted over the gulley and washed herself – she splashed and rubbed until she was quite clean of the humiliation. It was dark now, but she knew she could not face going back. Her boots and skirts were soaked and she was beginning to shiver with cold. Determined not to cry, she bit her lip and set off for Betty's house.

Betty received her former mistress without questions. With a few words of Gaelic she sent Calum off and helped Lizzie out of her wet clothes and into a stiff blanket which smelt of animal. If she noticed the raw skin where Lizzie had scoured her thighs in the icy water, she did not let on. For a long while they sat quietly by the fire, looking into the weak flames. Every now and again Betty would feed it a piece of dried turf – it didn't give off much heat, but there was no other fuel at this time of the year. Lizzie pulled the blanket closer around her shoulders.

'Betty,' she said, very quietly. The young Highland woman looked up. 'Do you ever think of home?'

'Home?' Betty thought it a strange question

'Why, my home is here, isn't it?' After a pause she added, 'They sent me away, didn't they? My pa said they had no choice. So no, I don't think of home. How could I, now that I know that it was for the best I left. I was sad to leave the little ones, but I know they are better off without me and one more mouth to feed.'

The two women continued to look into the glowing embers as if they expected them to reveal some deeper sense.

'The world back there was getting wider, filling with worries and sadness. Almost every month somebody would get up and leave for Canada. Here everything is contained and people keep close.' As she talked, the faces of Betty's parents and siblings returned to her blue gaze and the mainland felt suddenly close. It made her feel peculiar, minding them in that way, and she was grateful to the fire for offering distraction.

'What is wrong with me, Betty?' Lizzie's voice was suddenly lucid. The light from the tired fire was tracing the side of her face like an old lover.

'There is nothing wrong with you,' Betty replied fervently, 'but you expect too much of life – you seem to think it will explain itself to you, but that will never happen.'

Lizzie nodded slowly. 'There are times when I feel so insignificant, as if I'm about to disintegrate. Like pollen on the air.'

Betty stirred the embers, which gave off their heat like a truth. 'Is that why you were drawn to the stranger?'

Lizzie looked up in surprise and blushed. How could Betty know? Had she heard those whispers in her heart? She hesitated but decided to reply honestly: 'He saw me, he gave me purpose and he let me touch him – that was all.' The fire was alive again; she was feeling hot and her cheeks were aglow. The blanket had loosened to reveal a naked shoulder. 'It was a short period of folly, a few weeks of madness. And yet I felt more alive in that brief passion than I have done before or after. What is my life now?'

Betty was not used to speaking in such terms and it was not a question she could answer. She made an effort to bring the conversation back into their confined world. 'But your husband – he is a fine man and all?'

'Since the children died my husband has removed himself from me. He writes in his study and preaches in his kirk; he eats his dinner and takes his pleasure. That is all. I am of no consequence to him.' She broke off and smiled sadly. 'But you know, his betrayal hurts my head more than my heart – it sits like an iron band across my temples. I pray only to be rid of this pain that comes from being so irrelevant to the only person I am bound to love.'

Betty still did not quite comprehend, but she had enough imagination to feel a rush of pity. She

251

moved closer and held her friend's hand. It was surprisingly thin, almost childlike.

'Oh, Betty, the worst thing is that I have let myself become so insignificant, so badly used!'

'The minister, Mr MacKenzie, perhaps he is lonely too,' Betty suggested. 'He doesn't have any other loved ones, does he? It can do strange things to a man, losing his kin and bosom friends – it can turn a good one into a bad one, it can. Men, you see, they haven't got no words for all that grief – and nowhere to put it, like.' Betty's fair curls frizzed around her head like a halo. 'Can you not see that it is not *you* he has wronged, it is himself. You *must* talk to him!'

'Don't you think I have tried?' Lizzie flared up but settled quickly again. 'I just can't seem to get through. Solano, on the other hand –' she looked up to see if Betty had registered the secret of the name, but the younger woman seemed unperturbed – 'he let me come close. His passions are different and he was not ashamed to make me feel his heat. He looked at me and made me feel wanted and alive. And now I have lost him too.' Lizzie could feel a tide of anguish rising inside her. *But then, does it not hurt the sea when it rasps against the beach?* she thought. *What is my ache in comparison to the pain as it wears itself thin against the pebbles on the shore – or the agony of the nestling as it pushes out of its jagged shell or of the bud on the hawthorn bush as it bursts raw into the cold air?*

Betty looked at Lizzie's closed face with eyes full

of concern. 'You must think of your children. All this talk of you wanting to be this and wanting to be that – what about them needing their mother to be jolly and strong?'

Lizzie looked up in revelation, as if the thought had just dawned on her. 'O God, what have I done?' At last she started crying.

'Shh, it is not easy, I know. But this is your life now. You must try to come to terms with it.'

'But how?'

'It is not for me to say. You need to find out for yourself. We all do.'

Lizzie woke by the hearth where she had fallen asleep. The fire had gone out and the room was cold and damp. She could only just make out the sleeping forms of Betty and Calum in the recess in the earthen wall. Quietly so as not to waken them she pulled on her clothes, which had been placed across the *tallan* to dry. They were still damp and there was a bad smell around them as of greasy fleece. She stepped out into the brisk dawn. It was very early and no one was about in the *clachan*. A single gull moaned overhead – it may have been chasing through the sky all night. There was a strong wind from the sea and Lizzie abandoned herself to it, letting it reset her features into a recognisable face.

Neil, inconsolable, had been up all night preparing a speech for her. He had been writing to her, letting his failings take shape as he added word upon word until they flowed into sentences like rivers across a great plain. His desk was strewn with crumpled, discarded paper. How carefully he had been perfecting his redemption! But as he looked out the window and saw her crossing the glebe, her face so white in the drab morning, it all vanished and he was repulsed by himself anew. Yet he somehow found the courage to walk out to meet her, bringing a warm coat because she looked so cold.

Lizzie looked up, startled, as he came towards her. She stopped and appeared as if she would turn, but he said her name softly and she stayed. Cautiously, as if approaching a wild animal, he walked up to her and reached out, arms straight, to put the coat over her shoulders. She tensed but let it happen. She was shivering and kept her arms crossed over her chest, pretending it was the cold.

He spoke first. 'Lizzie, why . . . ?' But it came out like an accusation rather than a plea and he had to start again. 'This island, it is deforming us – me,' he quickly corrected himself. A memory raced through his head – the scent of the tanned skin of her neck on a summer's eve. 'We must not let it enter our hearts in this manner.' Why, he wondered, were they no longer able to share the simple gifts that the island offered: the intense deepening of the skies reflected in a tarn, the blinding splendour of the summer dawn across the sea, the streaks of fulmars sailing home from the west on the rays of the setting sun?

She had not been prepared for this and did not know how to react.

'Can it be repaired?' he asked, and the dread filled the morning air around them.

'I don't know, I just don't know, but we must try.' Her voice was surprisingly steady.

He opened his arms to her and as he embraced her he lifted his eyes over her head to the summit of Conachair, as if expecting to see their love still walking there, hand in hand. Suddenly, as he scanned the top of their island world, something seemed to fall from heaven – or was it just a gannet diving out of the sky for the first catch of the day?

1836

When she had a moment to herself Lizzie would sometimes make her way to the little graveyard which had been fashioned out of a piece of land on the gentle slope above Village Bay. Today she had brought a bunch of snowdrops which she had picked in the manse garden. She had woken early that morning out of a dream that was full of light. The dark bedchamber had still been intense with the relief she felt every new day when she woke up knowing that her children were alive.

Now as she crouched by the low, grassy mound that marked the grave of the twins she was struck by how exposed people became when their children entered into the world. She was powerless in the face of the love she felt towards her own children, but she had to carry on in spite of this crippling vulnerability. She knew she could keep them safe only by keeping the fear alive.

A while after the stranger left the island she had given birth to a little daughter – they had called her Jane, after one of the twins they had lost. Lizzie smiled now as she remembered a moment the previous summer when she had been feeding the baby – a blackbird had sung in the hawthorn by the open door, and as Lizzie had looked into the face of the nuzzling infant she was certain the baby was listening to the song. A true daughter of the island of birds!

Eliza was very excited to have a baby sister, but James Bannatyne, whose world was still confined to the manse and the glebe, seemed a bit confused about the newcomer. One day he had found the shell of a kittiwake egg by the garden wall and brought it to Lizzie and asked if they could not put Jane back inside. What view of the world will my children get here? she wondered. She remembered the scents and colours of her own childhood, the smell of the broom in the valleys and the gleam of dew on the gorse. And the way the approaching rain would bring the smell of lush green regeneration. It was strange to think that her children had never felt the fresh smell of budding trees. Here every green smell was tinged with blue. The deep breath of the sea defined their senses. The mists brought salt distilled from the waves of the Atlantic, and when she looked closely at her children's smooth faces she saw lines of salt crystals in the fine down above their eyes and lips. At times she feared that the sea was slowly eating into the core of them. Sometimes she would worry about what the children would think of the outside world – their landscape here amongst the towering rocks was vertical rather than horizontal, and they were sure to get quite dizzy when they set foot on the mainland. But such a scenario seemed so unlikely. Their entire world was here. Lizzie put a hand to her stomach and felt the swelling of yet another pregnancy.

She placed the snowdrops on the kind grass and blew into her hands. The dark months had not quite loosened their grip of the island yet, and the wind was raw. On days like these the grey hills and soaked valleys were numb and motionless – only the skies moved. At other times the island was so alive that the sky struggled to contain it.

Absent-mindedly she picked up the flowers again and divided them into two bunches. She rested on her knees and looked around the enclosure. Nathaniel, the first born, first dead, was also buried here somewhere, but his grave had not been marked. She could feel the old anxiety coming over her and struggled to keep it at bay. Looking closely at one of the snowdrops she could see the tiny green footprints at its core, from which three white petals fell like tears.

Some days she could feel them on the wind – like dry leaves they rustled past. Some nights when the wind settled she would put her ear to the wall and listen for them on the other side: for her dead children – and for him. With her husband sleeping beside her she would strain for a sound in the dark silence that would remind her of happiness.

But over time she had learned to let her thoughts be light on the wind that blew and blew. She didn't let them weigh down her head into darkness. Light as feathers, heavy as peat.

The Manse at Hirta, May 1836

To The Most Venerable Dr MacDonald of Ferintosh

Forgive me, Preceptor (or dare I say friend?), for delaying writing to you for so long. Believe me when I say that I have not forgotten my mentor. On the contrary, I often call on your wisdom and advice in my prayers (without ever neglecting to be grateful for His supreme advice, naturally). How I wish that you were nearer so that I could sometimes speak to you about my most pressing concerns.

I have been very busy these last few years. You may remember that I told you in my last letter that I had decided to move the village and reform the farming system on the island. This reform is now well under way and the earthly lives of my people are much improved. I have also had to deal with the care and accommodation of a number of shipwrecked crews and the birth of a daughter. Jane is now a year old! I now have three children on earth and three in heaven – a cruel symmetry – and although I know I ought to worry about the perfection of the living ones, the dead ones weigh heavier on my conscience. But forgive me for such talk of simple private matters. You need not remind me, Preceptor, that I have received a call from God and from the poor people of St Kilda and that my parish and myself are bound to one another in bonds of love.

I mentioned that the physical lives of the St Kildans have greatly improved. However, I am afraid I am still struggling with their spiritual redemption. Notwithstanding all my labours and prayers, I have not seen any real spiritual fruit for several years. For although they have acquired much knowledge of the facts and doctrines of Christianity, it does not seem to enter their hearts or do much to influence their lives. It is true that open and gross sin is less frequent, but it is only in a few cases that the heart seems to be at all touched, or that there awakens any real anxiety about the salvation of their souls. Am I then worthy to guide them towards salvation? I hear of your successes amongst the Highlanders – they call you Ministear Mona Toisidheachd – the Great Minister of Ferintosh. I am not surprised by this epithet, Preceptor, nor entirely satisfied as, if I had a say, your name would be accompanied by an even grander title. I remember well how the love of the Redeemer gleams inside you and how it shines out at the people as you preach to thousands at a time. I, on the other hand, can only aspire to enlighten the hearts and souls of my small congregation. Am I worthy? I ask of you again, as I ask the Lord every night. Perhaps it was a mistake to focus all my efforts on reforming the village? Nay, I will not believe it! Before they can properly understand and profit by preaching they have to be taught, step by step, and in the simplest way possible, the leading facts and truths of Christianity and the basic rules of modern life. My mind may fill with doubt, but I will not give up, and I will take inspiration from you and preach with new zeal and conviction! I often read the words of the apostle Paul, as he speaks of 'the glorious Gospel of the blessed God with which I have been entrusted . . . I thank Him who has given me strength, Christ Jesus our Lord, because He judged me faithful, appointing me to His service' (1 Timothy 1:11–12).

These, then, are some of my present concerns.

I read in an old newspaper brought to me by the factor about the Great Assembly last year, when the Evangelical Party gained new ground. I rejoice at the thought of religion being brought back to the people. The teachings of the Church of Scotland have become too refined and aloof for people to understand – it fosters superstition and oblivion. I

261

read of Thomas Chalmers's great work amongst the poor of our cities. You, Preceptor, ought to be similarly celebrated for your work in the Highlands!

I must finish now and send you this letter from these shores that I know you cherish. The island is beautiful today as summer has arrived and we have all forgotten the hardships of the winter (we had little fuel and were close to starvation before the birds returned from the west). Here is always the quick transition from light to darkness, from darkness to light. From my window I can see the gannets diving into Village Bay. They too are God's creation. Does He guide their wings as they fly high and low across the ocean and save lost mariners to our shores? What does He tell them – what do they know?

Blessings,

From one who strives to be your friend,
N. MacKenzie

The Manse at Ferintosh, June 1837

To the Rev. Neil MacKenzie of St Kilda

Dear brother,
We are indeed friends, and I think of you as a brother, or perhaps a son. Yes, a son is more

appropriate as you are still young and I have had the privilege of instructing you in some fields. So I pray you to be less formal in future correspondence.

I only just received your letter and hope to reply by returning mail as I also received a note from Mr Bethune saying that the factor will be visiting St Kilda one more time this summer – so forgive me if the letter is brief and my thoughts unstructured. Your letter betrays the very special concerns which can be expected in your parish – one which demands more than ordinary grace, and more than ordinary learning. Your calling, my son, was furnished by Christ Himself. I will say to you what I said to my own son when he was recently ordained: 'The day on which you received your licence constituted an important date, and inaugurated a new era in your life. The rise or fall of some in Israel may depend on the event which then took place – nay, so far as instrumentality is concerned, the eternity of your hearers may turn upon it. This, I confess, is a solemn, and at times may prove an overwhelming, thought. But be strong in your Redeemer; for He is mighty to save and rich in mercy.'

I often think of St Kilda and her inhabitants for which I felt such pity and responsibility. As I was walking amongst the people on Hirta on my last visit. I was overwhelmed by a feeling of despair and the fear that I would not have time enough to salvage those poor souls for His Kingdom. The fact that you are there now makes me sleep easier at night and I pray for the improvement of that vulnerable island community for which I felt such sympathy. They are amongst the last remaining kin of Ossian who brought to us the world of the Gàidhealtachd.

You ask if you are worthy. None of us is worthy to speak the words of God, but it is our duty to walk on, to the end of the world, like the apostles did and administer salvation where we can. We must be present amongst people whose Christian lives, and even humanity, is in question. So I ask you not to worry, my friend, your work is not in vain. You will see that in a place such as St Kilda, where the skies open to His Kingdom, the subject will suggest itself to your sermons and the same circumstances will give it greater force with its hearers.

I must haste now as I have to appear before a court of sorts. There was a young girl who was especially devout and whom I instructed last year. She has given birth to a baby boy and they say I am his father. Nonsense, of course – this is just another trial sent to us. Pray for me brother, friend, son.

MacDonald of Ferintosh
Post scriptum: Did you hear that our

Evangelical Party now holds a majority in the Great Assembly for the first time!

The Manse at Ferintosh, April 1838

To the Rev. Neil MacKenzie of St Kilda

Dear brother,

By now news may have reached you of the recent developments in the national Church of the Scottish people. The recent case of the rejected minister of Auchterarder, brought as far as the House of Lords, proves that the inherent rights of independence and the spiritual jurisdiction of the Church of Scotland are gravely threatened.

I ask myself now whether there shall not be a disruption of our Church in the near future. If this is indeed the case, I ask you, brother, to be ready to stand by the evangelist side for which you were chosen by our Lord. The common people and the middle classes are largely on our side, I would say, but we cannot hope for much support from the higher classes in this revolution. The Free Church will try to create associations in all parishes in Scotland, so that if we were forced to go out we would still be able to make a living preaching the Lord's Gospel, and unless the State decides to persecute us, I am sure we will get on. We must be prepared to go from house and home to serve our Lord under His sky!

I bless you, brother, and remind you that He alone knoweth the end from the beginning. Let us therefore look to the Lord for providence and grace.

Macdonald of Ferintosh

Betty and Lizzie were baking and Eliza was helping to shape the dough into bannocks for the griddle. Anna, who was always full of play, had taken the smaller children down to the beach. For a moment Lizzie worried about little Nigel, who was only a year old and could easily come to harm. She had heard all the stories of the big birds taking off with babies. But she put the worries aside – she knew that Anna would not let anything happen to the children; they were like siblings to her. Little Jane and baby Nigel were both born in April, two years apart, and they were children of that month: still tightly furled but full of possibilities.

Lizzie straightened her back, carefully keeping her floury hands over the trough, and rubbed her head against her shoulder to get rid of a strand of hair that had escaped from under the headscarf. She looked at Betty and Eliza, who were giggling at a shared joke in the floury dust. Lizzie smiled to herself; it is a strong bond which ties the three of us together, she thought. Betty was the one who had assisted her at birth, and the first one to lay eyes on the girl.

But the happiness of the morning, as she watched Eliza so full of joy and life, was tinged with sadness and loss for Betty's little boy who had died the previous month of the eight-day sickness. Lizzie felt almost ashamed to have been blessed with the good fortune to have four children alive when her friend had none. However, she thought, Betty is a strong girl and so full of forbearance and hope that she is convinced she will have another child soon.

She could hardly remember now what it was like not to have children in the house. Over the last few years she had witnessed the death of so many infants in the *clachan*. She tried her best to support the women in their grief but increasingly, as her own children survived, she noticed that they shied away from her compassion.

'Betty,' she said suddenly, 'do the women in the *clachan* resent me for the children?' She realised too late that the question was unfair – Betty was one of them.

Betty, however, did not seem disconcerted as she looked up – there was still mirth in her blue eyes. 'I believe they think you pleasant enough – although perhaps a wee bit prim.' She laughed the question away.

'I worry about the filth in the *clachan* – it cannot be healthy for the little ones.' Lizzie, who kept the manse clean and well aired in the hope that no ills would settle, shook her head at the thought. Some families even kept the latrines inside the houses in the winter in order to gather valuable manure for the fields.

'Ah,' Betty laughed, 'we cannot all be as trim as you; look at your hands – they are all red and coarse from all the scrubbing and washing. After all these years on Hirta, you should at least have grown used to the stink like I have!'

Lizzie felt a pang of hurt at being singled out like that, but there was no malice in Betty's mocking.

'*I* will *never* get used to the stink – it smells of old fizzy piss and horrible poo!' Eliza squealed delightedly and they all laughed.

But underneath all the gayness and delight Lizzie realised that the subject of the dying infants was unmentionable. She watched Betty's face and wondered if the light in the other woman was not turned up too high. Was she trying to hide the truth of her feelings from those she loved?

PART V

JUNE 1838 – LESSONS

There was a film of green on the black velvet, a vague colouring like fresh birch pollen on the still surface of a tarn. Below the velvet collar, on the shoulders and back of the coat, the fabric was shiny with wear. The boy Duncan was reminded of a greasy pot left out overnight to collect the rainwater – the way the grime would settle around the rim and in oily streaks across the surface. He wanted to taste the green on the collar, to draw his tongue through the velvet and leave a dark trail like the wake of a snail on a moss-covered stone.

The coat was hanging from the tip of a ram's horn which had been stuck into the wall of the new schoolroom. Duncan was sitting at the desk opposite the minister. The room had been attached to the kirk like a misshapen vestry, and it could not host enough students to form a seminar. It was about nine feet by eight, with a small canvas-covered window facing the bay. A wooden tube of the minister's own engineering served as a chimney in the winter and a ventilator in the summer. On this day the door had been left open to let in the summer air. It was a warm morning and the minister's coarse linen shirt was sticking to his back. Duncan could smell a sharp scent rising from the older man; it was of crushed cardamom and musk and not altogether unpleasant.

The boy's fair hair had been cut close to the scalp. His mother had used the small shears and called him her little lamb while she cut away his winter locks. His ears burned in humiliation when he thought about it. Why could she not understand that she was embarrassing him? He was not a child any more. In the slow afternoons, when he learned and improved, he sometimes came to believe in himself as somebody else, somebody older and slightly better. This is what the minister had promised – that he would be enlightened by the lessons and rise above his kin. The sounds of the schoolroom were contained and small compared to the noise of his world outside, where the acoustics were set against the sky. But in the mornings and at night, when feathers stuck to his dew-sodden feet and his mother prepared the *guga* over the hearth, he was Duncan again, and his mind would wander off into the old stories and songs. At such times he could hear the voices of the ancestors and his heart was full of the rocks and the sea. The calls of the birds re-formed in his mind until he could decipher their coded messages in the same way a traveller would slowly come to understand a foreign language. He kept a close watch on the movements of the birds and he would speak to them like he spoke to the sea.

Over the last few weeks his cropped hair had bleached in the sun like a cornfield after harvest, until it glowed almost unnaturally white against his bronzed forehead and temples. Now, as he sat on the hard stool in the sparsely furnished room, his thin brown legs were moving restlessly as his bare feet swept the rough floorboards under the desk.

'For goodness' sake boy! Can you sit still for one moment and concentrate on your task?' the minister said crossly in a voice that was thick but precise within the box-like room. His forehead was furrowed but his eyes, as he looked up from the papers in front of him, smiled at the boy. The minister had started giving Duncan special tasks and lessons shortly after Hogmanay a few years previously. In the beginning the lessons had been set to straighten his mind and quench any super-stitious tales that may have hovered on his tongue. Duncan could see that this was justified. He had fabricated all those stories and told them to the others in such a way that he believed his own words. He had been too young to understand back then – just a child with a child's mind – but every-body had wanted to listen to him and so he had got a bit carried away. The minister had been very cross with Duncan after this episode, and at first the lessons had been all dark and terrifying. He shuddered in the hot room as he thought about all the perils he had so narrowly escaped when the minister saved him from superstition and fables. After a while the nature of the lessons had changed and the minister had started telling him other things – things about the world and all the different countries, about kings and heroes in history, about the apostles and their adventures, and of philosophy and the monk Augustine. He talked of explorers and new worlds, and those were the stories Duncan liked the best.

By and by the man and the boy had become used to each other's company, perhaps even dependent on it. They would sit for hours in the lamplight and trace the wanderings of the apostles on the globe the minister had ordered from the mainland. This was called geography. The minister would point out large green and yellow areas which were called the Americas, where Christian missionaries had risked their lives in order to save the savages and bring them into the light. Another such explorer was Mungo Park, who had set out from Scotland a few years previously to find Timbuktu. Mungo, who was named after a saint, and as such was almost an apostle, had befriended Negroes along the way and learned to speak their language. It seemed as if their communication was just like the white man's. But mostly the savages were unimprovable and therefore outside humanity. This, explained the minister, justified the colonisation of the American prairies by the white farmers. The savages had forfeited their right to their parcel of God's earth as they had shown no intention of improving it or making it more productive. It was obvious in this light that Hirta must continue to change and improve. After the land reform that he, the minister, was putting in place, the land would no longer be held in common but each individual tenant would pay rent for his own croft. 'Why can the land no longer be held by the islanders like it has been since the time of the ancestors?' asked Duncan. 'Ah, the ancestors – tell me about them, boy,' MacKenzie had said.

The minister did not seem to understand that the ancestors were part of the land and that the intricate web of kinship tied the fields, meadows and fowling rocks to the community. The birds would have told him, if he had been able to hear them; they had been there since the very beginning, sharing the rocks with the men and women whose names were still given to the newly born and whose blood fuelled the souls of those who grew old. Just like the day moved east over the world to return each morning, climbing the steep cliffs of the Gap and entering Village Bay between Conachair and Oiseval, so would the St Kildans live on from generation to generation with the birds watching over them.

There were white patches at the top and bottom of the globe. These were very cold and largely unexplored, the minister explained. Duncan would often think of them at night and envisage himself walking across all the green and yellow and blue areas until he reached the white patches, which even the apostles and the missionaries had avoided or been defeated by. These white patches were the ends of the world and no one really knew what happened there. Duncan had his own theory that this was where the sky met the earth, and the white was the clouds and the wild storms that would gather there before being sent off across the seas to reach the shores of Hirta. Early on he asked where Hirta was, and the minister explained that it was not on the map but if it had been it would have been there, and he had put his finger in the middle of the blue which was ocean. It was strange, Duncan thought, to learn geography when your place in the world was still unmarked.

Once the minister told Duncan about swimming – how it could save people who fell over the rocks. Duncan had never known a human being to swim and the idea of it thrilled him. And so the minister and Duncan made a pact; the minister would teach Duncan to swim, and in return Duncan would tell the minister about the old beliefs and about all the songs and stories.

So for the last couple of weeks they had not looked at the globe. Instead the minister had asked Duncan to write down some of the old Hirta songs in a book with blank pages. Duncan would hum the songs to himself quietly so as not to disturb the minister, and as the song ran through his mind like a bright burn Duncan would put the words on the paper in front of him. Duncan thought this was an odd and boring task. Why would anyone want to have the songs on paper when they were supposed to be sung and everybody knew them anyway? Once there had been pipes and fiddles on the island, which the ancestors had played. This was before the missionaries started coming. The songs were the links to that time, the time before the pipes were taken away and the drums were buried and forgotten. But Duncan could still hear the music as he walked over the island; he would hear a fiddle being stroked by a burn after rain and the whispers of a song rising from a spring. Perhaps the minister knew this, but Duncan was loyal and unsuspecting and, unknown to himself, he was spiriting the Reverend's work, recording and mapping the souls of his people and exposing their hidden lives.

'When will you teach me to swim, sir?' the boy would ask every now and again, and the minister would lift his head from a book or a paper and smile absently. 'What? Oh, soon enough, my lad, soon enough.' 'When is soon?' The boy was eager, but the minister knew how to keep him occupied. 'When you have learned not to test my patience.'

But these thoughts alone were not the cause of Duncan's restlessness on this summer's morning. No, something much more exciting was going on. For the last couple of days, as the afternoon light lingered warmly into the white night, Duncan had felt them coming. He had felt it in his blood as surely as the return of the birds in early spring. He even thought he could smell it on the air, like the thickening scent of the first snow. And then at last, this morning, they were there. Even before he got out of the dwelling he knew that they had come. He had heard the birds calling to each other and telling of their arrival since the sun rose. He had been expecting them for days. The summer was warm, and green algae were growing around the island. And sure enough, when he reached the new sea wall that morning, Village Bay had been boiling with an enormous shoal of mackerel. As the morning wore on he had seen some of the older boys through the open door of the schoolroom as they walked in pairs and groups towards Dùn or the Point of Coll. It was insufferable to be indoors today. Duncan glanced longingly out of the window and thought of his rod, which was leaning against the kirk wall. He had worked on the rod and the line all winter and he knew they were perfect. His bare feet were drumming the floor now and although he tried to keep them still he would forget and sometimes his knees would hit the desk and rattle the ink bottle so that it shook dangerously.

The minister looked up again and shook his head. 'All right, Duncan, off you go before you spill the good ink all over my sermon.'

'Thank you, sir,' said Duncan as he pushed out his chair and caught it just before it toppled over.

'It is the mackerel come back,' he said at the door without turning.

'Yes, my boy, I know,' said Mr MacKenzie quietly as he watched the lad depart through the open door. 'I felt them coming too.'

Duncan loved fishing: the long wait for the sharp thrill, the delight of getting something for nothing, but above all the mystery and adventure of it. Adventure is as inherent to the nature of a boy as procreation is to a man. Adventure is the breeze becoming wind, bright, primary colours and the smattering of flags; it is dark shadows of purple and blue and a deep smell of earth and mystery. The very magnificence and beauty of adventure makes you braver as it offers the possibility of love, and of death.

As he climbed over the glebe wall Duncan could see a couple of older boys walking quickly ahead of him towards the Point of Coll. His heart was racing fast now, and for a moment he was afraid that they would get to his rock before him. He decided to try to reach it from above. For days during his free late afternoons he had been climbing around the point looking for the perfect ledge from which to cast his line. He had found it just on the other side of a rock which cut into the sea so that a narrow ledge was formed about six feet above the water. As he climbed the slope behind the kirk Duncan thought of the savages in America and how they would sneak up on their prey, or on the white men who had come in carts with women and children and clocks and bibles and cultivated the land on the great grass plains, which were like the seven seas but green. As he reached the right height he started running across the slope on a path trampled by sheep. He ran just like a Sioux or a Cherokee, crouched and thrusting the rod like a spear in front of him until he reached the edge of the sea, where he started to descend towards the ledge. He could see the other two boys below. They had stopped about a hundred yards from his ledge. A few puffins were dozing on the slope below him. He stopped and crouched behind a stone while keeping his eyes on the puffins. 'I will get you palefaces – there will be no surrender,' he whispered coarsely in what he thought might be a savage voice. He raised his imaginary bow and fired a couple of swift arrows – *phew! phew!* – before charging forward and grabbing the closest puffin by the neck. He twisted the neck with practised hands before facing the other birds. A few of them had been disturbed by the commotion and tumbled off the rock, but a handful remained and they were looking suspiciously at Duncan and grumbling in protest. 'I will tie all your bloody scalps to my belt,' he hissed to the bewildered puffins, and added, 'That will teach you to stay off my land!' He killed another three puffins and tied them to his belt before reaching his ledge safely. The ledge was not large enough to accommodate two boys or even a full-grown man but Duncan was not yet thirteen and his thin body sat comfortably on the stony seat.

Everything was still. There was a slight swell and the sun would sometimes break through the thin veil of clouds around the island. Further along the rugged coast, barely within earshot, the other two boys were throwing their lines into the sea, jigging for the precious catch. Duncan rested his head against the rock and let out a sigh of pleasure and the wind replied. He liked the warm granite at his back; a scent of salt and sun radiated from the pink rock and mixed with the sharp smell from the dead puffins around his waist. He was used to these smells and they comforted him. He watched the line as it disappeared into the deep – the water was very clear, and every now and again he thought he could see the bait glinting far below. The surface of the sea was still, but Duncan knew that they were down there, shooting back and forth in one great body. He closed his eyes and listened to the soft wash of the waves. It was the sound of his mother's hand gently stroking his temples just before falling asleep.

He woke when he felt a tug on the line, which he had tied to his big toe. He jerked his foot and felt the resistance. The fish had caught, and as he wound it in he waved triumphantly to the other boys, who did not acknowledge his greeting but stood watching grumpily as he pulled in the first catch of the day. It was a beautiful mackerel; its underside was the colour of clouds and the back still wore the colours of the sea, cut through with ribbons of grief.

As the morning wore on, the wind picked up and the fish ran too so that the boys were pulling them out until the bait ran out and they had to start using mackerel flesh on the hooks. The rock around Duncan was slippery with blood and gut, and the puffins gave off their strong smell. A new group of boys had assembled at the point. Clouds were gathering with the wind and would sometimes cover the sun, the sea darkening for a moment into threat. Suddenly Duncan heard a peal of laughter. He stood up quickly – too quickly – to see what was going on. As he stood one of his bare feet slipped on the slimy ledge. He tried to grab hold of the rock above. His hand clawed and grasped, looking for a tuft of grass, a solid piece of the island he had always known and never left. Because he could not believe it was happening, the beginning of his fall was horribly slow. He saw too much; he saw the safe rock falling away from him, the shimmer of minerals in the sun, a clump of violets in a crevice and next to it a cheerful bed of sea-campion, thrift and scurvy grass. He saw, or perhaps he did not, the boys look up at his shrill cry and start running, shuffling amongst the boulders and rocks towards him.

The punishment that inevitably followed the fall was severe and the boy was shocked by the chill of the water as it closed around him. As he bobbed up to the surface Duncan spat out the vile water he had swallowed. He found that he was still hanging on to the rod. Blinking away the cruel salt, he saw his friends on the rocks. They were calling to him but he could not hear. One or two were reaching out their rods for him to catch, but the current around the point had already carried him too far out, and in any case he did not want to let go of his own rod. He clung to it desperately, wide-eyed. The whole thing surprised him; he could not swim and yet he was afloat – how could it be? But none of this was imaginary, and the truth could not be reconciled. But just when disaster presents itself, in that moment when the horror is unveiled, there is a space where you are untouchable, and perfectly safe because it has already happened. The trick, unpreventable perhaps, but still so *unnecessary*, has already been played on you.

Because of this, Duncan was not afraid. He looked calmly at his golden arms that held on to the rod in front of him. Still he was not self-possessed; the adventure was obviously over now and nature had taken charge. He was not in control and the current was tugging at him, nibbling at his legs like dogs of the sea, hungry for the kill. The dead puffins at his belt were still full of air and carried him on the swell, but slowly, one after the other, they started filling with water, sinking as their broken necks were flushed and straightened by the rush of the water forcing itself into the damaged hulls of their bodies. As his life raft gave way, cruelly, slowly, Duncan went under for the first time. But the air in his own lungs saved him, and as he resurfaced he thought he saw the minister on the shore amongst the boys. He focused his eyes on the black figure and thought he saw him cupping his hands around his mouth. The minister was shouting something. What was it? It must be important, Duncan thought, and with all the curiosity and keenness of his age he strained his ears and with his last strength pushed once more out of the water to receive the tuition from his master – surely now he would be told how to swim. 'Pray, Duncan, remember to pray . . .' Was that really what he called? Was that all? But Duncan did not pray, and this time he sank for good, his eyes still open, staring into the underwater world until his lungs filled, the last pocket of air abandoned him and his eyes burst and saw no more. The spirit left the body it had worn and might have escaped with the last bubble of air that reached the surface. Then the shapelessness of the sea was again unbroken as it closed above the boy.

Lizzie had witnessed the terrible scene from up the slope of Oiseval. She had seen her husband arrive at the shore and she had shouted to him at the top of her voice, willing him to go in after the boy. Distraught, she hurried back to the manse and waited for Neil to return. When he did, she found it hard to look at him, and although she knew the time was not right – that it was too brutal – his dry clothes made her demand of him, 'Why did you not go in after him? You are the only one here who can swim.' The voice came from somewhere deep and dark inside her.

He looked at her, stupefied.

'Oh, Neil . . .' Her powerless rage was mixed with pity – she knew the boy had meant a lot to him. Perhaps he had awakened in her husband's heart a memory of a lighter childhood?

'Can you not see? I would have failed! They would all have watched me fail and they would have lost faith in me.' It was hard for him to speak; her words had skewered him deeply.

A memory of a distant summer's evening surfaced in Lizzie's head. George Atkinson's accusing voice from somewhere outside the open window, saying, '. . . as you take authority of their souls and minds they will turn to you as to a God'. She shivered in the hot room.

'You sacrificed a child's life, a beloved child's life, in order to keep your command – because you are too proud, too afraid of losing face.'

Her words made him flinch. He held out his hands as if to ward her off.

'Proud? No. NO!' He shook his head in agony. The grief and the guilt were closing over him like damp earth.

'What then? Tell me why!' she shouted.

Pushed into a corner, he had to strike back in

order to get out. 'Don't you talk to me about letting children die!'

'What is that supposed to mean?'

'You know very well what I mean.'

'No, you'd better explain it to me.' She was furious.

He didn't have the strength to go on; he knew he was losing ground. 'No bother,' he muttered weakly.

She tried to calm herself down. 'No bother – is that all you can say?'

'Be quiet!'

'Is this all part of your so-called mission? There are things that must be sacrificed for the cause, is that it?'

'You don't understand – I am the mission – there is nothing else.'

His words, although made blunt by his grief, cut through her like knives.

'Living changes us,' he continued. 'This island changes us – it eats into you and won't leave you alone.'

Lizzie shook her head miserably. 'It is true that you have changed, but you cannot blame the island. You must try to master your own life rather than the lives of the islanders. That is your main duty to God – and to yourself.' She thought about what Betty had told her a few years previously, that everyone was responsible for coming to terms with their own lives.

★ ★ ★

A few nights later the moon brought him home and the tide – that lunar mistress – carried him into Village Bay in her swelling arms. The bloated, gas-filled birds were still attached to his waist, like a funeral wreath of wilted white lilies. The village was asleep as the sad hearse settled in the shallows. Everyone slept soundly, exhausted by grief. One or two of the young boys may have woken up during the night. Perhaps they sat up abruptly in their beds, only to realise that the bad dream was not theirs, that they played no part in it. They went back to sleep saddened but secretly relieved. The death of infants was understandable and therefore almost acceptable to the St Kildans, who realised that the death on the eighth day was beyond their control. But the death of a child who had lived and survived the dangerous years of infancy, who was prized and treasured by the entire community . . . The young were their insurance from the end of the world; they were the ones who would make sure the sun rose on another day. They would preserve the age of man that was the time and space of their island world. Duncan's death was unnatural and inexplicable and he was mourned like the other young dead throughout time, with intensity and fear.

Neil MacKenzie knew this and understood that the web holding the past and the present together had been somehow damaged. It was like when you hear a crack in an old pot but the damage is invisible to the eye. In a similar way, Duncan's death seemed to herald a dark downturn of events which made the minister shudder, although he was still unaware of just why. Nor could he make himself recognise the nature of his betrayal.

Just as everything was coming together so perfectly, he thought. The new village was progressing well, the land had been shifted and he had arranged to be picked up – the boat was due any day – in order to travel to Glasgow to collect the furniture and windows for the new houses. And it had been decided that he should travel back with the Rev. Drs Dickson and MacLeod, who were going to inspect the congregation on St Kilda and decide whether any of them were worthy to be taken up in the Church. MacKenzie had been preparing a number of the cleverest islanders for this purpose, and Duncan had been one of his brightest and most promising pupils. For a moment it all seemed hopeless to the minister. And he missed the boy, whose company had been a comfort to him. His young strength and formative mind had been a source of hope to the minister. He remembered the face of the boy as the current pulled him out to sea. How he had looked towards his friends on the shore and never uttered a word as he clung to his rod. No one had jumped in to try to save him as no one on the island could swim. Except for MacKenzie. It had never crossed his mind that he should go in after the boy. His mind darkened as he recalled his wife's accusations. Anyway, Duncan was too far out when he himself had reached the point. *There was nothing I could do.*

Duncan's was not the only ghost that kept the minister awake this night and haunted the blackest, furthest realms of his mind. He had woken up in a sweat after a dream, a memory that kept surfacing these days, horrendous and real in all its detail, of the night, so many years ago, when he had been near death by drowning himself. A terrible storm had overcome them as they had been trying out a new fishing vessel a few hours out of Arran. The boat had not been properly loaded and it did not last long in the heavy seas. They had been thrown into the sea, William and he, and as the vessel was torn to pieces by wave after crashing wave they tried desperately to keep their heads above water. Most of the floating debris was useless to them, but suddenly they spotted a part of the wreck which looked sturdy enough to carry the weight of a young man. They pointed it out to each other, shouting above the roar of the ocean, but even as they did so they realised that the insubstantial raft would carry one man, not two. This undeniable fact must have occurred to them both at the same time and soon the youths, who had competed against each other so many times in the past, always in play, were engaged in their final race. Neil reached the raft first and clung to it, exhausted and spent. From his safe point he watched Will as he looked around in desperation for another piece of wood substantial enough to bear him. Will's frantic splashing was exhausting him, and Neil could see that he was now struggling to breathe above water. At that moment Will turned to look at him and it was those eyes, pleading and hopeless, that Neil kept remembering – that moment that he relived – in his dreams. *What could I have done? I would have died too if I had tried to save him. It was God's will. THERE WAS NOTHING I COULD DO.*

But in his darkest moments, when his faith and his confidence were failing him, a thought might occur to him: what if I was not chosen? What if I survived merely because I was stronger, because I saved myself and left Will to die? What if there is no afterlife, no heaven for the young dead? What if I have deceived myself.

PART VI

JULY 1838 – TRAIL OF FAITH

They had all been called into the house to get changed; Eliza and her brother James and Jane, who was not much fun yet according to her sister, and Nigel who was sweet but only a baby. Mother and Anna were dressing them in their Sunday clothes, although it was a hot and sticky day just before the Sabbath. The fabric was thick and itchy against Eliza's skin, which had already got used to the cotton summer frock. How hateful, she thought to herself. Jane was crying as Anna tried to pull the tweed dress over her head, and Eliza sighed and shook her head so that the dark curls bounced against her cheeks. What a crybaby! James was eager to get back to his game with the village boys and stood obligingly as Mother pulled on his stiff jacket and combed his fair hair. Eliza did not play so much with James and the boys any more. At six she had started to have secrets, to hide treasures in little caches in the drystone wall and tell stories to the dolls she made out of twigs and discarded wool. In the long, green afternoons she would lie in the high grass behind the glebe wall and smell the violets and chamomile. If you lay on your back and looked up into the sky the birds would make you dizzy so that it was difficult to stand up again. That dizziness was light and pleasant like Anna's kisses. In the mornings she had to sit in the new schoolroom and do the lessons her father set for her and the other children. He was not like Father then and she had to call him 'Sir' in the classroom. 'Sir' seemed taller and he had chalk dust on his sleeves and he got cross if you did not sit still. She tried to sit still, but her feet did not reach down to the floor and it was difficult to know for sure if they were swinging or not because sometimes, when she did the lessons, her mind would wander.

Her siblings were such a burden to her, except for Nigel whom she liked to dress in pretty frocks and kiss until he pulled his benign little face away and pushed his chubby hands on her chest. She hated her green Sunday outfit, but Mother insisted that they all had to dress up today as Father was due with the very important people from Glasgow. She hated Mother for making her wear the suit and she hated Jane for her hot red face and James for being so good and getting all the praise from Anna. It was all hateful and she had had quite enough of it. She skipped out of the kitchen, first on one leg, then on the other, and on to the porch. 'Don't go down to the beach, Eliza, you will ruin your dress,' Mother called after her. 'No, I won't!' Eliza called back with the conviction of all her years. 'Wait for me,' cried James, who had finally escaped from Anna's care. Eliza felt the irritation rise as he came running after her. 'Go and play with your own friends,' she called to him, but he did not seem to mind. 'Leave me alone, James,' she said furiously to his grinning face. 'Why?' he leered. 'Where are you going? I want to come too.' 'No!' She started running and he followed. As soon as they were out of sight from the manse she stopped short and turned towards James, who came charging after her down the slope. As he reached her she pushed him hard in the chest so that he fell on the grass on his hands and knees. 'There!' she said, already regretting the violence. She saw that his knees had scuffed on the grass and were green with the kind of dirt that does not wash off easily. She could sense trouble. 'If you tell Mother and Anna that I pushed you I will kill you,' she hissed, and left him sobbing. She went and hid behind a boulder by the shore.

She had been irritable and frustrated ever since she had seen Duncan's body on the beach that morning at the beginning of the summer. She was not meant to have seen it, she understood; *it was not for children*. At first she had not been quite sure what it was that she was looking at, hiding behind a boulder as the men and dogs gathered at a respectable distance from whatever it was. It took a while for her to realise that it was a boy, but once she did it was too terrible. Had she really seen one of Duncan's feet sticking out of a torn trouser leg, a foot that was blue and black as if it had been alive and beaten? Had she really seen blood around his eyes and nostrils? It had not been at all like the Duncan she used to see every day at school and sometimes in Father's study at night. He had been all fat and a strange colour, like a sheep's stomach filled with fulmar oil. Father had been the one to remove the horrible belt of bird carcasses and lift him up. He had carried him with the horrible puffy baby face resting against his chest, all the way up to the village, where he had left Duncan's body with his mother, who had lost her only child. Duncan's mother had screamed at first and then blubbered in a way that made her look ridiculous, and it had scared Eliza.

At night when the light could not protect her, her mind's eye had opened again to the horror it had seen. It had made her wonder and it had kept her awake until she could never go back to sleep and her hands and neck were sweaty and all she could see when she opened her eyes was darkness and the end of life. She could not envisage heaven, and when she tried to think of angels and green pastures there was only dark nothingness and loneliness. She panicked as she thought that one day she, Eliza, might not be any more. Could she be dead? Just a name like the little Jane who had died to give way for our Jane, the one who lived (for what purpose Eliza was not sure), and Margaret who had also died without even giving way for another little Margaret. 'I don't want to die,' she sobbed into the night, her heart racing. When Father went away, shortly after Duncan went over, she cried every night until she dared ask Mother if Father was dead too. Mother just laughed and said that she was a silly girl and of course he wasn't. But how could she be so sure? Eliza wondered. People went away and did not come back; that is how it happens. Death. But it was day now, and during the day she forgot about the night, and Mother had told them that today was the day when Father might be coming back.

At that point Eliza heard shouting from the village, and as she looked out from her hiding place she saw the men come running towards the beach. 'There is a ship on fire!' they shouted. 'Bring out the boat. We must assist them!' Eliza stood up and looked towards the sea. Far out on the horizon she saw a cloud of smoke. Suddenly there was a flash followed by a terrible sound, like a giant wave crashing against Dùn in the winter storms. The air seemed to shake as the sound echoed against the rocks. Everyone on the shore was screaming in alarm now. Mothers were collecting their young and ushering them back towards the huts while the men were shouting orders as the boat was launched. The sky was full of gannets and fulmar who had been disturbed by the noise and left their rocks to circle Village Bay. In all the commotion Eliza started running back towards the manse. She entered the kitchen short of breath and had to stop at the door for a second before she could bring the news. James, still red-eyed and snotty, was sitting on the kitchen table, and Anna was kneeling in front of him, nursing his knees. Mother was standing by the window and looking out with the baby on her arm. Eliza could not understand how they could be so calm.

'Mother, Anna, there is an enormous ship on fire and it shouts like a storm!' she cried with her regained breath. And then a terrible thought hit her: 'What if Father is on the ship? What if he is being eaten by a monster?' She started crying violently. To her great surprise Mother started laughing. How could she laugh when Father was in mortal peril?

'Come here, sweetheart,' said Lizzie, and put the baby in his high chair. Eliza hated her mother for laughing when Father was in danger but she could not resist the comfort she offered. She ran over to Lizzie and hid her face in her skirts. At once the familiar smell filled her nostrils. It was the smell of baking and potato peels, of warm wool and something altogether more mysterious which reminded Eliza of the hawthorn bush in spring. This space in her mother's skirts seemed private and wonderful – a secret that bound her and Mother together and excluded the others. As Mother stroked her hair she could not stop crying – she felt so sorry for herself. No one cared about her, and one day she might be dead like Duncan. Would they even miss her? She wished she had died instead of Duncan and they could all have been missing her and thinking: if only we had loved her better while she was alive. She would not have died like Duncan though, and she would not have looked so grotesque. She would have been pale and composed and her hair would have curled prettily around her face and been slightly darker than in life. The tragedy of her thoughts made her cry even harder. 'Shh, shh,' Mother whispered, and kissed the crown of Eliza's head. 'Listen to me, Eliza, the ship is not on fire; it is a steamship and it fired its cannon to tell us it is here.' Eliza had almost forgotten about the ship. She did not want to leave her mother's embrace so she cried a bit more, but her eyes were quite dry now and the noises she made sounded a bit artificial, even to her own ears. Anna offered her a glass of milk and then they all went out on the porch and watched the ship as it approached. It was the largest ship any of them had ever seen. It looked new and shone in the sun; the iron hull was painted green and the rigging was brightly polished. As it drew closer, the terror of the villagers gave way to a general sense of amazement as a brass band started playing on deck. The music carried on the summer breeze and made the day somehow seem brighter, as if somebody had opened a window. There were lots of people on deck, some of them in hats and fine clothes.

As soon as the ship reached the bay the village boat came up alongside it and a couple of the men were lifted up on deck. A name was painted with large red letters on the green hull. Mother said it read *The Vulcan of Broomielaw* and that was the name of the ship. She said it was a most appropriate name as a Vulcan created clouds and explosions just like the ship had.

Neil MacKenzie stood by the bulwarks on the quarterdeck and watched as his island home drew closer. He was trying to sort and define his feelings at that moment. He had actually quite enjoyed being away for a couple of months, and this made him feel guilty. His visit to Glasgow had been a success from his point of view, and he felt encouraged. There, in the church meetings and salons, he had been appreciated and revered. Churchmen and scholars had flocked to see him, and even women had shown a keen interest in him. Some of them, he had realised, were very agreeable both to look at and to speak to. Their white smooth faces had beamed at him and their bosoms had heaved in their corsets. The doubts and inadequacies he sometimes felt on the island were removed and he had felt strong and elevated. On the island he never knew if his efforts would be enough but there, in the candlelit parlours of Glasgow's rich and famous, he was encouraged to believe that his work on St Kilda was unique and spectacular. *That he was interesting.* Even during the journey he had been hailed by some of the more distinguished of the passengers as somebody intriguing and admirable. Lachlan MacLean, a young writer who had travelled with the party on the *Vulcan*, had been interviewing him about the island on several occasions. MacKenzie found him rather tedious and affected, but it was clear that the young man's zeal and enthusiasm were genuine. There was a certain Miss Thomson on board who had charmed many of the gentlemen, he believed, and especially Mr MacLean.

His expedition, his errand of mercy to Glasgow, had paid off. With the assistance of the kindly Dr MacLeod and a few generous gentlemen in Glasgow he had secured forty-seven bedsteads (two for every house that paid rent, one for each of the widows), also twenty-four chairs, twenty-one stools, twenty-one tables, twenty-one dressers, twenty-one glass windows, and numerous pieces of Delft ware. The manager of the Glasgow Steam Packet Company, Mr MacConnell, had agreed to warrant the company in advertising a trip, thus providing a commodious steamer for the expedition, if a sufficient number of tourists signed up.

Arrangements having been completed, the steamer *Vulcan*, with about forty passengers, left the Clyde on the twenty-fifth day of July. It had been a rather pleasant journey and Mr MacKenzie had enjoyed the attention that he received from the other passengers, who were curious about St Kilda and her inhabitants. The ship had stopped at several places on the way in order for the tourists to get the full value from their fare. At the Giant's Causeway one of the passengers, a most respectable tradesman, who had manufactured the household articles that were being given to the St Kildans, enquired of Mr MacKenzie, in real sincerity, if there was 'any history of the date of its construction'. MacKenzie shook his head in exasperation; how could good citizens still believe in giants? But the journey had not been short of wonders, and he had been fairly aghast himself when they cast anchor in Loch Maddy and at the inn he had seen a Negro waiter, who spoke and sang in Gaelic!

He looked up towards the island and suddenly he made out a group of people silhouetted against the whitewashed manse wall. He recognised the outlines of his children and his wife and the maid. He loved his children dearly, he was sure of that, but he had not given them much mind while he was away. Nor had his thoughts lingered on their mother, more than to compare her with the young ladies he had met in the city. But now as he sailed closer he could feel a new sensation rise within him, and he was suddenly very impatient to meet them. He thought with tenderness about how simple and uncomplicated they were in comparison with the beautifully made-up people in town. He watched his family with pride and waved at them. To his amazement they saw him and waved back.

At that moment Dr Dickson came up and stood beside MacKenzie at the railing. He wore a fur hat pulled down over his ears and royal-blue knee breeches with white silk stockings; his stomach was bulging under his coat. His face was rather fat and settled in the haughty beginnings of a smile, which made him look like a statue of some long-forgotten hero.

'Ah, at last we reach the enchanted island!' This exuberant remark clearly conveyed some relief; the journey had been rough, and the *Vulcan*'s passengers had waltzed helplessly around the deck as the Atlantic waves set the steamship rolling. The Rev. Dr Dickson was the minister of St Cuthbert's church in Edinburgh, and his pastoral care rarely brought him outside the capital. He was used to drinking claret in the genteel homes and salons of the New Town and generally mixed with the right sort. Only a few years previously he had had the honour of orchestrating the funeral of Sir Walter Scott. Normally he would not have bothered to undertake *this* kind of journey, but engagement in the Gaelic hinterland had become rather à la mode lately and he wished to stay in touch with current affairs. Besides, he considered it a charitable cause that would benefit them all in one way or another.

'Yes, I have rather missed it,' MacKenzie answered dreamily. 'It is my cathedral. The kirk is humble enough, but to my mind the island itself is as awe-inspiring as any temple built to God. Would you not agree when you look at it this morning, sir?'

Dr Dickson, who generally felt rather uneasy

around the intense younger man, could not decide whether his remark was appropriate or not. He cleared his throat:

'As examiner of the Society for the Propagation of Christian Knowledge, I have to express my grateful sense of what you have done for the comfort and advancement in civilisation of these sea-girt inhabitants, not least for promoting their spiritual welfare and for taking this initiative to administer to them, for the first time, the hallowed ordinance which commemorates the infinite love of our dying Redeemer.'

'It was the task you set me – I was only doing what was expected.'

'Hmm.' Dr Dickson pulled off his hat and scratched his sweaty scalp. 'I presume that you are satisfied that your people are fit to be admitted to communion; that they are ready, without any further preparation, to join in the service; and that you can, without prior communication with them, determine which of them should or should not be at once allowed and invited to join that high privilege?'

'I have a good idea, yes.'

'That is excellent, man, splendid!'

Suddenly he gave a short laugh and pointed towards the shore. 'Look how the natives run, like a flock of goats scrabbling for their lives, barefooted, bareheaded and coatless.'

'Yes, but so full of expectation and the longing to see their minister,' MacKenzie added quietly in a tone of voice for a private prayer.

Dr Dickson flinched at this strange remark. He strongly suspected that this bareheaded minister was getting a bit above himself. 'I am sure they are fairly devoted to you, sir, for their lowly state is the most favourable condition for worshipping the meek and lowly lamb in *truth*, and they will naturally get very attached to whomever takes it upon himself to deliver the Gospel in this place.'

With this remark he excused himself and left in search of Mr Buchanan, a gentleman of considerable influence, beyond the boundaries of Europe, whom he had befriended onboard and found to be most agreeable company.

MacKenzie sighed when Dr Dickson left him to himself. He was generally unaware of any effect he had on other people but he wanted to be admired. He wondered if he would ever shake off that part of himself that doubted his own abilities, the part that wanted to impress this important clergyman, a man he disliked for his obvious disapproval. He wondered what they were saying behind his back; what names did they call him? *The poor miller's boy who killed his only friend.* Were they laughing at him? *I will not be humiliated.*

He felt much more at ease with Dr MacLeod, a Glaswegian who spoke Gaelic and had grown up in Morvern. MacLeod was a true man of the Church, and he had convened the Great Assembly two years earlier. The previous night when they had landed at Loch Maddy they had seen a ship bound for Cape Breton, and Mr MacKenzie had asked Dr MacLeod if he wanted to accompany him onboard to speak to the émigrés. Dr MacLeod had replied solemnly, saying that he could not bear to see those unfortunate souls; he knew all too well what famine and malady had done to his own kin. Mr MacKenzie had nodded. He understood. It was all greatly disturbing; times were getting harder. Crops were failing in the Highlands, and with more and more of the best arable land enclosed and used for sheep farming, the situation was becoming alarming. The stories of starvation and misery he had heard told in Glasgow had only strengthened the minister's resolve. He had felt the same since his own family were forced to leave for Canada. He was no Utopian, but he saw clearly that the possibilities of the modern world were limitless. If he could remove the obstacles that had hindered the natural progress of social order on this island for so long, St Kilda could be different and its inhabitants would at last develop into better and more ethical beings. It would be a moral outpost, a true exemplar of the good of man and an island refuge away from the wrongs of the world. Today was the first day of this new era on the island. *Redemption was near.*

The village boat had reached the *Vulcan* and MacKenzie was lowered into the dinghy along with MacLean the writer and a few others. The villagers were still scrambling towards the beach, and he frowned when he saw his eldest daughter running along with them. Where was his wife?

Could she not keep the children in control? He did not want to be embarrassed in front of all these important people. With a hot rush of irritation he remembered how she had been when he first brought her here, so aloof and distracted. She had not offered any of the support and encouragement you should expect from a young wife. None at all! And now she had turned from him towards the children. She was always occupied – never any time for him. Had he not seen to it that she had a maid to help her so that she could be more involved in his work? Where was that lanky girl anyway? He could never quite trust her; had she not lied to him once?

While the St Kildans rowed the dinghy towards the shore the fresh-faced Mr MacLean was babbling endlessly about all the things he wanted to do on the island. He was rather effeminate and over-eager, MacKenzie thought, and forever scribbling in a waxed notebook. The minister silently hoped that the young man's writing was not as exasperating as his speech. Mr MacLean too wore knee-breeches and silk stockings and a bonnet that matched his coat. He had a fair, open face with slightly protruding eyes, and a loud, annoying laugh which reminded MacKenzie of the call of the herring gull. A nuisance, all in all.

'Ah, look at the bairns,' cooed Mr MacLean. 'Aren't they the bonniest you will ever see? So innocent and pure and not marked by starvation or conflict!'

MacKenzie glanced uncertainly at the writer, trying to discern a note of sarcasm, and then looked again towards the shore where his daughter Eliza and her brother James were tumbling down towards the beach with the other children. Their green tweed outfits matched the fresh sorrel and bracken on the slope, and their little faces, brightened by Atlantic mist, were open and eager. How he had missed them!

The rowing was too slow; he leaned forward in the dinghy, willing it to go faster. As soon as it hit the shelving beach he jumped out, not minding his nice new boots and trousers. He saw Eliza running ahead of her brother towards him. As she reached him, his own flesh and blood, he forgot himself and fell to his knees to embrace her. He kissed the soft, hot skin at the nape of her neck and felt tears well in his eyes as her hands held on to his ears, kissing him wetly on the nose. He was suddenly full of hope. Perhaps in time he would be able to convey to his daughter what was brewing in his own soul. She was the one who was most like him. Surely she would be the one to understand him. He tried to look deep into her eyes (would his soul not be mirrored there?), but the girl was rambling now about explosions and volcanoes. He couldn't quite understand and tried to shush her. 'Do you love your father?' He blew the soft question into her ear. She was wriggling in his arms, squealing in pleasure for Father was back and all was play. There was happiness in her dark curls again. 'No, no, I hate you, I HATE you! You went away and never came back,' yelled the elated child, and laughed into the sky. The minister suddenly stiffened and withdrew from his daughter. What was she saying? Could she really mean that she did not love him? He was making a fool of himself; his daughter was making a fool of him. It must be his wife who had influenced the child against him while he was away. Ever since Mrs MacKenzie's withdrawal into preoccupation with the children he had suspected that she resented him. Hardening his heart, he closed his face again and stood to greet the rest of his family. Eliza, bewildered and rejected, stepped back and bit her lip.

Lizzie watched her husband as he was welcomed by their eldest daughter. She was confused about her feelings at that moment and she suddenly realised that she had not missed him while he was away. He seemed slightly taller than before he left, and his shadow was longer. He reminded her of a guillemot: his black minister's coat sharp against the white collar and his eyes black and blankly lit by a hectic fire. His manners too were different, and she imagined that they might have been shaped by a desire to please these other people who suddenly filled the shore.

During his absence she had grown even closer to the children. As she had read the stories to them in the nursery at sunset, her children had nuzzled in around her like hibernating cubs around a mother bear. Once or twice she had fallen asleep in one of their beds after finishing the story, only to wake up an hour or so later, her heart brimming with happiness and purpose.

Through her own thoughts she heard her daughter's outburst, saw her husband stiffen and turn away, and suddenly aware of the rift between them she stepped in to save the situation: 'Oh, Neil, have reason – she is just a child.' She said it lightly so as not to scare her daughter. 'Of course Eliza has missed you, haven't you dear?' Eliza nodded, staring down at her stiff boots, tightly laced for the occasion, as her mother continued: 'She has been beside herself with worry! It is only a short while ago that I had to wipe away her tears.'

She smiled then, and he saw that there was no malice, no irony. For an instant they stood facing each other on the landing rock where the waves lapped idly at barnacles and seaweed. And for a second they were reunited again, husband and wife, shyly one in their shared world. Without a thought of the people around them Neil lifted his hand and placed his palm against her cheek. 'Oh, my lass – I miss you and the way we were,' he said under his breath as she inclined her face towards his warmth.

Just then Eliza entered the space between them, tugging at her father's coat. 'I picked you some flowers to stop your crying, Father.' She held up a clumsy fist of thrift. The moment of tenderness was broken, but Neil blinked and smiled as he picked up his daughter in his arms. 'I am not crying, darling. I am just so happy to be home again.'

It took a couple of hours to land all the passengers from the *Vulcan* on the beach. The sea was still choppy, and the passengers who were waiting on the ship to be taken ashore were tossed around the deck. The Rev. Dr MacLeod, who insisted on leaving the ship at the very last along with Captain M'Killop, was embracing the mainmast like Ulysses at Anthemoessa.

Finally, just after one o'clock, when the last of the passengers and all the goods had been unloaded onto the beach, Dr MacLeod seemed to regain his command and insisted on giving a service to the islanders. All who understood Gaelic made their way to the kirk. Many of the tourists from Glasgow followed suit, their curiosity fuelled less by the prospect of the sermon and more by the chance to get a close-up look at the natives. A handful of the less pious tourists decided to go for a bathe in the shallows of Village Bay.

As the visitors entered the kirk the islanders were all standing up listening to the *maor*, who was giving a prayer. MacKinnon was barefooted as usual and clothed in his coarse jacket and cropped wide trousers. He had removed his cap, and his curly hair sat like a mat on his head. He spoke in a low, firm Gaelic that compelled the visitors to stop their chattering and listen to the strange character who prayed so ardently with his eyes closed to the world. He did not stop to look up when the two churchmen entered the church but delivered the message to his kin calmly but with an intensity that surprised the newcomers.

Mr MacLean, wide-eyed and excited, was one of the last to enter the kirk, and as he did so he caught the last of the prayer:

> . . . *Bless those into whose hearts Thou hast put it to come and visit us – not to mock us, but with hearts running over with love, with the message of the Lamb, who taketh away the sin of the world. This we seek for His sake. Amen.*

Later that afternoon, on the other side of the island, Lachlan MacLean was striding ahead of a small group of visitors up the slope of Gleann Mòr. He had taken it upon himself to guide them on an excursion of the sublime island. MacKinnon, the *maor*, had offered to take the tourists to Glen Bay in the village boat. Mrs Ramsay was struggling in her silk mantle and Miss Thomson had to offer her arm as support. Messrs Goppy and Buchanan were walking a few steps behind, discussing the morning's sermon and agreeing that the Reverend Doctor had prayed with an unusual fervour and unction, possibly exceeding his usual eloquence. The natives had been moved to tears, and Mr Goppy insisted – and Mr Buchanan was not slow to second him – that no one could possibly close their hearts to such a sanctifying service, nor could anyone doubt, in that instance, that God was present on St Kilda.

'This is a great glen,' Lachlan shouted over his shoulder to the others. 'It could be put to good use!'

'Good use indeed!' Mrs Ramsay muttered as she stepped into some cow dung. 'I am certain no human could live here.'

'There seems to be little means for that, indeed,' Miss Thomson agreed.

'Look at this good grass, how lush it is – this soil could yield a plentiful crop.' Lachlan turned and walked backwards as he spoke to them.

'It is green,' Miss Thomson acknowledged.

'And fresh enough,' added Mrs Ramsay reluctantly.

'You are most observant, madam,' said Mr Buchanan gaily as he caught up with the ladies. 'Allow me,' he added, and caught Mrs Ramsay's elbow from Miss Thomson's grip.

'If I had a farm here . . .' Lachlan was still walking backwards, facing the ladies.

'You would be doing more good than playing the fool like this,' said Mrs Ramsay disapprovingly. She was panting harder now.

'You could plant some tobacco and trade with the natives,' Mr Buchanan suggested helpfully.

'If I were the lord of this manor, how would I run it?' His cheeks were flushed now.

'You would talk your servants to death, that is for sure.'

'Oh, Mrs Ramsay!' Miss Thomson giggled.

'There would be no classes; all would be equal, innocent and pure.'

'And yet you would be the lord of the manor.' Mrs Ramsay stopped to dab the sweat from her brow with a lace handkerchief which she kept tucked in her sleeve.

'And there would be no parties and no weddings – how perfectly dull!' Miss Thomson's shrill voice protested for once.

'A land where everything is held in common, where crime and war are unknown and where there is an abundance of food to feed my people and no one would have to work too hard.' MacLean was beaming. His dream had carried him off and he was quite oblivious to his fellow ramblers.

'And yet I doubt very much that there would be such peace, with you around.'

'Come now, Mrs Ramsay, where is your sense of charity?' Mr Buchanan said sternly, his eyes smiling.

'I would be such a fair chief and lead my island world beyond the Golden Age!'

'And long may he live!' shouted Mr Buchanan, and threw his hat in the air.

'Hail Caesar!' snarled Mrs Ramsay, and sat down to rest on a boulder.

Fatigued by the steep climb, the group stopped and turned to look back towards the bay below. The sun was still high in the west, but the light was thickening and sent long shadows along the length of the green valley. A couple of streams cut through the face of the glen like scars lit on either side by flaming gorse. The grass itself seemed illuminated where millions of dandelions burst from within it and the sea beyond was impossibly blue.

'Oh heavens! If I was not so hot and weary I would think I had reached the afterlife! Did you ever imagine paradise such as this?' MacLean cried in exultation.

'Here we go again,' said Mrs Ramsay below her breath. 'The emperor has died and gone to heaven – although it would rather resemble the other place, with him in it.'

The others, taken by the scenery, ignored her.

'God is truly in this place,' sighed Mr Buchanan, who could afford to be romantic.

'Would it not be a splendid idea if we named this bay after Dr MacLeod, who showed himself to be such a great benefactor to this island and its inhabitants this morning?' said MacLean excitedly.

'Oh yes, in commemoration of his most humane visit to the island!' shrieked Miss Thomson.

MacKinnon the *maor*, who was hovering a few yards away, trying to understand the gentlefolk's conversation, suddenly spoke up: 'But, sir, it has a name already. It was always *Loch a' Ghlinne*. The ancestors named it when they first arrived.'

One or two looked up but took no particular notice of this remark.

'Indeed . . . Indeed, what an excellent idea!' they agreed and congratulated each other on being the first to discover and name MacLeod's Bay.

As it happened it was only a matter of time before Dr Dickson got himself a bay too. It was the following morning, just after the communion service where Drs Dickson and MacLeod and the Rev. Mr MacKenzie interviewed the fifteen St Kildan men who had been chosen for – and seemed fit to receive – the Sacrament of the Lord's Supper. The communicants were all rather elderly and they shuffled in eager anticipation; their matted hair was greying on their bent heads and their bare feet were worn and twisted like the roots of old trees. The examination, conducted by Dr Dickson himself, took some time as his questions concerning the Scripture had to be translated by Mr MacKenzie and then reinterpreted by Dr MacLeod. After many hours the learned gentlemen from the mainland had satisfied themselves that the men were all worthy of receiving into their hands the symbols of the love of their crucified Saviour. Dr Dickson, on behalf of the Society, had already presented the humble kirk with a silver communion cup, a salver and a font. Everything was decent and in order. The fifteen St Kildan men who had been chosen to enter the Church of God were moved to tears by the ceremony and kirk-session that followed, witnessed by their kin.

Cheered and encouraged by this blessed event, Dr Dickson decided to go back to the *Vulcan* to preach a sermon from the ship's deck. The first mate offered to take him in the small boat, but on entering this dinghy a trick of nature was played on the portly Dr Dickson. The tired swell – which had been resting against the beach all night and all morning – yawned and a lazy ripple swept the dinghy away from under the feet of the Reverend Doctor. And so it happened that this man of God, as witnessed by a congregation of near savages, toppled over and somersaulted into the cold swell of Village Bay. Swiftly retrieved from those uncon-secrated waters, Dr Dickson was hurried aboard the *Vulcan* to change out of his wet clothes. Unfortunately he had not brought an extra pair of breeches and so had to wear a pair of trousers belonging to the first mate. The officer was a tall and lean man and it was plain to all that the trousers were an unusually bad fit. They could not be pulled up properly and so left a gap of about six inches, which Dr Dickson tried to cover up by tugging down his waistcoat.

From the shore MacKenzie watched Dr Dickson's fall with increasing dread. What was supposed to have been the most joyful day of his career had turned into a shambles. It must not develop into something unworthy and ridiculous. He had wanted it all to work out well. Would the great churchman's tumble undermine his own authority? He had worked hard and diligently towards this day for years. The thought that one of the islanders might in some way put him to shame in front of the guests had crossed his mind and worried him, but he could never have imagined that the action of the Rev. Dr Dickson would threaten to spoil the day. Eight years! For eight years he had strived to alter and better the minds of his congregation in order to prepare a handful of them for entry into the Church. And had he not, simultaneously, worked alongside his parishioners until his hands bled and the shirt tore from his back? Had he not broken his body to change the land and reshape the island so that it might be presented to the Lord's missionaries on this day? And what now? Was it all in vain? He heard a peal of laughter and froze. Who was laughing? He was starting to feel nauseous. *Stay calm. No need to work yourself up about this. No need. I will not be held accountable. There was nothing I could do.*

He looked around for his wife. He wanted her next to him; he needed her to reassure him and to tell him that it was all right. *It is all right.* He turned but could not see her anywhere. *Where has she gone? She is supposed to be here when I need her!* Eventually he saw her amongst a group of people on the shore. She was laughing and talking to Anna and Mrs MacCrimmon as if nothing had happened. Or were they talking about him? His own wife! He wiped the sweat from his eyes with the back of his hand and looked again. She had done her hair up in the St Kildan fashion; her frizzy locks scraped back from a centre parting straight as the flight of the solan geese, and gathered at the nape of her neck. And she had neglected to wear her bonnet. How had he not noticed it before, on the landing rock? When did she start wearing her hair like this? Why had he not been consulted? *So she thinks she is one of them now!* He felt a sudden rage rising inside him and strode towards the group of women. 'Mrs MacKenzie, I need you to see to our guests and make sure they are comfortable,' he said formally. His voice sounded strange and too loud and he faltered when people around looked up at him and stopped talking. He felt his face redden a bit. *Ridiculous hair.*

Lizzie looked up at her husband. She could sense the anxiety in him and studied his face for a moment or two, trying to work out what to make of it, how to react, before looking away. The hustle and bustle went on around them. She sighed.

'Of course, dear,' she said lightly, and walked up to him. She linked her arm through his and led him away from the group of women. She smiled at people around them and leant in to whisper in his ear, her lips brushing ever so lightly against his neck, 'It is all right, darling. You are doing fine.'

'No, Lizzie, I feel peculiar – dizzy.' Perhaps there was fear in his voice. 'My mind is not strong. I feel torn and I don't know any more what matters.' He was sweating in the hot day.

Lizzie stopped and turned to him. 'Look at me, Neil.' She knew how important this day was for him and she mustered all the strength inside her and made him see it there inside her eyes, which were the colour of blue steel. 'You made all this happen; you must follow it through.' He relaxed noticeably at the tone of her voice. 'Do you hear me? You must not fail now.'

He straightened and gave a short laugh. 'Ha, how foolish of me to get into such a state. It must be the long journey and the rough sea.' He drew a deep breath and let it out slowly, staring beyond her out to the bay.

She let go of his arm then and moved off towards Mrs Ramsay and Miss Thomson, who were busy handing out a donation of black silk scarves amongst the local girls. There was a great commotion as the St Kildans tried on the new scarves. They had been donated by one of the passengers who owned a textile factory in Paisley. The factory clerk had miscalculated the production of goods for the national mourning at the King's funeral the year before and they needed to get rid of some of the stock to make place in the warehouse. The excitement amongst the girls, however, was undeniable and they carefully arranged the scarves so that the merchant marks which had been left on were exposed like ornaments. Miss Thomson was helping them to tie the shawls over their hair or muslin caps while Mrs Ramsay was smiling benevolently from behind a lace handkerchief which she kept pressed against her nose. She had donated some of her own old dresses. They were only slightly frayed and torn and could, with advantage, be worn by some of the more mature ladies of the community. 'On special occasions, such as for a ball,' she shouted at one of these ladies. 'Ah, please, Mr MacLean, can you translate? I do not think they understand what I am saying.' She turned to the writer, who was loitering nearby with an amused look on his face.

MacKenzie watched his wife as she walked through the crowd and stopped here and there to chat with the visitors. He could still feel the warmth of her body along his side and the dizzy spell had passed. He felt much better and straightened his back and drew a hand through his hair as he smiled at Miss Thomson's sister, the pretty one, who was lingering nearby. *Still, I must remember to tell my wife not to wear her hair like that – it really makes her look ridiculous. She is not one of them.*

As the sun began to set and a crescent moon appeared above the ragged crenulations of Dùn, the visitors prepared to leave in order to meet the tide in the Sound of Harris. Mr MacKenzie walked with Dr MacLeod towards the boats.

'I wish to thank you, sir, for your kindness and generosity. I am much obliged and very grateful, naturally.' MacKenzie bowed slightly to the older man.

'Not at all, not at all, my friend.' Dr MacLeod

patted MacKenzie's arm absent-mindedly. 'We should be thankful to you. You have done an excellent job here.' He stopped and looked out over the *clachan*. 'They are far, far behind in the more ordinary arts of life; their huts are still not better than those of the Kaffirs, but their moral and spiritual condition is the most marvellous feature in their history.' Dr MacLeod smiled at MacKenzie. 'I believe that there are not of their number more holy persons on earth. As to this Sabbath day, it was one to be had in remembrance. I thank God I was here on this day. I have not passed a sweeter day on earth. Poor people – farewell – God bless them; we have added much to their comfort, and I hope to add more!' Tears were welling in the old man's eyes at this point.

MacKenzie, suddenly overwhelmed, could think of nothing to say.

Dr Dickson, who seemed to have regained his dignity while spending the afternoon and early evening aboard the *Vulcan*, pulled out a deckchair and placed his bible on it like on a pulpit.

It was an incredibly beautiful summer evening. Village Bay was framed by the looming hills of deep green; the peaks and crags seemed rounded and softened in the slow light and sent their velvet shadows far out on to the mirrored sea. The staccato laughter of a lonely herring gull briefly punctured the air. In the glowing evening it seemed too brutal; like a stabbing at night. Then silence was restored once more, only to be disturbed every now and again by the light sighs of the resting sea. The ship's steward raised the flags in the rigging and their gay colours opened like a rainbow as the last of the sun broke and fell over the ridge of Conachair.

With his back turned on the setting sun and facing the Atlantic, Dr Dickson beckoned to the voyagers to sing Psalm One Hundred as the *Vulcan* rocked gently on her anchor. At once the song rose through the air and the birds around the bay woke again to give their own concert. In this manner the voices of men and birds joined in a rare song of praise to God and nature. The sermon that followed started with the words 'I have set the Lord always before me'.

That July evening in 1838 was the pinnacle of the Rev. Neil MacKenzie's mission. For one brief moment it all seemed perfect. The arched stretch of the new village along a proper street smiled at its future inhabitants. The sea fowl exulted as fifteen of the islands' brightest souls were welcomed into the Lord's family. The waves at Village Bay lapped warm under the setting sun as Dr MacLeod told him that he had succeeded, that his work was indeed an important part of the Lord's mission. The stars' silver shone out of the summer firmament as the *Vulcan* weighed anchor and sailed off into the world. And on returning into that other world, to Buchanan Street and Queen Street, to Moray Place and Charlotte

Square, the voyagers would dine with the great and the good at tables dressed in damask and silver and they would remember the handsome minister of St Kilda and his zeal and enthusiasm. For a little while they would remember him and his extraordinary predicament.

But what happened on the island when the ship had sailed, when the prominent guests had departed, when all the tables, chairs and teapots had been distributed and when the glass windows had been fitted, one into each new earthen house? What then?

What followed was a harsh winter when the St Kildans, whose hearts had been full to the brim of God's warmth that summer, turned cold and unenthusiastic. The ancient community which had thought itself complete, perfect and self-sufficient suddenly realised that it was nothing of the sort. Faced with the prejudices of the outside world they understood they were lacking in something important, something that would make them human in the eyes of the world.

The gales were severe and started just after the harvest. The sea sprayed salt over the newly shifted fields, and sheep were blown off the cliffs like drifting snow. The minister's elder son lost his hearing to a howling storm. His senses did not recover until the following spring, when the birds returned and reached into his consciousness with their calls that carried the red heat of the African savannah and the fragrant winds of the Atlas

Mountains. The minister continued to instruct the communicants still more fully in the doctrines of the Gospel. He held communion every Friday in order to inspire greater piety. He tried to force faith into his people, and in this way, every other Friday, a newcomer was added to the number of communicants. The significance of the newly bequeathed communion vessels filled the dull kirk, and soon their shining surfaces misted over with the breath of the congregation. But in spite of the minister's fervent prayers his communicants' hearts remained closed to the Holy Ghost.

The bad weather continued through the summer, and a series of gales prevented the ship from the mainland setting out. When it did eventually try the hazardous journey the seas around the island were so wild it had to turn back and did not attempt another landing that year. That autumn supplies were scarcer than ever. Had it not been for the visit of a privateer seeking shelter in Village Bay during an autumn storm, the islanders would have been near starvation. The St Kildans were no strangers to pirates and happily offered to trade with the armed villains. The women washed battle-worn clothes and the men mended ropes in exchange for dried meat and ship's biscuit. The minister watched in horror as his parishioners traded with Satan, but when the captain of the vessel presented him with a case of smuggled wine, the gift was reluctantly accepted. The wine, mixed with hot water, made a fair substitute for tea in the manse as the winter approached.

In spite of this welcome visit, spirits were unusually low as yet another winter approached. The new village structure seemed to have upset the ancient social patterns of the community. People had been uprooted from the houses the ancestors built and in which kin lived so closely together as to become of one mind. The new houses were also heated by the beasts that shared the accommodation, but property was more marked and with property comes individuality. In this new village, as food and fuel grew scarcer by the day, superstitions, mistrust and jealousy festered amongst the St Kildans.

On Mullach Geal stood a group of ancient stones – a game of hurling hastily abandoned by jaded giants. One of these megaliths was cleft in two – children would often play around it, crawling through the secret passage.

One winter's day Anna came running into the manse rosy and breathless, 'Ma'am, you must come quickly. Oh please hurry! She is in trouble.'

'What is it that you are saying, girl? Who's in trouble?'

'Betty, ma'am. Do come! She is stuck in a stone!'

'Stuck in a . . . ?' Lizzie, who realised that she would not get any sense out of the girl, picked up her shawl and hastened from the house.

There was a bitter chill. Slight sheets of ice had broken up in the bay and were washed against the frozen sand on the beach. It made a surprisingly beautiful sound of thin crystal notes. Lizzie was tempted to stop for a moment to listen, but Anna was obviously very distressed.

She followed the girl, who was already clambering up the steep slope behind the *clachan*. The wind-stripped broom and heather were sapped of life, mud-coloured, miserable. Lizzie soon got warm; she was breathing hard now but continued upwards, using her feet and sometimes her hands. Every now and again she would stop briefly to wipe her nose on her woolly sleeve.

'Not so fast, Anna! How far now?'

'Not far, ma'am, hurry, please!'

They were high over the bay now and for a while she lost sight of the girl, who had disappeared amongst some large boulders.

'Over here!'

Lizzie rushed on but stopped abruptly in her tracks when she saw the strange form in front of her.

'What in God's name is this?' She moved closer, hesitantly. There was something large and white wedged in one of the rocks. 'Betty?'

'Oh for pity's sake! Don't just stand there – help me. I have been stuck here for over an hour!' Lizzie had never heard the former maid talk in such a way.

It was quite clear that Betty had somehow got jammed in the cleft stone. She had tried to crawl through, and when she got stuck she had tried to reverse, which had only resulted in her skirts being pushed up around her waist. Her naked thighs were pinking in the winter air. Lizzie, who was greatly embarrassed by the sight, walked around the megalith in order to face the unfortunate Betty. The younger woman was hanging over the stone, face down, like a child waiting to be spanked. She looked up at Lizzie from her wretched position, her face purple against her fair hair. 'Don't you dare tell anyone about this!' she hissed.

Lizzie didn't answer but grabbed hold of Betty's arms and started pulling. 'No, no, that won't work!'

'What then?' Lizzie felt a wave of irritation. This whole situation really was quite ridiculous.

'You've got to try and get my skirts back through the cleft and pull me backwards.'

Lizzie felt her heart sink but obeyed and walked around to the other side of the rock. By and by, with Anna's help, she managed to pull the coarse fabric of Betty's winter skirts through the cleft, tearing off a large piece of ragged tweed in the process. Once Betty was decent again Lizzie took hold of one leg and Anna the other. On the count of three they both pulled as hard as they could. Betty moaned but did not dislodge.

'Betty,' Lizzie said sternly, 'you have got to try to make yourself thinner.'

'Aw,' cried Betty gracelessly – she had long since lost her dignity.

'Suck your breath in!'

Betty did as she was told and this time Anna and Lizzie managed to pull her free from the trap. The three women lay on the ground puffing and gasping.

'What were you doing getting stuck in that rock?' Lizzie asked between breaths.

'I didn't get stuck on purpose, did I?' Betty snapped. She was rubbing some heat back into her stiff limbs.

Lizzie smiled at that, but bit her lip when she saw Betty's angry face.

'Ah, you might just as well know all of it,' Betty said quickly, her eyes to the ground. 'My grandmother used to tell me that pulling a woman through a cleft rock would make babies stick to the womb and grow good and healthy.'

'Did you really believe that?' Lizzie asked incredulously.

Betty looked up defiantly. 'Well, there is no harm in trying, is there?'

Lizzie shook her head slowly but said nothing.

'Maybe it is the bairns I should have pulled through the rock – not myself. All the babies I have carried for the full nine months – and none have survived but a few days. It can't be right!'

They were all quiet for a while. It was getting dark and the cold was seeping up through the ground. Clouds were gathering below them, hiding the bay from view.

Betty spoke first. 'Please don't tell Mr MacKenzie. He doesn't look kindly on such things.'

'Oh, I don't know . . .' Lizzie said gravely. 'I thought you looked rather becoming – I am sure a number of people would have enjoyed the view,' and suddenly she could not hold it inside her any more. An ugly, snorting laugh that had been kept in for far too long burst out of her like an undammed stream.

Betty stopped rubbing her thighs and looked up in fury. But presently her face changed and all of a sudden she was laughing too. She tore off a tuft of dry heather and threw it at Lizzie, who ducked away expertly. 'Ooh, petrifying!' she cooed.

Anna, who was standing by, nervously chewing the end of her braid, could not quite see what was so funny, but she laughed all the same, relieved that the two grown-up women were no longer quarrelling.

'This will teach you not to be lured by superstition and devilry,' Lizzie giggled, mimicking her husband's ministerial voice.

The dreary afternoon was suddenly alight with their laughter, which echoed between the strange stones and rang across the valley. If anyone had been about in the *clachan* at that moment they would have wondered at the strange witchy sound that seemed to fall out of the frost-fed sky.

To the minister, however, the superstitions that brewed all through that bitter winter seemed altogether more sinister.

One old woman stopped coming to the kirk on

the Sabbath, and when the minister asked her why she replied forthright that she must stay at home to protect her newly thatched roof from the ravens which had been picking at it, keeping her awake with nightmares and disturbing her work by day. The minister asked her why she didn't ask God for assistance, as He would surely look after her roof if she prayed sincerely. When the old woman insisted that this was not so the minister grew irritated and asked how she could be so sure. The reply came without fear or hesitation: 'I asked Him before and He did nothing about it then.'

A couple of months later, three men who had been fowling on Stac an Armin caught a great auk and tied her up inside a *cleit*. Then an unexpected storm blew up, preventing the men from leaving the stack. The storm raged for three nights and three days and on the third morning the men agreed that the storm had been caused by the great auk, which must therefore be a witch. They pelted her with stones until all that was left of the rare bird was a bloody mess. Once they threw the carcass to the sea the storm subsided and the men could return to Hirta. Uneasy and starved minds invested such events with feverish significance, and the minister began to feel powerless and exposed.

But a more serious incident occurred the following spring while the harsh winter struggled to decide whether it ought to withdraw from the land that it had harried for so long. One evening, in early March, when the people of Village Bay had started to starve and were forced to boil seaweed for tea, old Finlay found a keg of whisky in a disused *cleit*. The golden liquid poured down his throat and heated his empty stomach until the ancestors spoke to him. In the cold, cold night he set out towards the manse to tell the dark minister to leave the ancestors alone. Oh yes, he would tell him a thing or two! He would show him not to move old Finlay from the house of his kin! Swinging the half-empty bottle in one hand like a wrecker's lamp, he staggered through the sleeping village, but he skidded and slipped on the ice that had formed in the puddles between the houses and in doing so became disorientated. The frozen ground poured him down the slope towards the beach, which was still covered in snow. The shallow water by the beach was hard, but further out the ice thinned to a skin. Confused and enraged, Finlay walked on to the ice in the starless night. He heard a loud crack but plodded on, oblivious to any danger. When his feet went through the ice he could still stand as the water was not deep. But it was hard to walk on, and after a while he sat down next to the hole in the ice up to his knees in water. He was tired and worn out. The sudden cold had drained some of his anger; a wave of shame washed over him and he whimpered miserably. But soon his senses were benumbed and a great tiredness seeped into him. He rested his face in his hand against his knee and smiled as a strange warmth overcame him as the temperature dropped.

This is how he was found the following morning – covered in a glistening layer of frost. The rising sun fired its beams at the perfect human sculpture in the ice. The St Kildans walked out the twenty feet and gathered around old Finlay. They watched in awe as a clear drop of thawing frost fell from one of his ears and trailed along the frozen cheek towards the blue shadows around the mouth and the core of the mystery. 'It is a miracle!' whispered MacKinnon's wife, and crossed herself. A film of saliva, as thin as a hymen, had frozen across the dead man's mouth. MacKinnon leaned over and looked closer at it. 'I wonder . . .' he said, and prodded at the thin sheet of ice with his finger. 'I wonder if he managed to let his soul out in time.' They all stood quietly and pondered this for a while. 'Should we leave him here?' somebody asked reverently. MacKinnon shook his head authoritatively. 'No, no, we will cut him out and bring him home, and once he has thawed we will stretch him out for his grave.' Some of the younger men went back to the village to fetch a couple of axes and a saw blade from the saw pit by the manse. No one could think of anything to say as they considered the end of the old man's life. The young men returned with the tools and started cutting a perfect circle around the man in the ice. 'He looks so handsome,' remarked Mrs MacKinnon. 'He was never handsome when he lived. God must have had a meaning with this act of mercy.' The people gathered around her nodded in agreement. Once the ice had been cut through, the men took hold of Finlay and hoisted the whole sculpture out of the water. The cylinder of ice that had grown around his calves was about six inches thick. The white idol of the sitting man was carried respectfully on the shoulders of four men towards Finlay's house. No one acknowledged the empty bottle that was left behind, embedded in the ice.

Once inside the house, they put him down by the hearth. At first he would not stay put but eventually they managed to attach him to a stool with the help of one of the climbing ropes. Somebody lit a fire in the grate while somebody else placed an open bible in the hands which lay stiffly in his lap. This is beautiful, they agreed. This is a good way to go.

At that moment the minister's shadow filled the small room as he stooped across the *tallan*. 'What on God's earth is going on here?' His voice was hoarse and his face was enraged. No one moved except for Mrs MacKinnon, who put a comforting hand on the dead man's shoulder.

MacKinnon cleared his throat. 'Finlay's a stiffy, sir – we have brought him home to his hearth.'

'For Christ's sake, you don't have to tell me what's happened, man – I saw you from the manse.' MacKenzie looked in fury at the strange effigy by the fire. 'Now, all of you fools and heretics, get out before I do something I may regret!' He started to usher them towards the *tallan* with his arms, but Mrs MacKinnon stayed put.

'With respect, sir, you shall not call my kin such names, and nor shall you tell me to leave my uncle alone. No one can persuade me to let my own blood reach purgatory in a sitting position.'

'MacKinnon, tell your woman to obey my orders,' the minister shouted.

'If she doesn't obey you, sir, she sure as hell won't obey me. Now, I think for all our sakes that you should go back home to the manse and we will call you when old Finlay here has stretched out properly and is ready for his grave.'

The minister suddenly felt very tired. 'You must not fight against me – the Lord sees you even when you are hiding in your hovels.' He was overcome by an urge to cry. His eyes watered and his voice was unsteady as he pushed passed them to get out.

PART VII

MARCH 1841 – EXPOSURE

Early morning, with a damp fire in the hearth, all alone, in the mists of dawn. Loneliness was without hope, and the dread of it increased in the spring when desire returned. It was possible to hide the malaise in company, to look around and smile at well-known faces that offered no comfort. But at other times the empty skies closed around Lizzie and nothing entered her still life; the colours had faded. What sustains me? she wondered as she watched the sea through the mist, or perhaps it was a whisper of rain.

Lizzie was pregnant again. For the last three years, since the twins Mary Anne and Margaret were born, she had been spared. But now, in the spring of 1841, it was time again. She thought about her children. She had six children alive. Eliza was already eight years old and James Bannatyne seven. And then there was Jane, Nigel and the twins. She did not want to think of the other three. *The ones she let slip away.* The two lost girls had been replaced, reincarnated in the new Jane and the new Margaret. But the boy

Nathaniel, the gift of God that she had never seen, could not be replaced. He had lived silently by her side, reminding her of herself as she was before she got to the island. She remembered seeing the reflections of the stars in the sea one summer night and thinking that it was her lost children showing her the way in this new world. Since then she had been lost many times. I have forgotten the stars, she thought.

She was not in control of her life, she did not master it, but she had come to terms with this. Her body had brought forth six healthy children, who had moored her to the island. She swayed gently around their anchors like a ship in a calm sea.

Suddenly, as her thoughts ebbed and flowed, a distant memory surfaced in her mind. She felt the warmth of her husband as he put his arm around her while pointing towards the cradle with the mark of the MacLeods, the embossed twig of juniper. And then a voice: 'We shall be happy here,' – hearing the doubt in her own voice from so many years past.

That was such a long time ago. In all her terror she had wanted to trust him. How she had adored him! Not with passion perhaps – for what had she known of passion then? – but with all the expect-ations of a young bride standing at the threshold of adulthood eager to meet life as a real woman. But since the loss of Nathaniel the feeling between Lizzie and Neil had changed subtly. He would withdraw from her and rarely look her in the eyes. Somehow she knew he resented her for losing his firstborn son: the son that should have been born to herald the beginning of his mission on the island. He had rarely touched her outside the bed. She had tried to bring him back, to keep him in the world of human touch, but he had been so occupied with his mission. And for years now she had not known him enough to love him. He had changed – his authority had altered and she could no longer make herself look up to him. She pitied him, and that was the saddest thing. Lately he had weakened terribly and she had come to fear for his mind.

Her thoughts would often stray to the stranger and that brief touch . . . but that too was long ago now and she refused to be drawn back to that mystery. What was the use?

An extension had been added to the manse to house the growing family. Lizzie looked through the open door at her children asleep in bed. She could see Anna, a tall and lanky girl ready for marriage, in bed with the younger ones. Eliza and James were getting too old to share a bed; she would have to ask for another one. She sighed again and returned to the window in the kitchen. Eliza was a serious girl. She kept to herself and wrote secret poems and framed her words with garlands of purple and blue flowers. James on the other hand would still play with the local boys. His hair and skin stank of fulmar oil and worse.

Suddenly she saw a figure amongst the boulders by the landing rock. The morning mist was still clinging to the ground and the figure seemed cloaked in smoke. Whoever it was seemed to be hiding from the view of the village. Lizzie looked again and recognised her first maid, Betty Scott. Betty was moving once more, and it was soon clear that she was making her way towards the feather store. The feather store was kept locked, but a recent storm had torn a hole in the wall that faced the bay, and this was where Betty was heading.

In this place where men and women were quite separate Lizzie had learned to converse with the women. She still did not speak Gaelic, and they spoke little or no English. They communicated through small services and acts of kindness. But if she was honest she knew she was not close to anyone on the island. She was completely apart. The only person she had ever spoken to at any length was Betty. But even Betty belonged to another world, and their meetings would always be conducted on neutral ground. She smiled as she thought of the golden girl with the bouncy curls who had come to help her in the manse all those years ago.

Betty, who had married Calum MacDonald, had proved to be very fertile. There was something almost animal-like about her sturdy body that smelt of musk and sweat. Her feet were broad like a man's and large enough to carry her strong frame, her hips were wide and low and her breasts were heavy. She had given birth to a baby almost every year since she married, but they had all been lost to the eight-day sickness. One after the other Betty had watched as her children were suffocated to death by that strange devilry. Lizzie shivered when she thought about such a fate. Betty served as the island's midwife, and so her time was spent bringing life into the world. But as so many of the babies died it was like a Sisyphean task. And yet Betty was ever cheerful and strong. Her fair curls bounced on the wind and her songs rang through the air, but when you looked at her, if you tried to seek her gaze, she would avert her blue eyes so that you could not see into their depths. How shall I ever understand Betty? Lizzie thought as she watched the woman disappear from view.

A queer feeling came over Lizzie all of a sudden. It was not like Betty to behave like that. Betty would never hide. And yet there was the sense that would come upon Lizzie from time to time that there was a dark side to that Highland strength. Lizzie turned to the stove where she was heating porridge for the children's breakfast. She laughed to herself as she stirred the pot with a wooden spoon. I am so silly to create mystery where there can be none, she thought. She looked into the oatmeal, which was beginning to erupt and sink back into little craters. It was almost the last of the oats, and the boat from the mainland was not due for many months. She worried about the islanders. They were starving and things were not good. Some of the children had bloated stomachs, and the old people were looking increasingly drawn and tired. Her husband told them to pray. He believed that Jesus Christ would save them, but she could sense that people were losing their faith.

Suddenly she dropped the spoon into the porridge and ran out of the manse without stopping for her shawl. Afterwards she wondered what it was that had made her act in that way. Had she heard something?

It took her a minute or two to reach the back of the feather store and the hole in the wall. Her hands were cupped over her pregnant stomach and her swollen feet hurt in her boots. There was no sound from within the building, and Lizzie felt an itchy sweat in her armpits. 'Betty?' There was no reply. She stooped to enter the building and remembered the last time she had entered the feather store. She had stayed away from the building since. She felt sick and her throat contracted in panic. 'Betty? Are you in here, dear?' Her eyes were not yet accustomed to the darkness. She could not hear anything but suddenly sensed a movement to her left. She fell to her knees and crawled along the floor until she felt a leg. The younger woman was slumped on the floor, seemingly unconscious. But as Lizzie's hands reached Betty's face she could feel that it was soaked in tears. 'Oh, Betty . . .' She held her friend in her arms and felt a strange cord around the younger woman's neck; the texture was dry and a bit oily at the same time. She moved around so that some light fell on Betty's slumped body. The ligature around her neck had snapped.

'It broke; they would not hold me,' Betty moaned feebly. 'Oh, my babies!'

The wailing tore through Lizzie's heart. 'Oh, Betty, what have you done? What is this?' She tore at the snare and tried to remove it from Betty's throat.

'Leave it!' Betty's voice was suddenly fierce and she pulled herself away from Lizzie while clasping the cord. Her eyes were wild in the dusky light. She moaned again, 'I thought they would help me, my babies, to come to them.'

Lizzie looked down at the end of the rope in her hands. It seemed to have been made of bits of some kind of organic material knotted together. Lizzie felt cold inside and swallowed to reduce the sick feeling that was rising in her. 'What is this?' she asked again in a hoarse whisper.

'I thought the life lines that we shared would take me to them. Through this cord they were attached to me, each one of them, and when they were born I failed them. I wanted to be pulled back to them . . .' Lizzie could not make out the rest of the sentence. She looked in horror at the dried umbilical cords in her hands. They had been preserved in oil and tied together, all six of them, into a rope that was about six feet long. What grief would drive a person to such madness? Carefully she moved closer to Betty and held her again in her arms. Betty's limp body rested heavily on her own pregnancy as she rocked her friend softly and cooed in her ear. 'Shh, it is all right, oh, sweet Betty, it will be all right.' To herself she thought, Not Betty! Not Betty who was indestructible. On whom can I rely now?

In his study Mr MacKenzie stood by the window looking out over the bay. He was resting his forehead against the windowpane. The glass was slightly concave, which made the seascape wobble and buckle. He frowned as a lock of hair fell over his face. It was definitely grey, in this light he was sure of it; he was ageing. Perhaps he was already old. He shuddered at the thought and tried to recall his youth. How could it have left him so deviously without making him aware of its departure? How had he not been told?

The illness came upon him from time to time. At first it had merely been a vague nausea, a need to sit down and rest for a while. But slowly the headaches and dizziness had turned into migraines which would send him to bed in agony. At such moments it was as if somebody had crammed an iron helmet over his head, tightening it around his skull like an instrument from the sweltering chambers of the Inquisition. As he lay in his bed in still darkness the pain would bring to his eyes tears that would well and spill over his cheeks and into his ears. The noise of his children's gay voices would beat against his poor brain like steely waves against the winter rocks. His daughter Eliza was the only one allowed into the bedroom at such times. She would sometimes come and sit quietly by his bed and hold her cool little palms against his temples. But if he heard his wife at the door he would wipe his face on the pillow and pretend to be asleep. Behind his closed eyes volcanoes would erupt and red-hot lava would flow and fill the plains of blue and green. This was his predicament. *This is what they have reduced me to.*

He watched his tired reflection in the glass a moment longer and then he sighed and closed his eyes. He stood and thought, his face resting heavily against the window. *Our heavens are brass and our earth is iron. I need to address their conscience in plain discourse and show them the difference between those who truly fear our Lord and those who are mere formalists and hypocrites. They must listen now. They must understand!* It was suddenly clear to him that what was needed was a revival of the senses – an outpouring of the Holy Ghost! He stood straight and snapped his fingers. Why had he not thought of this before? He reached his desk in two strides and pulled out sheets of paper and his inkwell. He pushed the fringe out of his eyes and smiled to himself. *Just when our faith is weakest the Lord shows us His power.* The timing was good, as the men were away on Soay for a few days and he knew from experience that the women were more easily persuaded.

He set to writing his sermon. He would start with explaining the meaning of the petition 'Lead us not into temptation', and then, when he was sure they had understood, he would apply it in the most inspired way to their own consciences. He would describe in the most vivid colour what evils waited if they continued to give way to temptation and superstition. Ah, the demons and snakes of fire, the infernal torment! But oh, when they were thus terrified of the dangers to which they were exposed, he would turn their feeble thoughts to the power of the Saviour, the wise, powerful and merciful Christ who alone has the ability to save souls.

There was a knock on the door. Irritated, he looked up from his papers to see his wife enter the study.

'Yes?' She stood there in the dull light. Her face was red and she seemed fat. Had he really touched that body enough to impregnate it? The thought suddenly repulsed him.

She remained by the door, with a hand under her stomach and the other against the doorpost.

'Well?' His irritation was mounting. Had he not told her never to disturb him at work?

'Something has got to be done, Neil; the islanders are suffering!' Her voice was strong and calm and she ignored the look in his eyes.

'How so?' He yawned and stretched in his chair.

'They are despairing. They have been too long without food and fuel and we cannot cope another year without additional supplies. Their minds are weakening.' She did not want to tell him about Betty. He must never know about what had happened. Lizzie had brought Betty back to her house and put her to bed. She was sleeping now after drinking a brew of St John's wort, but Lizzie had been terrified by the incident. How would they be able to stand against the storm if the strongest of them all could be crippled into such weakness?

To her surprise he sat up and smiled at her.

'You are right. But there is no need to worry, I was just about to address the matter!' There was a strange light in his dark eyes and she was suddenly afraid.

'They need food and warmth, Neil, not words and prayers. That will not ease their suffering. They need some basic comforts before they can listen to your sermons.'

Suffering! What did she know of it? And what did *they* know of it? None of them could know what true suffering was like. Only he knew. Oh yes, he knew! 'Watch your blasphemous words, Elizabeth!' The broken spell of her Christian name, so rarely used, rang through the room like shattered glass. 'It is in their power to save themselves if they turn to the Lord!'

What could she say? She did not have his faith, but nor could she meekly leave it at that. Her heart was suddenly cold and serene. 'If nothing else, you must think of our own children, of your sons and daughters. They would be better off in a place where they could get proper food and schooling. Perhaps we ought to send them over to my relatives on the mainland when the next boat arrives . . . ?' She broke off. The thought had just occurred to her but she felt a great discomfort at uttering it. She was losing her balance, and her grip hardened on the door frame.

The man who was her husband turned away from her in silence to look out of the window. He had a vague smile on his face as he continued to ignore her. Lizzie, her face ashen, let go of the lintel and turned to go. MacKenzie, in a tone that was calm, said to her back, 'Who are you to speak of the welfare of our children, you who let our firstborn die?' She swayed but steadied herself and did not turn as she walked away from him.

That autumn the Holy Ghost was poured into the hearts of the St Kildans like molten lead. The prayers which had at first been forced down their throats were coming back up in an overwhelming flood of piety and emotion.

It began in September when most of the men were away on the islands fowling and the kirk was attended mainly by women. On such a day MacKenzie decided to describe the dangers to which they were exposed because of their temptations. At great length he expounded on the theme of evil, and when the fear of God had taken a hold in their bosoms he turned to outlining the greatness and nature of the love of Christ. He explained, in considerable detail, about the sufferings of Christ – their duration, their intensity and above all the glorious end for which they were endured: to save sinners. He urged and beseeched his parishioners to come to Him for safety and protection as there could be no other salvation.

He preached from Luke, chapter twelve, and concluded by talking about what must be done to bring forth the Holy Ghost:

It is quite certain that every man, woman and child on this island might be converted now if God, the sovereign judge of all, would only send out His Spirit. God alone has this power, and I, your humble preacher, your books and catechisms will not be of any use to you now. You must open your hearts to the injection of God because only then will the Holy Spirit be abundantly poured forth. You must each of you throw out your books and rely upon and honour the Spirit! Let us meet and pray, and if God doth not hear us, it will be the first time He has broken His promise. But if the Lord does bless us, all the ends of the earth shall fear Him. And then, just before the sun is turned into darkness and the moon is turned into blood, the Spirit of God will be poured out upon all your flesh. O Lord, lift up Thyself because of

Thine enemies; pluck Thy right hand out of Thy bosom, O Lord our God, for Christ's sake, Amen!

When he had finished the minister staggered and slumped against the pulpit. His face was pale and sweat was pouring down his forehead as he looked out over the congregation. At that precise moment, after so many years of struggle, the Lord showed his power and the St Kildans believed. Oh how they believed! Feeble and starved women and the few men present wept and cried aloud in agony and distress. The minister, when he recovered, could hardly make himself heard and proposed a psalm to calm the congregation, but the precentor was overcome with extreme feeling and could not sing so the minister had to lead the song himself. Only a few sobbing voices joined in. He continued to sing until the excited feelings subsided a little, at which he grabbed hold of the pulpit and, as they all thirsted for more, resumed the preaching.

The meetings continued throughout the winter. Every other night somebody new was penetrated by the Spirit. Even the most hard-hearted would suddenly start breathing quicker. Their hands would be raised above their heads, reaching into the air as if they were drowning. Some of the afflicted would cry out and faint, others would fall to the floor and twist in the dust, others again would scream vehemently: 'O, my overwhelming burden! . . . My sins! . . . Relieve me of my woe! . . . Have mercy on my soul!' In the end some would sit up and cry out in a superhuman voice: 'I have found Him! . . . I know that He will pardon my sins!' One or two would beg the Lord to take them home at once so that they would not sin again. At the end of such a meeting, the kirk looked more like a battleground than a sanctuary.

The minister was utterly exhausted. His body and mind were working as one during those long winter months. He preached almost every night. Sometimes he would go home for supper and a quick prayer for guidance before he felt compelled to go back into the church and preach again. His migraines became ever more frequent and he hardly saw his family. Mrs MacKenzie refused to let the children take part in the meetings and would only visit the kirk on the Sabbath.

As the birds returned and food was once again available the evangelism amongst the St Kildans became much less intense. The minister was greatly alarmed when he realised that the hearts of some of the St Kildans had remained hard and that they had only been imitating their neighbours in the winter excitement. He feared that some of them might be mocking him behind his back, and the arrogance of such blatant refusal of the righteousness of the Son of God infuriated him. However, he was well aware by now of the deceitfulness of the human heart and the power of Satan over feeble minds.

And at the same time he was able to rejoice at the progress of some of the islanders. Old sins were freely confessed; sometimes crimes that had been buried for over forty years were brought to the light and atoned for. Indeed some of the natives were so keen to air their guilty conscience and profess their hatred of all evil that the minister had to set up a surgery to receive them during the day. Envy, cunning, theft, uncleanness, Sabbath-breaking (including singing of profane songs), laziness and general loitering, excessive talking and chattering, swearing and irritability were some of the sins noted and carefully recorded in the minister's black book. That summer, instead of gossiping about each other and their daily toil or bragging about the deeds and wonders of the ancestors, the St Kildans would be overheard discussing the state of their souls. They would frequently be seen, in the fields or on the rocks, to fall to their knees to utter a prayer. Holy conversation was conducted behind walls, in *cleits*, out of the wind and in the shadow of an outcrop.

That summer of 1842 the taxman brought a thick bunch of letters for MacKenzie. Their stamps bore the marks of the Society for the Propagation of Christian Knowledge and of other Church dignitaries in Edinburgh and Glasgow. It seemed that the ten-year conflict within the Church of Scotland was coming to a head. The Evangelical Party formed in 1834 was now strong in the

Assembly and its followers called for reform of the ancient system whereby the laird selected the minister for his parishes. The evangelicalists wanted community elders and the parishioners to have the right to reject a minister nominated by a patron. The ministers were being asked to choose between staying within the established Church or walking out with the evangelicalists to form a new Church. This would mean leaving the churches and the manses behind to preach in chapels, barns and village halls and live amongst the parishioners.

When MacKenzie had finished reading the letters he went to bed with a fever that roared at night and simmered gently during the day. His gaze was slow and his limbs were slack. At times, when he thought no one noticed, he cried. It went on for weeks.

She felt the spirit around him going hot and humid and it frightened her. She had avoided him for so long – had she hated him? Now as his weakness finally showed it frightened her. Desperate, she got into bed beside him, her body forming a perfect S around his, and she folded her arm protectively over his chest. Hesitantly, almost reluctantly, as if forced to, she gently stroked the body of the man she had loved. Her health pulled out his sickness and her strength drew out his weakness. She remembered the young man she loved all those years ago: the man whom her young self adored; the firm body that would arouse her;

the eyes that aspired to know her. How she loved him then; she would follow him anywhere. He seemed to walk ahead of her, opening all the doors and letting in the light. She had followed him here, to this life. Did I follow the man or the love? she asked herself as she rubbed his damp limbs.

Now she stroked his sagging muscles and coarse skin, hot and humid. For all the old love she stroked it – wanting it to go cool and dry again. The body she had once loved. His grey hair. Remembering the strong thighs and the narrow hips.

He is turned towards the wall, a child again, needing somebody to love him. He is confused. Oh his despairing mind, the agony! Who was it that loved him well? He is too weak; he loses the thought; he cannot remember.

She breathes into his hot neck. She blows cool breath just where his dark hair meets the skin. In that soft place where youth lingers, where tenderness can still exist.

He dreams of birds. Of wings and noise and air. White wings batting the air. The noise! Island of wings. He hears a curlew's call. Or is it a man laughing? And then another dream; somebody is pulling him underwater.

She watches the thin lines around his closed eyes, the blue veins on his eyelids that will not rest. She puts her lips to his temples to still the pulse and the demons who pump it.

Her smell fills his nostrils. She is in the bed next to

him. Her arm is slung across his chest and one naked breast is pasted to his damp skin. He tries to pull away, embarrassed. Has she noticed that his body is sagging? That the hair on his body is grey? How much does she know? How much of his failure . . . of his betrayal?

Once she puts her hand between his legs to cup his testicles and hold his slack penis. With gentle hands she cradles it as if it was a fledgling fallen from its nest.

And being in an agony he prayed more earnestly; and his sweat became as it were great drops of blood falling down upon the ground.

Is he bleeding or is the damp on his pillow just sweat. He has dreamed again of a monster, a dusk-born devil. He is alone in the bed and the room is cold.

He was suddenly awake and knew that he had to make a decision. In his last letter the Rev. John MacDonald had explained the situation to him clearly and in all its brutality. Ever since Lord Brougham's declaration against the evangelicalists in the House of Lords in 1839, the evangelicalists within the Presbyterian Church had realised that they would have to break away from the established Church. A date had been set for this historical event; the General Assembly in Edinburgh on 18th May, 1843. MacDonald knew he had the elders on his side, and he reckoned that almost two-fifths of the ministers would walk out with him and leave the moderates to remain under the domination of the state. MacKenzie knew all too well what this meant. The ministers who left the established Church would also have to leave the manses and the kirks. In his own case it would mean moving his family into one of the dwellings in the *clachan* and preaching in the darkness of the sooty hovels of his congregation. The alternative was to give in to the lairds and the establishment, thus betraying his calling and everything he had achieved on Hirta. He would disappoint his mentors as well as his flock. The thought was unbearable. The elders on the island had grown strong through his instruction – they were sure to join the Free Church.

Perhaps his work on Hirta was finished? The past two years had been very difficult and his labour had told heavily, both on his health and his mental vigour. He had endowed the St Kildans with thoughts that made them human in the face of God. Many of them had passed from darkness into light, from being servants of Satan to being sons of God. Might he not be more useful elsewhere? And besides, he needed a time of mental rest and refreshment. He had always thought the laird kind and generous and had no wish to oppose him.

He had prayed for guidance. 'I can trust God to show me what will be most for His glory,' he said to himself, and the remark gave him some strength.

He got out of bed and threw a blanket over his

shoulders. The house was quiet but he could hear the voices of children somewhere outside; they reminded him of the reassuring bells of cattle in the hills of his own childhood. Baby Patrick must be asleep, the last of his children to slumber in the cot with the carved sprigs of juniper. Quietly, so as not to disturb the blessed silence, he opened the door to the parlour. The light from the window was even and bleak, barely strong enough to distinguish shadow from darkness. She was squatting on the floor, going through a drawer. There were some old letters on the floor next to her and a silver and amethyst brooch which he thought he recognised. Her head was bent, and the light that fell through the window seemed to stroke her neck and wrap it in silk. Her breasts were large inside the badly fitting dress which made her look slightly absurd, ugly even. Looking at her he felt lost and betrayed. She had lost her firm body and there was something dusty about her. Had he brought her to this? He tried to remember her as she had been when they were first married – but it was impossible. But still he knew; he knew that she had been beautiful and that he had been able to love. That she alone had made it possible for him to love.

'Lizzie, I am tired.' The words slipped out before he could stop them.

She gasped and looked around for she had been far away.

He cleared his throat. 'I have . . .' He did not

know how to put it. 'I have not been quite myself lately – you must not mind some of the harsh things that I say when my mood is dark.'

She looked at him in silence and wondered what guilt does to a man. He averted his eyes and looked around the room which he had once decorated himself. The carpet was still good, but there were patches of damp on the walls. Was it time to leave it all?

She nodded, that was all. Perhaps she wondered what she had given away.

He had never been able to recognise weakness as a virtue, and he could not bring himself to say sorry because the word was not substantial enough to express his shame.

'We are going back to the mainland.' There, it was decided. She nodded again. 'When?'

'I wish to be present at the next General Assembly in May, and my vote will make it impossible for us to stay on Hirta.'

'So soon.' She tried to stand up, but she had been on the floor for too long and her body would not obey her. He walked over in two long strides and helped her to her feet, lifting her tenderly until her face was close to his. He recognised her then for the first time in many years, and she gave him a quick smile. Together they sat down at the table by the window.

'My sole aim was to bring them to a state of penitence – to make them realise . . .' His voice faltered.

'Do not brood on words; you have prospered on this island.' Somehow she still could find the strength to be charitable.

He did not seem to hear.

'I have watched them as closely as a scientist looks at insects under a glass. I have been able to touch them, to heal them, to encourage them, to instruct them – but I still do not understand them.'

She made a sound that might have been a sigh. 'You have kept yourself aloof and apart from them. You saw them as a problem that needed to be solved. But they were never the problem.'

He shook his head, but she was not sure he was listening. She had suddenly had enough of him and his self-pity. There was intensity and some of the old spirit in her voice as she said, 'The only way we can come to understand other beings is by tainting them with a bit of ourselves. When we are all covered by the same filth it is possible to understand each other – and to believe in each other.'

He noticed there was a bit missing in the threshold – he had never had the time to repair it. Not a difficult job really, just the bother of finding the right wood. And there had been so little time. What had he ever believed in, apart from his faith? What else was there to believe in?

'Certainly, yes.' He did not have the strength to contradict her – but had he not understood Duncan? A print showing Jesus at the temple in Jerusalem had been damaged by the damp. Why had he not seen it before? Still, it was not the damaged print that made his eyes hurt, nor the memory of Duncan, all skinny legs and white-blond hair, picking up his rod outside the schoolroom.

'You seem, at times, to have applied the same approach to your own children.' Her voice was gentle but it trembled a bit as she continued, uttering for the first time what she had always known: 'Your mission was always most important, was it not? More important than me and the children.'

He shook his head quietly but did not look at her, nor contradict her.

She went on. 'I think at times that perhaps you were never really brave enough to love us'.

Such failing scarred the heart.

'They love you, you know, your children.'

He looked up. Was she teasing him? How could she say such a thing? She reached across the table to hold his hand because she would not yet let herself accept that her own devotion was wasted – she could not forget the words and the emotions he had never spoken. She looked into his blank eyes and tried to tell him, with the blue light of dawn and dusk, that she was still willing to believe in him: the bravest of churchmen and most cowardly of men. He pulled away his hand and covered his eyes.

PART VIII

MAY 1843 – DEPARTURE

He did not walk out. He had waited in such agony for the day when the historic dispute would be settled that when it arrived he could hardly believe in the reality of it. Might it not be, he asked of himself, that when it came to trial, the hearts of the men who had spoken so bravely, so foolishly, against the established Church would fail them? Surely the days of martyrdom were over? There was no need to walk away from manse, livings and pulpit. No need – just plain obstinacy! There was a rumour that over three hundred ministers had signed the protest. Three hundred! That was impossible. Forty perhaps, but none at all seemed more likely.

There was a fresh wind in Edinburgh on the morning of the Great Assembly. Representatives from all the parishes around the country had gathered outside St Andrew's church in George Street to see what their ministers would do. There were thousands of them, all hungry to know of the outcome. MacKenzie had struggled to get past the masses to take his seat. The church was already crowded with elders from all the parishes and members of the public, some of whom had been waiting since before dawn. He had felt slightly panicky, and sweat had been pouring down his face. The spectators had been shouting at him and the other ministers, 'Will you go out? . . . Will you stand up for the Church or the state? . . . Will you support the parishioners or the lairds?'

As they all sat down to council, Dr Welsh, the chair who had moderated the last Assembly, had stood up to open the proceedings with a prayer. The air in the church was thick with anxiety and purpose. Rising slowly, Dr Welsh looked out over the seated ministers in front of him. The church had never before seen such a congregation but, although men of religion sat densely in the pews, there was not a sound, no coughs or shoes scraping on the floor, no whispers or snuffles to break the silence of expectation. Dr Welsh, who was a short man but who seemed to tower over the crowd that morning, cleared his throat to address the ministers of the Church of Scotland. He gave a brief prayer, asking for the Lord's blessing, after which he declared that he could not go on with the business of the Assembly as it could no longer act as the Supreme Court of the Church of Scotland because its terms had been violated and its jurisdictions had been infringed upon by the secular courts. He then asked for permission to read out the Protest of the Free Church of Scotland. When he had finished reading he put down the document, bowed reverently to Lord Bute, Her

Majesty's Lord High Commissioner, stepped down from the podium and walked towards the doors. There was a moment of silence and confusion before Rev. Thomas Chalmers, who had been sitting next to Dr Welsh, picked up his hat and followed him back up the aisle. At this point, as if a signal had been raised or a horn had been blown, row after row of ministers and elders stood to leave. Solemnly but with raised heads they filed out after the leaders of the new commission. From where he stood at the back, MacKenzie watched with growing apprehension. He saw many of his old friends walk out along with some of the most venerated churchmen – there was Dr Gordon and Dr Macfarlane and Campbell of Monzie. And then he saw to his horror Dr MacDonald, the Apostle of the North, who had meant so much to him. As Dr MacDonald walked past he looked straight at MacKenzie and nodded his head ever so faintly. But MacKenzie stood still. Even if he had wanted to, he could not have moved: his limbs would not allow it. Paralysed, he watched as disappointment and contempt filled the eyes of his former mentor. He wanted to call out, to defend himself, but he could not speak. *There was nothing I could do.*

Four hundred and fifty ministers walked out, nearly a third of the total number and many of the most distinguished names within the established Church. For a moment MacKenzie thought he saw amongst them the ghost of a young man who had once set out to preach the Gospels at the furthest corner of the realm. He closed his eyes to disperse the image, but the emptiness in his heart did not subside. Through the open doors he could hear the cheers from the assembled crowd as the true evangelicalists walked down the hill towards the Canonmills and Tanfield Hall where the Free Church was to be set up. The crowd celebrated as if it was a public holiday, and the outgoing ministers had to file through in procession, three abreast. Those who remained seemed stunned, as if what had just happened was unreal. But the increasing echo of the emptying church made it all too real and, as they started to travel back to their manses, where their relieved families welcomed them, there was a piece of their hearts which knew that the days of the old Church were gone and things would never be quite the same again.

A month had passed since that day and MacKenzie had returned to St Kilda to take his farewell of the islanders. In reward for his loyalty to the established Church he had been offered the small highland parish of Duror. Here, he was promised, he could relax and regain his energy after his years of faithful service to the Society for the Propagation of Christian Knowledge.

Now, as he walked towards the Point of Coll for the last time, there was a strange absence in his mind. He could not put his finger on it. Over the last few days, as Lizzie and Anna had been packing the crates and boxes with their possessions, Anna overwhelmed and brought to tears from time to time by the thought of her house-folk going away, he had felt a sense of relief at leaving the island. He watched his children playing in the garden and knew it was the right decision for them. The only one he could not quite bear to look at was young Eliza. At twelve her once chubby limbs had grown slender and willowy and there was a new depth in her dark eyes. She was old enough to know this island as her home.

But apart from that there was peace. I am weakened, he thought. I can no longer feel the divine strength that used to fill my heart with action and fervour. The spell is broken and all I want now is to be released from this place. To go home to Argyll and end my days – content with my lot and without any demands or aspirations. There was a time when they were like puppets in my hands, impressionable and naive – I wanted to protect them from their misdemeanours and show them the purifying properties of the heart's sorrow. I moved their world when they did not think it possible; I waged war upon the ghosts of their minds and chased away the witches of their imagination; I have ridden the storm and relaxed in the eye of the wind. This was my art. I was strong once, and then weakness overcame me.

As he watched the waves break over the rocks, not far from the place where Duncan went over, he suddenly realised what the absence meant. He had lost his calling. His deed was done, and from now on he could retire.

The remaining days on the island were short and confused. When it arrived, the drab plainness of the morning of departure seemed inappropriately understated in comparison to the high emotions on the island.

Lizzie was alone in the empty manse. She trailed her hand over the crates and boxes which were piled on the floor ready to be picked up when the ship arrived. The spring had been cold and wet, and the rooms were soaked in damp, a cold stream of air flowing into the house from the sea. She thought of lighting a last fire in the grate but decided against it; what was the use? The manse and the kirk would soon be boarded up and left to decay. She winced as her hand caught a splinter from one of the crates. The piece was large enough to be pulled out whole, but it left an angry gash in the fleshy part of her palm. She studied her hand, her eyes smarting – it was an old woman's hand, she realised. And yet she was not yet old. At least I'm still learning, she thought.

Along the outer side of her palm ran a fine scar, a patch of silky pink against the roughened creases around it. She struggled to recapture the moment when she had received it, trying to ease her fall when the dark birds had hunted her off the Gap. They should have let me see my dead son, she thought. I will never be able to recall his face, only the happiness I carried under my heart.

What will be expected of me now? she wondered. Suddenly she felt the emptiness inside her fill up with all the lightness of her days and the darkness of her nights. Her heart contracted and her throat was tight. She could not breathe fast enough and had to inhale deeply. Blue light streamed through the sooty windows. She smiled to herself. *To think that I had to come all this way to know about life.*

Without realising why, she dragged her hand hard across a rugged box again and felt the pain as another splinter pierced her skin.

The St Kildans had all risen early to put on their Sunday best. MacKenzie had met them in the kirk to give a last service. Everyone seemed exhausted with grief, and MacKenzie himself, who was impatient to leave, was suddenly insensitive to the commotion around him. In his hurry to reach the landing rock he forgot his book. Turning to his eldest daughter he pleaded, 'Eliza dear, will you run and pick up my bible from the pulpit in the kirk, please?'

Glad to serve her father, Eliza ran again – for the last time – in her stiff new clothes up the hill, past the feather store and through the clusters of cowslip which were curtsying humbly to the breeze of the bay. She skipped over the glebe wall and hurried along the bed of sweet peas and mustard. At the gable of the manse she skimmed past the hawthorn and the lilac which were both just out. He watched her disappear around the corner of the kirk and wondered what her childhood had been like.

The MacKenzies were all quiet as the dinghy set out, each drawn to his or her own memories and thoughts. The St Kildans were kneeling on the rocks and on the beach. Lizzie saw Betty standing a little apart from the others. The sun, still kind to her, had flicked some silver into the waves of her hair. The two women had said their farewells and Lizzie had locked her friend into her heart along with all the other memories of the island, good and bad: memories she would hold for later – telling them back silently to herself, naming her loss.

MacKinnon started to sing, and soon the others joined in the psalm. Behind them, like a mocking grin along the slope, lay the tidy street of new houses. The fierce geometry of the village was softened by the green light which poured down from the hills.

Once safely aboard the cutter, Lizzie stood with the children at the stern. Eliza was a grown-up girl now and a great help to her mother. She was looking after her siblings, and Lizzie watched as they pointed out parts of the receding island to each other, shouting agitatedly as they caught sight of a friend waving or a well-known spot where they had played and which was therefore invested with mystery and meaning. Lizzie followed their gaze and wondered what it must be like for them to look at their home from the sea for the first time. Once again she asked herself how these children would cope on the mainland. They had never seen any trees or forests or great fields of wheat. They had never seen a town or a village with horses and pigs. She had been afraid at the beginning of what the island might do to them. Now she was afraid of the mainland. How could she protect them? She gripped the hand of Patrick, who stood beside her. At least he would be fine, as he was too young to remember anything from the island. She felt his tiny hand in hers and knew that she would not always be able to hold it.

She searched the green slopes for the little graveyard her husband had built and which enclosed the graves of her three dead children. She could not say if she was looking forward to returning to the world; nor could she imagine what life there would be like. She had a new purpose: to guide her children like an eider duck until they could swim on their own. Then she would tow them gently behind.

She looked up to see her husband standing alone at the bulwarks on the starboard side. His face was withdrawn and masked and she felt a rush of pity.

As the canvas was raised and the cutter fell off to the south-east, MacKenzie turned from the island, away from the wind and the yammer of kittiwakes in Village Bay, and faced the open sea and the Long Isle beyond. Fulmars were skimming the waves around the ship and a myriad of gannets coasted for a moment high over the mainmast before remembering their purpose and returning to their homes in the rocks. Only once did he look back, to see for the last time the sun riding over the ridge of Mullach Sgar sitting comfortably in the saddle of Ruiaval before arriving safely at the battlements of Dùn.

As the island subsided into the vanishing skies behind him he took out of his coat his Gaelic bible and opened it to the title page where his name had once been inscribed. For a moment he looked at the browning ink that spelled out his past before he closed the book and, leaning over the bulwarks, dropped it into the silencing sea.